"*I heard you're a widow*,"

Cole said. "Is it true?"

Jordan froze. She opened her mouth to speak, but no sound came out. Here's your chance to wipe the slate clean—to stop living a lie, she told herself.

Finally she whispered the untruth. "Yes, it's true."

Cole clenched and unclenched his fists, anger coiling in the pit of his stomach. "And you had...have a child?"

Jordan tried to swallow her fear. She nodded.

"Whoever he was, Jordan, did he make you happier than *I* did?" Cole asked sarcastically.

"He gave me something I needed."

"Security. Love," he said, his voice ragged with emotion. All the things he couldn't give her.

"No, Cole. A baby." *You* gave me *your* baby, she silently added.

Dear Reader,

Once again Intimate Moments is offering you a month filled with terrific books, starting right off with Kathleen Korbel's American Hero title, *A Walk on the Wild Side*. J. P. O'Neill is an undercover agent for the DEA, but when he's framed for the murder of his partner, he realizes his own agency has set him up. The only thing to do is take off in search of the truth himself, and the only way to escape is in the company of his lawyer—who's handcuffed to his arm! Theirs is a rocky beginning, but the end will be terrific—if only they can live that long!

In *The Hell-Raiser*, author Dallas Schulze pens a powerful tale of lovers reunited after ten long years. Jenny had always been the proverbial good girl and Mitch the bad boy, but now he feels it's time for her to let go of the guilts of the past and let him take her for a whirl through life.

Linda Shaw's *Indian Summer* takes a hero and heroine from feuding families and forces them into an alliance that is at first just business but eventually becomes something far more: love. As always, Linda plumbs the depths of her characters' hearts—and souls.

In *Run to the Moon*, talented Sandy Steen puts her own unique spin on the ever-popular "secret baby" plot, while Catherine Palmer's *Red Hot* takes you to chile farm country for a steamy marriage-of-convenience story. Finally, let new author Julia Quinn tell you about *Wade Conner's Revenge*. Driven from town by suspicion and unprovable accusations, betrayed by the silence of the woman he loved, Wade Conner returns with a score to settle. But suspicion begins to follow him once again, and now he needs the help of a woman he no longer trusts—to keep a murder charge at bay.

I think you'll enjoy each and every one of these terrific books, as well as all the exciting novels we have in store for you in months to come—books by such favorites as Rachel Lee, Marilyn Pappano, Paula Detmer Riggs and Justine Davis, to name only a few. Meanwhile, happy reading!

Yours,

Leslie J. Wainger
Senior Editor and Editorial Coordinator

RUN TO

THE

MOON

Sandy
Steen

Silhouette®

INTIMATE MOMENTS®

Published by Silhouette Books New York

America's Publisher of Contemporary Romance

SILHOUETTE BOOKS
300 East 42nd St., New York, N.Y. 10017

RUN TO THE MOON

ISBN: 0-373-07459-X

First Silhouette Books printing November 1992

Books by Sandy Steen

Silhouette Intimate Moments

Sweet Reason #155
Past Perfect #202
The Simple Truth #375
Run to the Moon #459

Silhouette Special Edition

Vanquish the Night #638

SANDY STEEN

spent many an hour daydreaming while growing up in the Texas Panhandle. Later, inspired by her husband of more than twenty years and her two children, Sandy decided to put her dreams on paper.

Although her family had some doubts when they first observed her method of plotting her stories, they are now her staunchest supporters. Sandy herself believes that if she can make a reader believe in the wonder of fantasy and feel the joy of falling in love, then she has, indeed, succeeded.

Chapter 1

"Sugar, you were the smash hit of the evening." Barry Clark's beaming smile almost rivaled the polished gleam of the sleek black, chauffeur-driven Lincoln as he handed the woman inside, then slid in next to her.

"One more bow in this dress and I would have been a hit all right. Of the Breckenridge vice squad." The dress in question was black satin, strapless and perched so low across Jordan Lockridge's breasts that a mere shrug of her shoulders, much less a bow, had caused more than one man in tonight's audience to wonder if the entertainment might take a decidedly X-rated turn.

Barry glanced at his friend and employer's obvious charms provocatively enhanced by the dress. "I did notice a couple of guys backstage taking bets on the possibility of one hell of a 'coming out' party. Bet your number put a hundred grand in the Make A Wish Foundation coffers if it put in a nickel."

"I doubt that."

"Hey, whoever decided you were perfect to pantomime 'Put The Blame On Mame' from that old Rita Hayworth movie was a genius. And I got every tantalizing second on film," he teased, patting the video camera that was never far from his fingertips no matter what the occasion. "Besides, it was for a good cause."

Jordan's teeth gently gnawed one corner of her mouth. "The only thing I'm perfect for is making a fool out of myself, but I'd gladly do it every day if it would help just one child."

Barry eyed the woman who not only paid his salary but had long ago earned his respect and friendship. "You got a big heart, sugar."

Her smile was both sad and sweet. "Or very little willpower when it comes to saying no." She sighed. "I just wish I didn't have to face this reception."

"Fancy food, good booze and hobnobbing with the snobs. Rough life, but somebody's got to live it."

Even though Jordan knew Barry was teasing, she was the first to admit her life was far from rough. Simple maybe, but definitely comfortable. And she had earned that comfort. The hard way. And alone.

From the time she was five years old and her parents died, Jordan had known what it meant to be truly alone. Raised by well-meaning grandparents who were ill-prepared to cope with a willful, imaginative child, much less one who harbored deep feelings of abandonment at her parents' death, Jordan was achingly familiar with aloneness. She knew what it was like to feel marooned on an island of loneliness surrounded by an ocean of love that never quite touched the shores of her heart. Jordan also knew what it was like to carefully construct, layer by layer, a self-confident, I-don't-need-anyone veneer of protection. She sought her solace privately.

As a child she had spent endless hours staring up at the starry night sky, particularly the moon. A symbol of love and magic, she even imagined the man in the moon smiled at her, that they were friends. Small comfort for a lonely child, but often it was all she had. She had wished on the moon the same way others wished on a star. And her childhood wishes were always the same: to live in the mountains forever, grow up beautiful, marry a handsome man, have lots of babies and live happily ever after.

Even as an adult, Jordan found comfort in the familiar, pale glow of the moon. As silly as it sounded, when the going got tough, the moon was as comforting as an old teddy bear. Jordan smiled to herself. Very few people knew about her childhood preoccupation with the moon and even fewer understood.

Jason had understood.

Jordan hadn't thought about Jason Cole, or whatever other fictitious name he was using these days, in months or maybe weeks. Okay, to be honest, it was more like days, but dwelling on thoughts of a man who had walked out on her without a backward glance was nonproductive. That, too, she had learned the hard way.

As in how many nights can one woman cry herself to sleep and how many billions of tears can she shed?

As in how do you live with an ache so deep in your soul that the mere effort of breathing was painful?

Don't! she cautioned herself. *Don't what? Remember?* She couldn't stop even if she wanted to. Jordan shook herself free of hurtful memories she had tried to escape but could no more dismiss completely than she could dismiss the sunrise.

Gazing out the tinted window at the clear June evening, she sighed. What she needed was a good night's sleep. What she wanted most was to go home, get out of this dress that barely allowed her a decent breath and...*hide*? Yes, she admitted, hide. Sometimes hiding was the only way she could deal with the memories of Jason Cole. And sometimes even hiding didn't help.

"Daydreaming?" Barry asked after her prolonged silence.

Jordan shook her head. "Dreading." She took as deep a breath as the dress would permit and forced her thoughts back to the present. "I have had about all the socializing I can stand for one night. If I have to plaster on one more smile and shake one more hand—"

"But you will and...if you should just happen to mention needing support for another very worthwhile cause, what could it hurt?"

Jordan rubbed the bridge of her nose and tried to tamp her rising irritation, more with circumstances than with Barry. She knew the last half of his comment referred to his inability to accept the defeat of their mutual efforts to protest a construction project that would spell ecological disaster to the area around Fairplay, Colorado, where Jordan lived.

"It's over, Barry. A done deal. The bobsled run and ski resort project is going ahead no matter how hard the Park County Ecology Society worked. The only thing we can do now is put all our efforts into minimizing the destruction of wildlife and the environment."

"Hey, it ain't over till the fat lady sings, remember? And there are going to be a lot of fat-cat ladies at this shindig."

"There will be no arm twisting tonight," she said firmly.

"Arm twisting? Me?"

"I may not be as militant as you, but I care just as deeply about what's happening and what's going to happen to our part of the Rockies. You're my best friend, Barry, but you're like a pit bull with a bone where this issue is concerned.''

"So what's wrong with a little determination?"

"Nothing, but you don't have to hit people over the head with your zealotry."

"My what?"

"A little tolerance, my friend," Jordan advised as the Lincoln drew up to the entrance of the Beaver Run Resort conference center, "goes a long way."

Tolerance wasn't Cole Forrester's long suit, and he was down to his last few ounces. Noise from the surrounding party buzzed around his head like dive-bombers looking for a place to drop their payload. Only Cole's well-disciplined mind kept the irritating racket pushed to the edge of intrusion as he swirled warm brandy around in a snifter, absently watching the amber liquid coat the sides then slide to the bottom. He was bored. Not simply bored, but alone, sober and fed-up-to-his-eyeballs bored. And for Cole Forrester, boredom of any flavor was a dangerous state of mind. It made him irritable, short-tempered and likely to speak his mind in biting expletives.

The black-tie reception was jammed with sparkling socialites and debonair do-gooders. Some, he supposed, were genuinely interested in contributing to the fund-raiser for terminally ill children. The rest, he suspected, were genuinely interested in being seen with the right people who were doing the right thing, discussing the right topics. And tonight's topic was the preceding variety show, specifically, a sexy pantomime. Fearing the boredom he was now experiencing, and knowing his appearance at the social part of the evening was unavoidable, he had avoided the benefit, but judging from cocktail chitchat, he had missed a showstopper.

Too bad, Cole thought, sipping the inexpensive brandy. He could use a little entertainment right now. And a lot more room. The ballroom of the resort, obviously intended to hold a lesser crowd, was packed literally wall-to-wall with people. He hated tight places, and this one was getting tighter by the minute. The caustic noise had finally perforated his mental barrier and intruded. Music played, glasses clinked, partiers pressed in around him. He felt as if the entire room, maybe even the whole damned hotel, was covered in shrink wrap, tight, airless, and he fought the urge to yank the precisely tied bow tie from his shirt collar.

Cole tossed the remaining brandy down his throat. Tedium, close quarters, plus the ever-present pain in his right leg kicked up several notches his desire to leave. His gaze scanned the crowded room for his hostess in order to make a donation and a socially acceptable apology, but the smiling blonde with the overdeveloped chest who had greeted him upon his arrival was nowhere to be seen. The ultra-high-tech security for Great Northern Construction's bobsled and ski resort was definitely a feather in his cap, and he couldn't simply disappear without a word, no matter how badly he wanted to leave. But the smell of cologned and perfumed bodies mixed with the aroma of champagne and smoke, plus an unimaginative exhibition of piano playing from the corner of the room, ground into his patience. His tolerance level was dropping rapidly, and if anyone in the world recognized his own tolerance-level danger zone, it was Cole Forrester.

Tolerance.

As in, how long can a man stand to be isolated, shut off from all sound but the beating of his own heart...in a space barely large enough to comfortably contain a small child, much less a powerfully built man?

As in, how long can a man stifle a scream while the bones of one of his legs are being systematically broken. Oh yes, Cole knew all about tolerance. He also knew, firsthand, just how far a man's mind and body could be pushed.

And what happens when he's pushed over the edge.

Glancing down, he realized his white-knuckled grip on the empty brandy snifter threatened to shatter the glass into a million pieces.

To hell with it, Cole decided. He shoved the snifter aside and turned toward the exit just as a smattering of applause started at the doorway and rippled across the room. The main body of the party crowded forward. Instinctively Cole stepped back, positioning his aching leg out of harm's way.

Now at the edge of the glittering guests he caught a glimpse of a woman at the center of the crowd. The intriguing recipient of all the attention had gorgeous dark auburn hair almost to her waist and was gowned in a long, tight black satin evening dress with matching elbow-length gloves. Someone in the crowd yelled "Encore!" and the piano player struck up "Put The Blame On Mame." Undoubtedly the star of the evening, Cole decided as the group of people directly in front of him parted, providing not a view of the star's face, but of her tantalizingly bare back and shapely hips. But as enticing as the body was, it was the woman's long, thick, wavy hair that caught Cole's attention. Considerably darker than Rita Hayworth's flame-red, the richly burnished dark auburn was every bit as eye-catching, every bit as sexy. The kind of hair a man could no more resist touching than he could resist drawing breath. The kind a man could imagine whispering over his body through long hours of loving.

In Cole's case, imagination gave way to vivid, bitter-sweet memory. A memory he had worked hard to eradicate without much success. A memory he both cursed and blessed, wondering if the day would ever come when it wouldn't be a part of him. In his mind and heart the answer rocked between hoping he would and praying he wouldn't. The same way his memories rocked between pain and pleasure, hurting and wanting. The same way he wanted to obliterate all recollections even remotely connected with the woman in his memories, yet would be satisfied if hers was the last name he called before dying.

Even now, after four years he could close his eyes and recall in haunting, exquisite detail the silken touch and seductive scent that belonged to the only woman he had ever truly loved. Cole's eyes drifted shut. He could see her face and hear her voice and respond as if she were standing next to him. At times, like now, her memory was so real he half expected to open his eyes and see her.

Regretfully Cole opened his eyes to the present and knew with a certainty forged out of a powerful, albeit brief bond, that the day thoughts of Jordan Lockridge vanished completely he would be dead.

Feeling sorry for yourself, Forrester? Perhaps he was, or perhaps merely being in the one part of the country Jordan had loved above all else had stirred the ever-simmering pot of recollections. A home in the Rockies had been one of her passions, and more than once since his flight touched down in Denver only hours earlier he had dueled with her memory. Thoughts of Jordan Lockridge juxtaposed with the word *passion* threatened a new assault of a less ethereal nature. Yeah, he was definitely on edge, and this party wasn't helping one damned bit.

Calls for an encore persisted, and even from Cole's position across the room it was obvious the entertainer was given little choice but to agree. Her back still to him as she went into the routine, Cole decided she didn't have to have a drop-dead gorgeous face. Pantomime or no, she was selling the song with her body, and every man in the room was buying. She tossed her head to the sexy beat of the music, then bent forward, sending the riot of the dark auburn hair cascading down, only to gather it back up on top of her head as she straightened. Slowly she let the soft waves slide from her hold and tumble down around her shoulders. The effect was predictable.

Cole's body tightened and he realized he had traded one kind of edge for another. The edge on his boredom might have disappeared, but thanks to his memories, the edge on his purely male response was hard and sharp. The pulse at his temple increased and he couldn't take his eyes off the lady in black. Completely entranced, he was on the verge of skirting the crowd for a better view when she started to roll a black satin glove down one slender arm. Cole stopped. He reminded himself he was only watching a performance, make-believe. But his body was more interested in dealing with reality.

Switching her hips to the pounding beat, the dancer slipped off the glove, grasped an end in each hand and slowly, sexily raised the now-taut glove above her head. With a flick of her dainty wrist she let go of one end of the glove and flung the swatch of black satin into the audience. Whistles and applause almost drowned out the music. Repeating the same mouth-watering process, she turned and flung the second glove into Cole's side of the crowd, then turned back.

For one heart-stopping second Cole had caught a glimpse of her face. A face out of his memories. And his nightmares.

A face he couldn't forget if he lived to be a million.

Fate couldn't be that cruel. *The hell it can't,* Cole thought, knowing full well how ruthlessly Fate could slice a man's life to ribbons, then leave the tattered shreds flapping in the breeze. Hallucination or a cruel twist of Fate. Either way he was getting the hell out of this room . . . now.

Like tolerance, hallucinations and Cole were on a first-name basis, but he also recognized reality for the ugly beast it could be. If he had been eager to leave before, now he was desperate. Working his way along the edge of the party heading for the door, he had almost succeeded when he felt a hand on his shoulder.

"Leaving so soon?" Cole spun to find Reed Sheridan, CEO of Great Northern Construction, longtime business associate and the closest thing he had to a friend these days, eyeing him closely. "At the risk of sounding clichéd, the night is young, what's your hurry?"

"Guess I'm more tired than I thought." Cole glanced in the direction where the entertainer had been, but she was gone. "Those, uh, contract negotiations this afternoon were a killer." It was a lame excuse and one he doubted Reed would buy.

"I've seen you go through days of sessions like that and walk away barely winded."

Cole shrugged. "To be perfectly honest, my leg could use a rest."

In the two-plus years he had known Cole Forrester, Reed had never once heard his friend complain about his old injury, much less use it as an excuse. The fact that Cole chose to do so now was telling in the extreme, informing Reed that his friend's need to leave the party was on the same level with a condemned man's need for a massive power failure. "If it were up to me, I'd say go. But Mayor Burke specifically requested we save him a few minutes."

"Make my excuses."

The terse response, indeed almost a command, didn't faze Sheridan. Well aware that Cole's behavioral norm was cut-to-the-chase abrupt, he had expected some resistance toward the necessary social aspects of this job. "I'm afraid he won't take no for an answer. Look, I'm not into this glad-handing stuff any more than you are, but this project is different. I had no idea when I bid for the job how hands-on the city government intended to be. Burke has hinted he would like for us to say a few words at tomorrow's—"

"No speeches."

Reed saw the muscles in Cole's jaw tighten, and wondered what on earth had his friend so uptight.

"I couldn't agree more, but it will probably take both of us to convince His Honor otherwise." Reed glanced across the room, caught the mayor's eye and motioned for him to join them.

Cole was caught.

Still flushed from her encore, Jordan was talking to one of the evening's largest contributors when Fairplay's mayor, Will Burke, swooped down like a bird of prey, looped an arm through hers and hauled her out of her chair even as he said, "Sorry, but I need to borrow the belle of the ball for a moment. You don't mind, do you?" Without waiting for an answer, he pulled Jordan with him across the room. "I finally caught Reed Sheridan and his hot-shot security fellow that arrived from Canada today, and I want you to help me convince them to say a few words at tomorrow's little ground-breaking ceremony. You know, how we're all working together for the good of the economy—"

"Me?" Jordan had to admire the mayor's determination, even if she didn't agree with his politics. "What makes you think I can talk them into making a speech?"

"Jordan, in that dress—" Burke eyed the clinging satin and his mouth went dry "—you could probably talk the devil into going to church."

As an old adversary in local and state politics, Jordan was used to crossing swords with the mayor over budgets and ordinances versus ecology and quality of life, but they had never stooped to using each other.

She pulled free of the mayor's light hold on her elbow and stopped. "No," she said flatly, firmly. So firmly that Will Burke recognized he had overstepped a private boundary. He switched to Plan B without missing a beat.

"Look, Jordan, you and your ecological troops have taken this defeat better than I hoped. And I'm not trying to rub salt into an open wound, but it's going to take more than a let-bygones-be-bygones attitude to close the rift between the people in this town. A few well-placed words from Sheridan addressing unity just might help the healing process."

As much as Jordan hated to admit it, Will was right. If she could help calm already-turbulent waters, what would it cost but a few minutes of her time? She owed the Park County Ecological Society that much. "Let the record show I'm agreeing under duress."

Will Burke smiled. "So noted. And thanks."

"Save your thanks until they step up to the podium."

His hand on her elbow, the mayor guided her across the crowded room, skillfully dodging well-wishers without ever losing sight of his objective.

Jordan had never met Reed Sheridan. In fact, she had seen him only twice, but even at a glance and from several yards away she recognized his imposing height and bulk. Imposing enough to almost completely obscure the person he was talking to. As they drew to within six feet of where Sheridan stood, he turned aside to speak to another guest, providing a clear view of the man in front of him.

Despite Will Burke's insistent grip, Jordan stopped dead in her tracks. For a moment she stood like a passenger on a roller coaster poised at the top of a death-defying climb, waiting, teetering, unable to stop the seconds-away terrifying plunge. Her stomach dropped to her feet; she couldn't move, couldn't breathe. Her heart hammering in her chest like a wild thing in captivity, she stared at the tall, dark-haired man now directly in her line of vision. *It can't be . . . can't be!*

She tried to force her mind to reconcile what her eyes were insisting was true with what her heart was saying had to be false. *Please, God, don't let it be him.*

After more tears and sleepless nights than anyone should have to endure, after months, years of bandaging an almost fatally wounded spirit, Jordan was face-to-face with her worst nightmare.

And her sweetest dream.

Disoriented, like a child spinning on a merry-go-round suddenly halted, she stared at the man she had known as Jason Cole. Her heartbeat had long since shot past racing. She tried to swallow and discovered her throat was high-noon-in-the-Sahara dry. *Oh, please, no—*

"Jordan?"

Just when I've put my life, my heart, back together again.

"Jordan?" When she didn't respond, Will practically dragged her the remaining few feet to where the two men stood.

Cole forced his expression to remain nonchalant, his eyes emotionless. It was his only hope of getting through this situation without betraying himself or her. Without breaking the promise he had made to stay out of her life. And the only way he could keep that promise was to pretend she meant nothing to him, to pretend he barely remembered her or their time together. Until two years ago, pretense had been a way of life for Cole, but he doubted even his experience would be enough to pull off the acting job of a lifetime.

"Mr. Sheridan," Burke said offering an overzealous handshake, "may I introduce the power behind tonight's well-organized benefit and one of our most attractive businesswomen, Jordan Lockridge. Jordan, Mr. Reed Sheridan, CEO of Great Northern Construction."

The introduction registered but only dimly as she fought the rising tide of bone-deep terror. Despite her alarm, she couldn't take her eyes off Jason Cole.

"Delighted, Ms. Lockridge." The touch of Sheridan's huge hand enveloping hers brought Jordan out of her trance.

And to the realization that Jason Cole had barely given her a glance. Not once had those eyes she had always thought so intensely sensual, eyes the color of dark velvety chocolate, looked her way. In fact, if she hadn't known better, she would think he was acting as if he didn't even know her. His indifference sent a wave of relief crashing over her, but it was short-lived. Wasn't he a master at deception? Hadn't he lied to her with honeyed sweetness? Hadn't he hurt her as no one had, before or since? A burning rage flashed through her, then simmered to indignation.

It took every ounce of Cole's considerable willpower not to look at her. Not to stare at her, not to drink his fill of the sight of her. Still, he hadn't missed the shock in her green eyes quickly followed by flashes of pain. And anger. The shock he expected. The pain he understood. And the anger he deserved. And why not? He would be the last one to deny her anger was justified. Her memories of him had to be less than treasured.

Cole certainly couldn't, in fact, never wanted to say the same about his memories of her. They had kept him alive when nothing else on earth could have, and those same memories had kept him from going to her when he finally healed enough to realize life did indeed go on. Seeing her now, seeing the remnants of her pain, Cole knew his decision to stay out of her life had been the right one. It was still right.

"Ms. Lockridge," Sheridan said, "may I present a business associate, Cole Forrester. Mr. Forrester's company will be providing the security for the bobsled project."

Cole Forrester? *Another alias, no doubt.* Memories bombarded Jordan like icy missiles from the past. Memories of countless telephone calls and questions, only to discover the man she had loved as Jason Cole didn't have a phone, or an address, or even a social security number. He simply didn't exist. For four of the most beautiful weeks of her life she had lived with... a phantom.

But he wasn't just a memory anymore. He was real, no matter what name he used. And he was here, now. A heartbeat away. Just as handsome. Just as dangerous to her peace of mind.

"Mr. ... F-Forrester," she said to the man who was neither phantom nor reality.

"Ms. Lockridge." His voice was every bit as deep and compelling as she remembered, its smooth resonant quality seductively slipping past some personal barrier. His very presence trespassed on her emotions. She felt invaded.

He still did not meet her gaze. Jordan was both relieved and, strange as it might sound, annoyed. Part of her was relieved that he had no interest in a trip down memory lane. Another part of her resented the fact that he didn't.

"Well," Burke said, highly pleased with himself and totally oblivious to the undercurrent of tension, "Jordan and I were just remarking on how well everything is going. Don't you agree, Sheridan?"

"So far, so good. I'm anxious to get started."

"Of course, of course. And we are anxious for you to get started, aren't we, Jordan?" When she didn't answer, Burke rushed ahead. "I mean, now that everything is official, I'm certain any previous opposition will simply vanish as though it had never existed. Isn't that right, Jordan?"

Never existed... never existed. The words reverberated inside her head like a kettledrum, and a suspicious moistness gathered in the corners of her eyes. She blinked back tears. *I will not cry! I will not—*

"Isn't that right, Jordan?" Will urged, floundering in her silence.

"Y-yes."

"In fact, we had hoped you might say a few words at tomorrow's ceremony."

"I'm not much of an orator," Reed stated flatly. "Besides, under the circumstances I'm not sure making a big deal out of the first day of construction is such a good idea."

"Nonsense," Will insisted.

The conversation bounced back and forth between the two men but Jordan barely heard a word. All her energies were focused on getting through the next few minutes... until she could get as far away from Cole Forrester as she could.

Suddenly she felt his eyes on her as surely as if he had reached out and touched her. Jordan looked up. And wished she hadn't. The roller coaster plummeted again and she felt as if she were falling, crashing. And if she had thought her personal space crowded merely by his presence before, it suddenly shrunk to a two-sizes-too-small fit. *Please don't let me make a fool out of myself,* she prayed.

Cole was relieved to see the resentment in her eyes had mellowed to a guarded expression. Guarded he could deal with.

What he couldn't deal with was Jordan in strapless black satin. If she had aroused him as a faceless dancer, her effect on him now was nothing less than dangerous. Every time she breathed, he half expected her to come out of the damned dress. The thought of dozens of pairs of lecherous eyes feasting on her soft, naked skin sent unexpected anger swirling through him like a whirlwind. An anger he had no right to feel. Where Jordan was concerned, he had no right to feel, period.

Right or wrong, he couldn't stop himself, because he knew just how soft her skin was, just how dewy and fragrant. He knew the answer to the question that had probably crossed the minds of half the men in the room tonight: What would it be like to make love to Jordan Lockridge?

Like paradise. Like reaching deep inside your soul and discovering an untouched, unmarred, perfect part of yourself that was only made perfect because you gave it to her. Like dying and being reborn into a world of joy and light so clean, so pure, it was almost unbearable.

Stop it, Forrester. You don't want this. You can't want this. Cole cautioned himself to play the role.

For an instant Jordan thought she caught a spark of something that resembled yearning in Cole's eyes. But that wasn't possible. Still there was *something* in his eyes she had never seen before, something . . . she almost said haunting, but dismissed that description as well. No, the only thing she now saw in his eyes was a coldness to match his dispassionate body language that fairly shouted how insignificant he considered the encounter. Against all reason, her ego suddenly sported a whooping bruise.

"And what do you think, Ms. Lockridge?" Reed Sheridan was speaking directly to her, and Jordan hadn't the faintest idea what he was talking about.

"I, uh . . ." They were all waiting patiently for her to answer. But answer what? The look in Will Burke's eyes said he was clearly annoyed at her hesitation, and suddenly Jordan decided she had had enough pressure for one night.

"You don't approve of the bobsled project?" Sheridan asked.

"Well," she began, relieved to once more have a handle on the conversation.

"Perhaps Ms. Lockridge doesn't care to share her opinion." Cole's voice held a vague hint of disapproval.

"No, it's not—"

"Or perhaps she doesn't actually *have* an opinion." His dark-eyed gaze slid away as the slicing insinuation, however slight, was delivered with the precision of an expert surgeon.

Jordan was dazed from her emotional roller coaster ride, up and down between fear and pain, tears and resentment, holding on for dear life. Jason's—or rather, Cole Forrester's—tone of voice, indeed his whole demeanor, brought the ride to a screeching halt a few inches short of rage. Stretched to its limit, Jordan's tension snapped, freeing her. Without thinking, she courted recklessness.

No wonder he changed his name, Jordan thought. The man before her was a cold imitation of the Jason Cole she had known. Her fear took a back seat to pride and self-protection. How dare he intimidate her? How dare she let him?

"Oh, I definitely have an opinion, Mr...Forrester, is it?" Out of the corner of her eye she saw Will Burke cringe. "In a nutshell, my opinion is that the quality of life is more important than money. And that's the bottom line here, isn't it? Money in your pocket. Regardless of how many lives you—"

"Uh, excuse us just a moment, will you? I see the mayor of Breckenridge trying to get our attention," Will Burke said, whipping Jordan around so quickly she almost stumbled. "Just what the hell are you trying to do?" he hissed in her ear as he practically bulldozed his way across the room, using her as a shield.

"Nothing."

"Nothing!" he squeaked trying to keep his voice low.

"He asked for my opinion."

"And he sure as hell got it. Whatever possessed you?"

Pain, fear and memories, Jordan wanted to say. Too much pain and too many memories. In the time between heartbeats she made a decision. She wanted to leave the party, the area, the planet if possible. "Have you seen Barry?"

"Barry? No. Jordan—"

"I want to go home."

"You what?"

"I'll call you tomorrow." At the pronouncement, Jordan turned and disappeared into the crowd, leaving a stunned mayor gaping at the empty space where she had stood.

When she finally found Barry he was knee-deep in an animated conversation with two women Jordan recognized as part of the militant faction of the ecological society. If she had to listen to another word on the subject of the bobsled run, she would scream. But Barry had provided the limo, and there were no cabs to take her the twenty-three-mile, thirty-minute drive over Hoosier Pass from Breckenridge to her cabin outside Fairplay.

"Excuse me." She tugged on Barry's sleeve.

"Hey, sugar, we were just—"

Smiling her best fund-raiser smile, Jordan looked directly into her best friend's eyes and said pointedly, "If you don't take me home this very minute you're going to have a corpse on your hands.''

Evidently Barry got the message that smile or no smile, she wasn't joking. He quickly made his apologies to the two women and escorted her out of the ballroom.

They didn't say a word to each other until Barry pulled into the driveway of Jordan's picturesque cottage. "You okay?" he asked.

"Fine."

"Wanna try that again?"

"No," she answered on a ragged sigh. "I'm beat, that's all."

When no additional information was forthcoming, he realized whatever had Jordan tied in knots, she wasn't in the mood to disclose the details. At least not tonight.

"Okay, sugar." He got out, opened her door and helped her out. "Call me if you need me."

As he watched her walk to her front door, unlock it and slip inside, Barry wondered what had upset one of the most grounded and well-balanced women he had ever known.

"Hi," the pretty, nineteen-year-old baby-sitter said when Jordan closed her front door behind her.

"Hi, Jill. Any problems?"

"Are you kidding? She was a little angel, as usual."

Jordan smiled. At least one part of her life hadn't changed in the past hour. She paid Jill, thanked her, but didn't release a sigh of relief until she heard the young woman's ancient pickup grind and sputter out of the driveway.

At the foot of the stairs Jordan slipped off the black satin-covered high-heeled pumps and carried them up the steps. Haphazardly she pitched them onto her bedroom floor as she headed for the room next to hers. Slowly, silently, she pushed open the door and crept across the soft, plush carpet to stand beside the single bed.

Nestled beneath a cream-colored eyelet comforter embroidered with tiny rosebuds, her russet curls and delicate cheek barely visible, was the thing that gave Jordan's life purpose and meaning. And too much was at stake for her to let memories of an old love, no matter how grand or passionate, make her careless with this most precious of treasures. This time she stood to lose more than just her heart.

Gazing down at her three-and-a-half-year-old daughter, tears misting her vision, she knew what she would see if those soft brown eyelashes fluttered open.

Eyes the color of dark velvety chocolate.

Just like her father's.

Just like Cole Forrester's.

Chapter 2

Jordan's hands were shaking, and it had nothing to do with the fact that she was consuming her fourth cup of black coffee in two hours. *Seven in the morning and my nerves are shot.* Seated on a high stool at a serving bar in her kitchen, she stared into the mug of coffee captured between her slender trembling hands as though the dark steaming brew might hold the answers to her dilemma.

Dilemma. Now there's a classic, understated definition of my situation if I ever heard one. Shoving a thick, wayward mass of curls away from her face, she transferred her stare to the scenery outside the glassed-in sun-room on the far side of her kitchen. Aspen leaves, dark green on one side, pale green on the other, twinkled in the early-morning breeze and rarely failed to draw her appreciative attention. Gathering her ancient, but so-soft-it-was-almost-decadent terry robe tighter, she barely noticed them today.

Dilemma didn't even begin to define the consequences of Jason's or Cole's—or whatever the hell his name was—

reappearance in her life. Debacle, disaster, devastation—now there were words she could grasp. Words that undoubtedly framed the picture of her future if...

If he intended to spend much time in Colorado.

If he kept crossing her path.

She closed her eyes. If he found out about Fancy.

Fancy. Fancy. My little miracle. Sunlight and laughter all tied up in a pink bow.

And until last night she thought no one would ever know the truth about Fancy's parentage. No one would ever know about her lie.

In the beginning she had told herself the lie was to protect her child. In truth, she needed the lie to ease her wounded spirit. When she learned the extent of Jason's deception, all the feelings of abandonment she had known when her parents died came crashing over her in wave after wave of heartrending pain. At the tender age of five she couldn't understand why one moment they were in her life and the next they weren't. But at the still-tender age of twenty-eight the loss of her parents paled to insignificance beside her lover's treachery.

Abandoned. Again.

At that point she thought he had left her nothing but pain. And memories. Memories of love words whispered on night sighs, and Jason stroking her body, moving in her, with her, to a glory and bliss that was almost too painful to bear. Memories of them lying heartbeat to heartbeat, savoring the last blush of loving, and Jason whispering that if it was within his power he would give her her heart's fancy, whatever it was. Unknowingly he had done just that.

Her heart's fancy. A beautiful baby girl.

Jordan's eyes snapped open. That night and the ones before it, were seared into her memory. Indelibly. Forever. The brief four weeks they had shared were so emotionally and physically hot that the memory still clung to her like thin cotton on a steamy night in the tropics. And, like a tropical breeze, Jason had swept into her life, caressing, whispering, then was gone. One night he was holding her in his arms, loving her as though there were no tomorrows, and the next morning he simply disappeared without even a goodbye.

So, born out of her desperate need to ease the loneliness, she fabricated a man who had loved her, married her and helped create a perfect child. And, God help her, the fairy tale had been a comfort. She *had* felt less deserted, less lonely. Her self-esteem was so severely damaged, only after the joy of Fancy's birth did she decide to "bury" the fairy-tale husband along with her pain. The only problem was that she buried a piece of her heart as well, vowing no one would ever hurt her again the way Jason Cole had. No one. Ever.

Jordan forced her thoughts back to the present. The anxious present. What if he had somehow found out about Fancy? But how could he?

She had never told anyone about Jason. Everyone thought Fancy's father had died before she was born because that's exactly what Jordan wanted them to think. Besides, she had covered her tracks well enough.

None of her co-workers at the Shreveport television station, where she had worked when she knew Jason, were intimate friends. She made it a point to keep her personal and professional life separate. Even though her on-camera persona as an interviewer was public domain, she made sure the names of the men she dated weren't ground through the gossip mill. She rarely dated anyone for any length of time and never took them to business-related social functions, choosing instead to go alone or with a group of her colleagues. Almost reclusive when it came to her private life, with little effort she was able to field the few questions about her manufactured husband. And with the aid of some stylish but deceptive dressing plus continuation of her exercise regime, she had successfully hidden her pregnancy until almost her seventh month, when she left Shreveport for a new business, a new life.

Jordan made up her mind that her new life would fulfill the childhood dreams she had wished for while gazing at the moon. And she had achieved more than a moderate success. She had Fancy, a cabin in her beloved Rockies and Video Images, Inc., her thriving business offering tourists videotapes of their vacations, river-rafting trips, hot-air balloon rides and ski trips. So, the husband of her dreams had been make-believe; she had been blessed despite that flaw. Perhaps she was tempting Fate to even ask for all her dreams to come true.

But Cole Forrester was no dream. And somehow she had to make sure he never learned about his paternity. She had lost too much; she couldn't, wouldn't lose Fancy.

"Mommy?"

Jordan's head snapped up. Barefoot, sleepy-eyed and clutching a bedraggled-looking stuffed clown in a loving stranglehold in the crook of one arm, Fancy Lockridge padded across the oak-planked floor toward her mother.

Jordan slipped off the bar stool, lifted her daughter in her arms, clown and all. "Good morning, sunshine." She planted a soft kiss on the even softer small cheek.

"I'm—" Fancy yawned "—hungry."

Jordan smiled, thankful for the temporary shift from adult-size problems to child-size normalcy. When it came to priorities, politicians, ecologists and the world at large could take lessons from three-year-olds. "And what—" she patted her daughter's flannel-covered stomach "—does your tummy say it wants for breakfast?"

At the signal to begin her favorite game, Fancy giggled. "You listen."

The Talking Tummy was a game they frequently played and one Fancy never tired of, whether she was the listener or the listenee.

"Hmm, let's see." Jordan scooted Fancy higher in her arms and put her ear to the small stomach. "Grumble, grumble, growl, growl, scrambled eggs." She lifted her head only to meet with a very definite frown. Her second try of, "Growl, growl, pancakes," received a more positive response.

"What else?" Fancy asked, pleased with herself.

Jordan repositioned her ear. "Uh... bacon."

Fancy held up her stuffed companion. "What does Winky's tummy say?"

Placing an ear against the well-loved patchwork clown, Jordan solemnly announced, "Winky says, don't forget the juice."

"Okee, dokee," the child agreed as she wiggled out of the embrace and raced around the serving island in the center of the kitchen, headed for the pantry.

The doorbell rang and Jordan groaned. There was only one person who would show up on her doorstep at that hour.

"Hi ya, sugar," Barry announced, as he and his irritatingly affable grin breezed through the door.

"Has anyone ever told that you're disgustingly cheerful?"

"Flatterer. Hey, what's this?" he asked, eyeing her rumpled appearance. "Fashionably mussed?"

Jordan raked a hand through her hair. "I just got up," she lied.

"One of the perks of being the boss. You sleep in while your lowly and humble employee—" he made a sweeping bow from the waist "—does the grunt work."

"What are you babbling—" Jordan stopped. Eyes wide, she turned to Barry. "The balloon shoot. We're supposed to meet the clients—"

"In about thirty minutes."

"Oh, Lord," Jordan moaned. She had been so deep in thoughts of Cole Forrester she had completely forgotten about the early-morning appointment to film a hot-air balloon ride. Thank goodness her memory had deserted her after she had asked Jill to come in early this morning. "I'll be dressed in five minutes. Tell Fancy I'm sorry, but Jill will fix her pancakes," she tossed over her shoulder as she raced upstairs. Ten minutes later, moisture from her shower still glistening on her slender neck, Jordan outlined her schedule for Jill, kissed Fancy goodbye and dashed out the door with Barry.

On the drive over Hoosier Pass they discussed the particulars of the impending shoot, plus the day's remaining appointments. Jordan was in the process of checking one of the three cameras they had brought along when Barry blindsided her with a question.

"What did you think of Sheridan and his buddy?"

"W-who?"

"I saw you talking to Reed Sheridan last night and that guy he brought in from Canada to do the security. Think his name's..." Barry snapped his fingers. "Forest—"

"Forrester."

"Yeah, that's him." When she didn't pick up the conversation, Barry urged, "And..."

"And nothing. Burke introduced me, that's all." If only that was true, she thought. If only last night's encounter had been nothing more than a polite introduction to a total stranger. *And if wishes were horses, beggars could ride.*

"Come on, sugar. Ol' Willy boy never does anything without an ulterior motive. He must've wanted something."

"I told you." Jordan tried to shrug off the inquiries. "It was nothing. He thought it would be a good idea for Sheridan and . . . Forrester to make a speech, so he asked—"

"You to do his dirty work," Barry finished for her.

She shot him a quelling look. "I'm a big girl, Barry, and I told you last night, there's no need to beat a dead horse."

Barry blinked. His mouth opened as if to speak, then he closed it again. By mutual, unspoken consent the rest of the ride to Breckenridge consisted of business conversation.

A short time later, as they checked last-minute preparations for the balloon ascent, Jordan suffered a twinge of guilt over her abrupt behavior.

She knew she had been too sharp with Barry, but lately his tenacious refusal to accept the inevitability of the bobsled project had gotten on her nerves. Never one to retread beaten ground, she had urged him to focus his energies on preserving as much of the environment as possible and to accept the reality that they couldn't save it all. Despite her insistence to the contrary, he had latched on to the issue with the tenacity of a pit bull. There were times, Jordan decided, when her friend's unquestionable expertise with a camera was all that saved him from an old-fashioned, sisterly tongue-lashing.

They used two balloons, Jordan filming with the clients in one, and Barry in the other, filming the first balloon to use in a promotion for Video Images, Inc. The shoot went well except for some minor in-air adjustments that entailed a complete change of direction because of a sudden and insistent wind. They had originally planned to take the familiar route toward Copper Mountain, but the wind forced them to head east instead. In Jordan's opinion, the view wasn't the most picturesque, but the client didn't seem to notice, particularly when the pilot took a sweeping dip over a small, breathtakingly clear lake set into the landscape like a sapphire nestled in lush green velvet. A couple of men, probably fishermen, glanced up as they drifted past. The client's wife even waved, but the men didn't return the friendly gesture.

The shoot having been declared a resounding success by the clients, she and Barry headed for the storefront offices of Video Images on South Main.

She was in the back of the shop, trying to concentrate on editing a piece of film, when Barry stuck his head in the door and asked, "Hey, am I still in the doghouse?"

She lifted her head from her task and met his gaze. "Am I forgiven for being a first-class shrew?"

He feigned shock. "My mild-mannered boss, a shrew? Unthinkable."

"I imagine there's been some pretty 'unthinkable' commentary on my behavior dancing around in that head of yours today."

"Figured it was PMS," he said and promptly ducked. A missile that looked suspiciously like Jordan's pencil sailed right past his ear. "Your aim is getting better."

She responded the way any former television personality and honor graduate of the University of Colorado would do. She stuck out her tongue.

"I know I'm taking my life in my hands by asking, but are you going to legend-in-his-own-mind Burke's official, super-duper, ribbon cutting this afternoon?"

At his question, the onset of what promised to be a warm smile died. If she refused, Barry might think she was still peeved with him. If she went, there was a very real chance she would run into Cole Forrester. Jordan had friends on both sides of the sensitive issue, and she honestly believed there was a solution, albeit undiscovered, that would appease almost everyone . . . just as she believed it was still her civic duty to show her support of finding that solution. So what if Cole happened to be at the event? It was a free country, and he had a vested interest in the project. As she had pointed out to Barry earlier, she was a big girl.

Jordan sat up straight in her chair and put on her best smile. ''Of course I'm going.'' *Going crazy. You really are tempting Fate. You've been a basket case since last night. How are you going to keep it together if you see him again?*

He wasn't going to see her again. He was going to get the hell out of town. Cole had reiterated that promise to himself at least three times in the past hour. Seeing her was pointless. Seeing her was useless.

Seeing her was all he thought about.

Don't do this to yourself, Forrester. Don't do this to her.

Standing at the window of his third-floor room at the Beaver Run Resort, Cole had a sweeping view of a good part of Breckenridge. The once-sleepy mountain-village-turned-successful-tourist-resort was bustling with summer visitors. Cole could easily understand why Jordan's business had thrived. In spite of his promise to stay out of her life, he had checked into Video Images and confirmed what he already suspected. Her reputation as an honest, experienced professional was as solid as her business.

Gazing down at the activity in the town, he wondered if Jordan was in her shop at this very moment. Or was she out in the crowds of people, maybe having lunch or meeting with a client? Perhaps she was on her way back to Fairplay in preparation for this afternoon's politically correct ceremony? Damn, he couldn't string two thoughts together without one of them being about her.

Cole stalked across the room, picked up a crisp stack of dress shirts fresh from the valet and hurled them into his open suitcase. They landed with such force that two bounced right back out. He never should have let Reed talk him into lending moral support to this afternoon's official commencement of the project designed for the media, and as soon as he could get a flight out in the morning, he was leaving. He didn't need to personally oversee security installations, and there was no reason for him to stay. No reason at all.

Except Jordan.

No. Not now. Not ever. She's better off the way she is.

The way she was, was hurt. Cole couldn't forget the look in her eyes when he had all but ignored her last night. Those cool emerald eyes. Eyes he had seen turned from frost to smoldering in the space of a kiss, a touch. His kiss. His touch.

Frustrated, he raked both hands through his coarse coffee-colored hair. Last night had been the second hardest thing he had ever done in his life. The first was not going to her after he was released, after he healed. Standing in the middle of a crowded ballroom, yet feeling as if they were the only two people in the world, he had been mere inches from her and it might as well have been miles. He could look but he couldn't touch. He could want but he couldn't have, and the not having would probably cost him his sanity.

When he succumbed to Reed's urging to bid for the security on the bobsled project, he had known it was in the area of Colorado that Jordan had loved so much. He tried to convince himself that fact had nothing to do with his decision to bid, but even then he knew it was pure self-deception. Subconsciously he wanted to be near the one place on earth she loved best. Never one to overanalyze his decisions, Cole had spent the better part of the morning doing just that. He had been asking for trouble to even think about joining this project, and he had gotten it last night. With both barrels. Right where he lived.

Seeing Jordan had knocked the props right out from under him, and it was no one's fault but his. Why couldn't he have left well enough alone?

Because *alone* was the problem. Alone was the place he had lived for so long that a few brief moments in Jordan's presence had seemed like a year of warmth in his otherwise cold world.

So, now he was caught between a rock and a hard place and he would just have to bluff his way out. He could do it. God knows he was a master of the bluff. No, Cole corrected himself, had been. He *had* been a master, past tense. But there are some situations even a master can't bluff his way out of. There are some situations where truth was inevitable. Stark, painful and unavoidable. And this situation called for every scrap of technique he had once used as skillfully as a dancer uses her body.

The image of Jordan, her sleek, sensual body encased in tight black satin, sent him tumbling back into the whirlpool of sensations and memories. Jordan, draped in a sheet, sated from their lovemaking and sleeping like a peaceful child. Jordan wearing nothing but a damp towel and a seductive look in her eyes that could have ignited granite. Jordan . . . Jordan . . . Jordan . . .

I'm losing what's left of my mind. No, he reassured himself, but he had lived on memories for so long his mind automatically sought their comfort.

Cole stared at the results of his maniacal method of packing and wondered if he was indeed missing a few brain cells. Regardless of his feelings about Jordan, he wasn't going anywhere until the project foreman showed up. Tomorrow. Or the next day. Cole groaned out loud. *Just a minor point you seemed to have forgotten.*

If mere thoughts of Jordan could tip the scales of his fragile rationale, what would happen when they crossed paths again?

Not if, but when?

Was his subconscious trying to tell him something? Like maybe he was his own worst enemy? Cole realized with an uncomfortable certainty that he would see Jordan again. He also realized if the ribbon cutting tonight hadn't provided a convenient opportunity, he would have found some other way to see her one last time. As hard as he had fought against the probability of another meeting, that same probability, indeed, the sense of inevitability, was comforting. So comforting, in fact, Cole had an overwhelming . . . and dangerous urge to embrace that inevitability and hang on for dear life.

Jordan was hanging on to the very last of her frayed nerves as she entered the smallish dining room of the historical Fairplay Hotel. A quick glance told her she wasn't the only late arrival. Cole was nowhere in sight.

Across the room Barry's wave caught her attention and he motioned for her to join him. "Hey, I was about to count you out," he said when she sat down at his table.

"Uh, some last-minute details at home." She could easily have defined last-minute details as an almost terminal case of last-minute nerves. She could also have added that since their conversation this afternoon she had changed her mind about attending the meeting no less than four times. Relieved at Cole's absence, she was on the verge of thanking her lucky stars when she heard Will Burke's voice behind her. She turned, and the intended greeting died on her lips. Will, Reed Sheridan and Cole were making their way toward the front of the room. Jordan's gaze unerringly went to Cole.

He was casually dressed in khaki-colored slacks, a shirt of the same hue but a lighter shade, and a double-breasted navy blazer. The jacket was open, as were the first two buttons of his shirt. A loosely knotted paisley print tie hung slightly askew. Despite his end-of-the-day-and-who-cares appearance, he was so phenomenally good-looking he almost took her breath away. Taller than Burke or Sheridan, he exuded an aura of self-confidence that defined the word *macho* at its best, the same brand of assuredness that had first attracted her.

Then she noticed the limp.

It was slight, barely noticeable in fact. But Jordan noticed, and in spite of good intentions to keep her feelings tightly reined, she fought an unexpected urge to cry.

He had been hurt. The simple explanation of the obvious stirred long-denied emotions that were anything but simple. Were, in fact, more complicated than Jordan could deal with. The only thing she knew for certain at that moment was that Cole had suffered, and her heart softened, more than she expected, more than it should.

What had caused the limp? A car accident? A fall? Was it recent? Had he narrowly missed death, or had he suffered the same kind of ordinary mishap endured by ordinary people? No, she suspected whatever the origin of the limp, it was probably anything but ordinary. Cole Forrester wasn't an ordinary kind of man. *Past tense. You don't know what he's like now.*

Questions, not unlike the one she had asked herself four years before, came rushing back. Who was Jason Cole, now aka Cole Forrester? Where had he been and what had he done? There was only one place, one person she could go to for answers, and Jordan wasn't certain she had that much courage.

She only half listened as the mayor made the obligatory speech, gesturing repeatedly to the scale model of the bobsled run displayed on a table before him. But as much as she hated to admit it, her lack of concentration had nothing to do with boredom. It had to do with Cole. She couldn't stop thinking about him. His reappearance in her life had dredged up all of the pain and confusion he had left in his wake, all of the questions and doubts. He had lied about who and what he was. Had he lied when he told her she was the only woman who had ever touched his soul?

Don't do this, Jordan cautioned herself. *You've put your life back together. Forget the questions. Let it be.* She knew her need for answers was emotionally unhealthy; yet a part of her refused to relinquish the past without them. She wanted answers, yet the thought of a repeat performance of last night's icy encounter filled her with dread.

Make up your mind. You can't have it both ways.

Jordan refocused her concentration just as Reed Sheridan finished his brief remarks to lukewarm applause from the sparse crowd.

"Wait until I tell you the latest dirt," Barry said as the gathering broke up a few moments later. The word "dirt" was spoken in a tone of voice that implied nasty little secrets Jordan wasn't sure she wanted to hear. "Guess who Sheridan's security sidekick used to work for?"

She shouldn't ask, shouldn't care, but she did. "W-who?"

"None other than good ol' Uncle Sam."

Barry responded to her quizzical expression with a grin that redefined self-satisfaction. "Until two years ago Mr. Jason Coleman Forrester was an active employee of the CIA."

Jordan stared at her friend as if he had just displayed blood-dripping fangs. "CIA?"

"Well," he said, backstepping slightly. "I'm not certain it was CIA, but he definitely belonged to one of our government's little *organizations* that either have initials or no names and probably trained thousands of James Bonds while Ian Fleming was still in short pants."

"You m-mean, an . . . agent?"

"Correct-ta-mondo, sugar. Now we know why Sheridan thinks he wrote the book on high-tech security. It would appear that our Mr. Forrester graduated from the school of practical experience with a capital *E*."

She couldn't believe her ears. No wonder the man she had known as Jason Cole had so successfully vanished into thin air. He had had the assistance of the United States government. "You're sure?"

"Hey, my sources are unimpeachable. Trust me, sugar. This guy is the genuine article, or used to be. Seems he got mixed up in something real ugly two or three years back. My sources didn't have details, just that he dropped out afterward, moved to Canada and went into business for himself. A very successful business, I might add. Our Mr. Forrester has a healthy six-figure income."

Jordan stared at Barry, trying to decide if she was more stunned by his wealth of data or the fact that he possessed such knowledge at all. Where had he gleaned so much information about Cole and, more importantly, why?

"How . . . how did you find out—"

"What can I tell you?" he said, smugness fairly oozing from every pore. "I travel in the right circles and I know people who can get just about anything on anybody."

Jordan thought back to the time, only weeks earlier, when Barry had unearthed some old accusations that Sheridan's construction firm had taken kickbacks. The allegations, although never proven, had caused enough doubt in several city councilmen's minds to almost cost Sheridan the bobsled project. She knew Barry still had contacts left over from his time as a news cameraman and that his sources had, for the most part, been accurate. But how could he have tapped into the level of information that Jordan would bet next month's income was confidential?

"What kind of circles have access to data that is probably highly classified?"

His eyes narrowed. "How did you know it was classified?"

"Since when does the CIA or any other nameless government agency hand out information on their agents, active or otherwise, to every Joe Blow off the streets?"

"Hey, I'm hardly—"

"What you are, is treading ethically questionable ground. Doesn't any of this strike you as invasion of Cole Forrester's privacy?"

"All's fair in love and war."

"War? Is that what you think this is all about, the good guys against the bad guys?"

"Damn right it's a war. And obviously your commitment to winning isn't what I thought it was."

"Not at the cost of a person's civil rights. Did it ever occur to you that Cole might have some very specific and *personal* reasons for not wanting his past employment record bandied about like a piece of cheap gossip?" Jordan sighed, weary of what had become a real bone of contention between the friends, and angry that Barry's narrow perspective had forced the confrontation. If the thought crossed her mind that she was defending the very man who could ruin her life, she ignored it.

"And as for my commitment to preserving the Rockies," she continued, "you know damn good and well it's every bit as valid as yours. But I can't, no, won't, condone this militant attitude, Barry. This project is going forward regardless of how much dirt you dig up, so deal with it. And I think for the sake of our friendship we had better consider this subject taboo." She sliced her hand sideways through the air in a gesture of finality.

The frown on Barry's face and the tension in the muscles of his neck belied his "Whatever you say, boss" retort. She didn't care; she hated losing her temper, but they had been headed for this particular collision for weeks and she was relieved it was over. Now maybe they could get back to being good friends instead of reluctant adversaries.

"I'll see you tomorrow." She paused then added, "Okay, friend?"

"Sure." Barry ducked his head and Jordan could already see the signs of his tension easing. Then he looked up and offered a fraction of his irrepressible grin. "Okay, friend."

Relieved, she was still smiling a few minutes later as she closed the hotel's front door behind her.

"Lovers' quarrel?"

Jordan's head snapped up. Arms folded across his chest, Cole Forrester was leaning against the railing that encased the wide porch. From his vantage point he had a clear view of the spot where she and Barry had been standing. She glanced over her shoulder, then back at him, realizing that he had obviously jumped to the wrong conclusion.

"No. Barry's just a—"

"Friend?" A light breeze stirred and he caught the fragrance of her perfume. Sensual, seductive and arousingly familiar.

"Yes."

Relief surged through Cole like a flash-flooded river. All the months of agony suffered at the hands of his sadistic captors paled in comparison to the burning pain that had lanced his heart as he watched the two of them. Slowly one or two of the fist-size knots that had formed in the pit of his stomach the instant he saw Jordan and her "friend" together began to unfurl.

Cole smiled. "I guess appearances can sometimes be—"

"Deceiving?"

With one word she had effectively stripped away the fragile veil of civility separating them from old hurts, old truths. Cole's gaze met hers, and he knew she would ask for the truth and he knew he would have to lie... again.

The word slipped out before Jordan could edit herself. But surprisingly, instead of the relief, even elation, she anticipated, she was swamped with a sudden, almost desperate urge to recall the word.

The full realization of Barry's information suddenly hit her with all the subtlety of a mule's kick to her backside. What if Barry's source was right? If Cole *had* been a government agent, that might explain why he hadn't told her his real name or the truth about where he worked. Maybe he had lied to her because he had no choice. Had she held on to an anger that was unjustified, at least in part? As much as Jordan hated to admit it, that possibility now existed. The admission rippled through her like a pebble tossed into a pond, pushing the boundaries of her dilemma ever wider.

Still, the very personal, very painful question of why he left without a word and never returned hung in the air like California smog.

Despite the emotional Pandora's box Jordan knew she was opening, she looked Cole directly in the eye. "Why..." *Did you lie? Why did you hurt me?* She swallowed hard. "Why did you... pretend you didn't know me last night?"

"Why did you?"

"You... surprised me. I never expected..."

"Neither did I. When I bid for this job, I had no idea you lived here. If I had . . ." His words trailed off but the inference was clear.

"I see." She glanced away, her hands nervously fumbling for the pockets of her skirt.

"And if it makes you feel any better, I'm leaving soon."

The simple announcement, words she should have heard years ago, twisted in her gut like a serrated knife and tossed her between relief and regret. Relief that her secret would be safe and a profound regret she didn't dare inspect too closely. In any case, Jordan doubted she would "feel better" for a long time after Cole left. Long enough to put her life back together one more time. Unwilling to trust her voice at that moment, she nodded.

"There's really no reason for me to stay."

Like there was no reason for you to stay four years ago? she wanted to demand. *Damn you, Jason Coleman Forrester.*

Cole looked into her eyes and knew he was damned if he stayed and damned if he left. She had every right to hate his guts and he wouldn't blame her a bit. All he knew for sure was that the next few minutes were probably the last ones he would ever spend this close to her, and the devil and a host of demons would have to drag him away before he cut that time short. Even if it meant facing her anger. Even if it meant facing questions he still couldn't answer truthfully.

Cole pushed himself away from the railing and took a step toward her, automatically favoring his bad leg. He *had* to be closer.

Jordan saw him wince slightly, reminding her that his life too had not been without pain, reminding her there were four years of Cole missing from her life, four blank years. She had to ask.

"Are you . . . did you have an accident?"

"Yeah." *The kind I was trained for. The kind I was sure would never happen to me.* "Car crash." The lie he used most frequently rolled easily from his lips. It saved explanations.

"I'm sorry."

"I survived." *Barely, and only because of you. And standing this close, feeling you so near but so far away is sure and slow death.*

She glanced away again. "Y-you look well."

"You mean besides the limp."

"No!" Her gaze flew back to his. "I wasn't even ... I just ..." Inhaling deeply, she tried to calm her wrangled nerves. "I only meant you look—" *More handsome than my most vivid memory. Good enough to make every woman over the age of consent drool.* "Fit."

"So do you." She looked better than anything he had seen in a long, long time.

They lapsed into a what-now staring match. Finally Jordan broke free of the almost hypnotic trance, took a deep breath and turned away.

Knowing he was playing with fire, he stepped closer. "Jordan."

The sound of her name on his lips was a caress. While her heart longed for more, her head reeled with confusion. He was a threat to all she held dear. She should run from him as far and as fast as she could. Then why didn't she? Everything had been so clear until Barry had dropped his little bombshell. Until tonight it had been much easier to hang on to her anger.

"I ... better go," she whispered.

He reached out to touch her hair, but stopped himself. His hand fell silently to his side. "Goodbye, Jordan."

The finality of his words vibrated through her, aftershocks of lingering pain that resurrected old defenses, plumbed the deep well of resentment she had struggled to contain. Jordan turned to face him. "Why didn't you have the decency to say that four years ago?" When he didn't respond except to stare at her, she added in a low voice, "You lied to me."

"Yes."

Chapter 3

Relief. Where was the relief she expected to surge over her in wave after consoling wave? Hadn't she waited for this, prayed for this? Why didn't she feel vindicated?

All at once reality, masquerading as the answer to her prayers, was an unexpected guest at her self-righteous party for one. For the first time, she questioned her motives in confronting Cole, and the thought was unsettling in the extreme.

Some fools never learn, Jordan thought, realizing she had underestimated Cole's power to hurt her. Even though she knew he had lied to her, hearing his admission out loud was more devastating than she had ever imagined. His single-syllable answer breached her anger, cutting straight to the heart of her self-confidence. She closed her eyes briefly, fighting to regain lost ground, fighting to hold on to her tattered dignity.

Cole was dying by degrees, watching her face, witnessing the pain he alone was responsible for, and deservedly so. He knew that the truth, or as much of it as he could divulge, would widen the chasm of heartache between them even more.

Jordan gathered what was left of her shredded pride, holding on to it like a shield. "Thank you for that much honesty, at least."

"Jordan…" Cole's voice trailed off. Nothing he could say would wipe away the years of hurt.

She had longed to hear him admit to his lies, but now it wasn't any comfort. She wanted to hate him, but couldn't. Nothing, not her anger, not his presence, *nothing* felt the way it was supposed to. She fought to keep her voice from breaking, fought to keep from drowning in her own confusion.

"I have to go," she whispered, turning to leave.

Before Cole's mind could counteract the command of his heart, he put his hands on her shoulders and stopped her. His breath hit the back of his throat. Her familiar warmth and softness burst through him in one explosive stroke.

My God, I'm touching her, actually touching her. But not in any of the ways he wanted to, not in any of the ways he had fantasized about. It was too much hell and not enough heaven.

"Not like this," Cole said, his voice husky with tension.

Jordan couldn't breathe. The available air felt trapped in her lungs, and the energy required to release it, indeed all her energies, were focused on one thing. Cole's touch. Achingly familiar and sensual. He had always touched her with such soul-stirring tenderness. Nothing had changed . . . and everything had changed.

"Not without your knowing I would never have lied to you if there had been any other way to—"

"To what?" Jordan's own breathy voice was as tremulous as her emotions. "Protect yourself?"

"No. To protect you."

She lifted her head and looked into his eyes. "Me?"

"I lied to you because those are the rules of the game. Because, believe it or not, I was doing you a favor."

"Rules of the game? What game?"

The inevitable question he still couldn't answer. "Just take it for granted that I'm doing you a favor by not answering that. Trust me, you're better off not knowing."

"That you worked for the CIA?"

Every muscle in Cole's body went taut. The tension shot from his body into hers, radiating from his hands like streamers of electric current. Then he released her. "Who told you that?"

"I—I..." She suddenly realized the implications of answering his question truthfully extended far beyond just the two of them. "We... the ecological group received some background information on you and Reed Sheridan... we don't even know where it came from."

"From someone trying to make trouble."

"Then it's true?"

Cole tried not to fall victim to the urgent need he saw in her eyes, the need to finally have some of the answers she had been denied. "My former employer wasn't hung up on names or titles. They were more concerned with results. If it makes you feel better to deal with a familiar label." He shrugged. "Suit yourself."

It did make her feel better. The relief she had anticipated earlier now flowed over and around her in a sudden sweet rush. And in spite of all the time before when she believed he had lied to her, she never questioned the truth of his words now.

Jordan sighed. "No wonder every avenue I pursued to find you was shut off. I looked for you," she stated simply, calmly. "Only to discover you had vanished into thin air."

Not thin air, Cole thought, another country and a four-day assignment that stretched into four weeks. An assignment he had intended to deal with as quickly as possible, then return to Jordan with the truth . . . and enough love to last a lifetime. Lifetimes weren't what they used to be and, instead, he had gone from one assignment right into another, then another, then into hell. But he didn't want to explain. Explaining meant remembering, reliving in vivid color, and one tour of duty in hell was all any man should have to serve.

"Jordan, I can't—"

"Tell me any more today than you could four years ago."

I could tell you that you're what kept me alive when death was a welcome alternative. I could tell you that right now I want you so much I can barely breathe. I could tell you a lot, but I'm not sure you could hear me. "No, I can't."

Jordan knew she could demand explanations from now until hell froze over and he wouldn't comply. Still so many questions. Had everything else he had told her been a lie as well? Like how she made him feel as no other woman ever had. Like how he made love to her so completely until neither of them could remember being separate, only one. So hell probably *would* freeze. So much for dealing with the past.

"I expected as much," she said. "At least now I understand why I was stonewalled at every turn. For a while I thought you were a figment of my imagination." *Until I discovered you left me something very real, someone to love.*

He looked into her eyes. "I was real." More real than he had ever been before or since, he could have added. More real than he ever hoped to be again. *But this isn't real. Holding myself away from you isn't natural, even if I have no choice.* Neither did he have a choice about the hot river of desire coursing through him like molten lava destined to build upon itself in layer after torturous layer.

Jordan's gaze met his, and her air supply was once again in jeopardy. So was her resistance to the dangerous but tantalizing sensation of drowning beneath a dark, powerful wave of sensuality. The same sensation that had once been her undoing and was, she reluctantly admitted, every bit as seductive now as then.

"Yes." She hated the fact that he could still reduce her to breathlessness with only a look. Worse still, she hated her body's response. Her heartbeat had escalated from keep-your-cool elevated to you've-lost-it pounding. And her body tingled with the first flush of an all-too-well-remembered passion.

As confrontations went, this one barely rated a C minus. The little flash points of revelation about herself were far more disturbing than anything Cole had disclosed. Most disturbing of all was the emotional bridge to the past she had unhesitatingly crossed at some point during the last few moments. A bridge back to old hungers, old desires.

"I, uh..." Why couldn't she stop thinking about the feel of his hands on her shoulders? The sweet liquid fire that only he could ignite. "I'm glad we finally...talked."

"Yes." So, this was how it ended, Cole thought. No more wondering what she looked like after all these years. She looked like joy and temptation in a satin-ribboned package. No more wondering about her life. Her life was fine without him. No more wondering how he would feel when he saw her again. He felt empty, hollow clear to his soul. For years he had lived on what-ifs, now he wondered if he might die from reality. She had gone on with her life. But no matter how many times he had told himself he hoped she had done precisely that, the actuality was a bitter pill to swallow.

"So, you're leaving right away?" She should turn her back and walk away. But she was unreasonably compelled to remain, just as she was unreasonably attracted to this man in spite of how badly he had hurt her.

"In a couple of days."

"But you'll return from time to time . . . to check on the project?" She held her breath, waiting for his answer.

"I'm not sure. My partner may do the follow-through."

"Oh," she said, hoping Cole hadn't heard the trace of disappointment in her voice. "Then we probably won't run into each other again."

"Probably not."

The brevity of his responses didn't bother her so much as the coldness in his voice. The icy tone delivered its own message. Clearly, succinctly. The past, their past, was gone.

For Jordan it would never be gone. It would live on in Fancy. And if she was honest with herself, even if Fancy had never existed, what they had shared would always live in her heart. With as much dignity as possible, she held out her hand. "Take care of . . . yourself."

Cole took her hand and wondered how in the name of all that was sacred he would be able to keep from taking her in his arms. More than he wanted tomorrow's sunrise he wanted to pull her to him, feel her slender body pressed against his and know again the singleness of heart, body and soul that only they had shared. He wanted to lose himself in her.

If she didn't make the break now she was lost and Jordan knew it. Reluctantly she pulled her hand free, turned, walked down the hotel steps and hurried toward her car.

Cole watched her walk into the dusky Colorado twilight, and it was all he could do to keep from calling her back. Back to what? The past? They couldn't reclaim the past and couldn't lay claim to the future. For Cole, living in the present was the only path through the jungle of unhappiness that was life without Jordan.

"Mommy, Mommy, Mommy!" Already dressed for bed, Fancy raced across the living room and wrapped her arms around her mother the instant Jordan walked through the door.

"She's been wound up like a top all day," Jill said, slipping into her jacket and preparing to leave.

"Obviously," a smiling Jordan agreed.

Now, standing in the opened door, Jill said, "She's had her supper and there's leftovers in the fridge. See ya' in the morning."

"Good night, Jill."

Fancy waved enthusiastically. "Bye, bye."

Jordan glanced down at her energetic daughter now babbling nonstop about the events of her day. "...and then we tookted—"

"Took," Jordan gently corrected.

"Uh-huh, we did. A loooong walk, and you know what we found, Mommy? We found teeny, tiny—" diminutive hands measured the distance between thumb and index finger "—nuts, and Jill said, stick'em in dirt and they grow—" standing on tiptoe, the child stretched her arms as high as they would reach "—this big."

"Sounds like you had a pretty terrific day." Jordan only wished she could say the same for herself. She listened while Fancy recounted the day in typical three-year-old fashion, that is to say, in bits and pieces worked together like a pint-size crazy quilt. Fancy ended the breathless run-on sentence commentary with, "Read me Charlotte."

Jordan laughed and tweaked her daughter's turned-up nose. "You got it, sunshine." Watching Fancy race to her room for the book they had been reading over the past few days, Jordan sighed and made a mental note to remind Jill about sugar intake. A few moments later, mother and daughter were snuggled on the couch with a well-loved and repeatedly read copy of *Charlotte's Web*.

Their last session had ended a couple of paragraphs short of the endearing spider's death, and as Jordan reached that poignant passage, Fancy asked, "Does Charlotte live in heaven now, Mommy?"

"I think so, sweetheart."

"And my daddy, too?"

Sideswiped by the totally unexpected question, Jordan's eyes misted, and she struggled to control her voice. Although this wasn't the first time Fancy had asked similar questions, tonight the inquiry was particularly bittersweet. Unable to speak the lie out loud, Jordan used the kind of diversionary tactic employed universally by parents since the dawn of time. "Hey, Miss Question Every Minute, you want to hear about Wilbur and all of Charlotte's babies, or not?"

"Okee, dokee."

Long after the story was finished, long after Fancy was sleeping peacefully in her bed, Jordan reflected on everything that had happened tonight, not the least of which was her daughter's innocently asked question.

Had she done the right thing by not telling Cole about his child? A part of her, still the most significant part, was certain she had been right. Another part, an ever-insistent part, was beginning to doubt the wisdom of her self-protective lie.

No! Right or wrong, I did what I had to. So, he had worked for the government. So, maybe he couldn't tell her the truth about himself. So what? Regardless of the fact that Cole had little choice four years ago, he had never come looking for her since then. If she had meant as much to him as he had to her, nothing could have kept him away.

Nothing.

* * *

Activity at the construction site was as brisk as Rocky Mountain air in September and had been for three days. During that time Jordan hadn't so much as caught a glimpse of Cole and naturally assumed he must have returned to Canada. While her head kept telling her she was better off without him, her heart kept insisting otherwise. He was gone. Thoroughly convinced it was for good this time, she almost dropped a handful of videotapes when he walked into Video Images.

"I, uh, thought you'd be gone—" she wrestled unsuccessfully with the stack of tapes "—by now."

Cole lifted the whole awkward mess from her hands and set it on the counter. In the process, his fingers skimmed over hers, setting off those familiar little sunbursts of sensations neither had forgotten from their last meeting. "So did I," he said quietly.

For a man who was supposed to be in a hurry to leave town, leave Jordan, Cole could have taken root for all his desire to be somewhere else at that moment. For three days he had existed in a war zone, battling himself, battling his better judgment. And now, using a semi-valid excuse, he had surrendered.

For a woman who was supposed to be happy that Cole had exited her life again, Jordan's smile was a far better definition of happiness.

Her smile went straight to his heart and almost obliterated his reason, at least his only *justifiable* reason, for being there. He didn't like quizzing Jordan, but he knew the high value she placed on truth. For all the uncertainty in this world, he would stake his life on her honesty.

He cleared his throat, reminding himself of the business at hand. "Out of the group of ecologists who fought the hardest against the project, are there any you would consider militant?''

Cole's choice of words, the same words she had applied to Barry only days earlier, jolted her. "What do you mean by militant?''

"Anyone so determined to save the planet that the end justifies the means.''

An icy fear inched its way up Jordan's spine. His question wasn't an idle one. "Has something happened?''

Tedious seconds ticked by before he replied, "A minor incident.''

"At the construction site?''

"A crate containing one of the main components for our security system was broken into and the contents damaged.''

The icy fear congealed into a dead cold certainty. "And you think someone in our organization is responsible?''

"My job is to check *all* possibilities. Including vandalism and . . . sabotage.''

"Sabotage?''

"More than likely the incident will prove to be vandalism. Teenagers probably, but I can't rule out the other. I'm looking for anyone with a motive.''

Jordan's mind was whirling with suspicions she didn't like, particularly Barry's comment that he thought all was fair in love and war. How many others shared Barry's opinion? And were any of them capable of acting on such opinions?

"Cole, I've known most of our members for over three years. They're all decent, hardworking people. Sure, they are willing to go to the wall to preserve our environment and wildlife, but I can assure you none of them would deliberately commit acts of vandalism.''

"Jordan, this isn't personal. It's my job.''

"I understand." And she did. But part of her was infuriated that Cole should question the actions and motives of people she trusted. "It's just that if you knew these people the way I do, you would see how unfounded your suspicions—"

"Speculations," he corrected. "No one has been accused, yet."

Why did the word *yet* have such an ominous ring? And why couldn't she stop thinking about Barry's recent attitude in connection with the problem at the construction site? No, Jordan assured herself, Barry would never go that far. And neither would any of the other society members. "To answer your original question, Cole, there is no militant faction among our members."

"If you say so." He appeared to be genuinely relieved and Jordan realized this part of his job must be as distasteful to him as to the people he had to question.

Cole had no doubt Jordan believed her colleagues were innocent, but he knew how cunning some people could be. Cunning and determined. Still, until he learned otherwise, he was willing to give Jordan and her friends the benefit of the doubt.

"What happens now?" she asked.

"Depends on what I find."

Jordan swallowed hard and licked her lips. "Then you're not . . . leaving?" she asked softly.

He shook his head, unable to pull his gaze away from her mouth. Soft. Lord, but the memory of those soft, willing lips beneath his was pure, blissful torture. Soft and sweet. Some flavors, like the first taste of homemade ice cream at a Fourth of July picnic, live long and beautifully in one's memory. Such was the taste of Jordan's mouth. Cole craved that taste and would until the day he died.

"Well, I, uh..." She bit the corner of her bottom lip, and Cole almost groaned out loud. "I've got an appointment."

"Sure," he finally said.

"Uh, a family wants their raft trip photographed."

"Good luck."

"You, too. I hope you find what you're looking for."

I did, Cole wanted to say, *but I can't have it.* But a husky-voiced "yeah" was all he could manage.

The rest of Jordan's day went downhill from that point. For all intents and purposes the family rafting shoot was an unorganized, soggy mess. So much so, she wound up offering the client a rain check the following day. Additionally one client canceled, another was justifiably displeased with the final edit on their video, and she had to agree to do it over.

And on top of everything else she couldn't stop thinking about Cole.

By the time she and Barry finished and she headed homeward to Fairplay, the sun had already slid behind the Rockies and the clear, moonlit night sky was filled with stars.

Fancy was sound asleep, and as usual when work kept her late at the shop, Jordan suffered more than a twinge of guilt at not being able to kiss her daughter good-night. For the most part, she considered herself a good parent, but on days like today, a severe attack of the am-I-really-a-good-mother guilts was a sure bet.

"Thank God for Jill," she mumbled, gratefully dropping onto the comfortable sofa. Wearily she stretched her long legs out and propped her feet, crossed at the ankles, on the rustic oak coffee table in front of her. "I'll make it up to you in the morning, sunshine," Jordan promised the sleeping child while trying to stifle a yawn.

Yeah, Jordan thought, closing her eyes and heaving a ragged sigh, this was not the kind of a day that produced what her grandmother used to call, "a good tired." It was the kind of day that produced a nerve-racking, clear-to-the-bone fatigue. Totally exhausted, she longed for sleep the way a lover longs for an embrace. Her eyes popped open.

Thoughts of lovers and embraces abruptly relegated fatigue to an inconsequential nuisance compared to the way her body responded. Every muscle tightened; heartbeats drummed a wild rhythm, and her breathing became shallow. She untangled her slender, jean-clad legs, walked to the kitchen, opened the refrigerator and took out a bottle of zinfandel. She poured herself a glass of the blush wine then returned the bottle to its former place on the shelf. She started to close the door, but on second thought, retrieved the bottle, tucking it securely under her arm. Oh, yeah, she was in fine shape except for one tiny little detail.

Cole.

She plucked a lightweight jacket from a peg by the front door, slipped it on and stepped outside. Slowly sipping the wine, she absently strolled the cedar deck that framed the first story of the cabin on three sides. She stopped outside the sun-room and gazed up at a fat, yellow, summer moon.

Jordan smiled despite her somersaulting emotions. Nine or ninety, people never outgrew the need for comfort, and hers had always been the moon. Memories of her parents were vague, almost like fairy-tale sketches of events except for a vivid recollection of her mother describing the moon as a symbol of love and magic.

So, Mr. Man In The Moon, what kind of advice can you offer me tonight? The luminous "sovereign mistress of the true melancholy" as described by Shakespeare seemed as oblivious to her quandary as it did the night wind blowing gently across her cheek. Strange, she thought, pouring herself another glass of wine, her connection with the moon was almost pagan, yet undeniably she felt better...more secure, after one of her moonlight therapy sessions. As a lonely child these one-way conversations had been the only safe outlet for her fears. As an adult, they afforded her the kind of peaceful time she often needed to regain a balanced perspective on her life. Tonight she needed to take a long, hard, *honest* look into her own heart.

Cole was back in her life, albeit temporarily, whether she liked the situation or not, whether she wanted it or not. Did she like it, honestly? A week ago she would have said positively, unequivocally, no. Today she wasn't so sure. So much had changed since the night he unexpectedly stepped back into her life. She had changed. And he certainly had. At least her attitude was different, Jordan assured herself, due in no small measure to the fact that Cole had been forced to lie.

And speaking of lies... what about the whopper you've hauled around all these years?

The period of depression that had given birth to her fabricated family was not one Jordan was particularly proud of, but at least she was honest enough with herself to realize the fairy tale had fulfilled a need. Looking back, she now considered that need to be a weakness. Perhaps that was why she had pushed her fictional husband to the back of her mind, almost completely forgotten, until she saw Cole again.

She took a drink of the fragrant zinfandel then gnawed on her bottom lip, wondering why in hell she couldn't sort through her problems and find a sensible answer. In the past five days, her world had been shaken like the San Francisco earthquake, and here she stood, expecting solutions from the moon. Some captain of her destiny she was. Some logical woman of the 90s she was. *Maybe that's the real prob-*

lem. *You're using logic when you should be listening to your heart.*

Her heart hurt. How could she listen when all she heard was pain?

Jordan had always taken pride in the fact that she was honest with herself no matter what. *And we all know what goes before a fall.* And fall she just might. For Cole, all over again if she wasn't careful. *No, he'll hurt you again.*

She pressed trembling fingers to her throbbing temples, massaging as though she could knead the confusion out of her brain. Confusion was the word for the day, the month, maybe the decade, the way things were shaping up.

Cole's reappearance frightened her. And thrilled her. Her tangled emotions were incredibly complicated. And simple. Fairness argued he had a right to know about his child. Her wounded spirit said he forfeited all rights four years ago.

He had lied to her. With good reason.

She wanted him to leave. To stay.

She wanted him. She didn't.

Now, that is a lie.

Jordan sighed, weary of her struggles. All right, she did want him. What difference did it make? Wanting wasn't having, any more than sex was love.

Finally the sixty-four-thousand-dollar question.

Was she still in love with Cole?

Automatically Jordan started to reject the question then stopped. Gazing at her old friend the moon, her eyes misted and she felt trapped within a moonglow spotlight, illuminating the secret part of her heart that held the answer. The truth stood sparkling in her heart like moonlight dancing, twinkling across a midnight-blue ocean. Was she still in love with Cole?

In truth, she couldn't remember a day when she had *not* been in love with him.

Chapter 4

Oh, Lord, what have I done? Jordan's hand flew to her mouth as if to trap any further confessions. She had just admitted she was in love with a man who obviously didn't care a tinker's damn about her. What kind of fool was she?

Gingerly setting her wineglass on the cedar deck railing, she wrapped her arms around her waist in a gesture of unqualified protection. Sadly the person she needed protection from was herself.

Out of her loneliness, maybe she was magnifying her emotions. Maybe she was in love with a memory. Maybe. But no matter how much less complicated her life would be if that *maybe* was a positive, Jordan couldn't bring herself to reduce what she felt for Cole to memory worship. The fact of the matter was, she was guilty of the worst kind of lies—self-deception. Since the day Cole disappeared, she had been working diligently to convince herself she could do very well, thank you, without him or any other man in her life.

And so much about her life was absolutely right it was tempting to believe everything was. She had a career she thrived on and people who cared about her. And of course there was Fancy. She had everything she needed. Cole was her past and that's all there was to it.

Then why had she dreamed about him for the past four nights? Dreams of Cole holding her, kissing her in ways no other man ever had. Dreams of the two of them lying among tangled sheets still damp from their unrestrained lovemaking. Erotic and intensely emotional dreams so realistic that more than once Jordan had awakened to find her body flushed and tense. Was that all there was to her current state of confusion? Hormones? No woman over the age of six and under the age of sixty could look at Cole and not be attracted to him. And Jordan knew all too well just how sensual and enticing he could be. Oh, how she knew! But her tender susceptibility to Cole went miles deeper than mere physical desire. It went all the way to her soul, nurtured there by a need as old as time and as new as the next moment.

Then there was the issue of Fancy. Was she being fair to Cole, keeping Fancy a secret? Even if he didn't want the mother, he might want the child. That thought was almost too painful for Jordan to bear, but she was trying to be objective enough to sort through her confusion. And was she being fair to her daughter to willingly deprive her of the kind of love Jordan knew Cole was capable of giving? What would happen if and when her beautiful, loving child discovered she had lived a lie of her mother's making . . . when a real flesh-and-blood father existed?

Jordan breathed a ragged sigh. All things considered, she had several options. One: remain confused, stick her head in the sand and hope Cole and her feelings just went away. Two: make up her mind to avoid at all costs any entangle-

ment or reveal any secrets, even to the point of avoiding
Cole completely. Three: confront the situation head-on; deal
with her emotions and Fancy's paternity, recognizing that
letting the chips fall where they may might be asking for a
second serving of the same kind of pain that had robbed her
of emotional sustenance for years.

Resolutely she mentally whittled away her options. She
had been confused too long and sticking her head in the
sand had never been her style. In all honesty, it was already
too late to avoid entanglements, whatever the cost, as her
aching heart could testify. That left her with only one clear-
cut course of action. Straight out. Head-on.

And pray her heart wasn't leading her straight into hell.
Again.

Jordan wondered if her trip to hell had already begun
when she woke up with a blinding headache the following
morning. How many glasses of wine had she consumed last
night? Whatever the number, it was obviously in direct
proportion to her state of frustration and the size of the
bottle, because her head had been invaded by a drum-and-
bugle corps the size of a third world country. One long hot
shower, two extra-strength aspirins and several cups of coffee later, she felt ready to carry out her decision. What was
it again? she wondered, her brain finally beginning to
emerge from the lingering effects of alcoholic fuzziness. Oh,
yeah. Charge! The opening lines of Tennyson's "Charge of
the Light Brigade" flitted across her mind, and Jordan
moaned out loud. Well, if she was riding into the valley of
death she'd best saddle up and face the day. The day, including her work schedule and the weather, turned out to be
almost more than she was prepared for and certainly more
than she expected.

Summer in the Rockies was the sparkling emerald forested gemstone of the seasons, enhanced with baguettes of golden sunshine and breathtaking blue skies and set in the strength and beauty of the mountains. Jordan was in her element. Standing in a narrow meadow of knee-high mountain grass, a stretch of the serpentine ribbon of highway leading south into Fairplay at her back, she focused her camera on a ridge about a half mile away. The ridge, paralleling Beaver Creek, the site of the bobsled run, rose in multicolored grandeur, the striations in its rocky side looking like exposed slices of Neapolitan ice cream. A gentle but steady midmorning breeze teased her hair and helped diffuse the heat of the sun's insistent, unseasonably warm rays. Her choice of jeans and flannel shirt had been perfect for the cool temperature when she left her cabin, but were now decidedly uncomfortable.

Still, out here, in the middle of nature's glorious technicolor statement of timelessness and beauty, she felt more alive than she had in ages and more certain that last night's decision was a good one.

Slowly swinging her camera in a panoramic arch, then back to her original point of reference, she zoomed in on the ridge and a lone rider that had appeared out of nowhere. He was scarcely more than a silhouette against the bright morning sky. Jordan watched, enthralled by the rider's agile grace and strength as he skillfully worked his horse across the rocky terrain and headed in her general direction. Less than a hundred yards away, the rider, now more substance than silhouette, pulled up on the reins, and the sturdy bay beneath him came to a halt. The unidentified and powerfully built man wore jeans and light-colored, probably blue, long-sleeved shirt, the sleeves rolled almost to his elbows. A black cowboy hat sitting low on his forehead shaded his eyes and obscured his features. He seemed to watch her for several seconds, then urged the horse forward in a straight line to where she stood.

A flicker of panic skipped up Jordan's spine as the face-less, muscular cowboy bore down on her at a steadily increasing speed. She reversed the position of the video camera, grasping the lens firmly in one hand. Not much of a weapon, but wielded with force it would do. Out in the middle of nowhere, her Jeep a brisk five-minute walk away, she could scream her lungs out and it wouldn't do one damned bit of good. *Easy does it. He's probably an accountant from Pittsburgh who got separated from a group of tourists.* Tall in the saddle, broad shouldered and a well-seated rider, he didn't look like any accountant she had ever met. As a matter of fact, there was something vaguely familiar...

Cole would have recognized Jordan at a hundred miles, much less a hundred yards. The chance meeting was almost enough to make him believe in Fate.

"Good morning," Cole said, dismounting with a fluid grace that nearly took Jordan's breath away.

"Good...good morning." The shirt that she had tagged light blue from a distance proved to be an incredible shade of aquamarine, and silk. Dusty boots, faded-to-white-at-the-seams, button-fly tight jeans, black cowboy hat...and a silk shirt. The eclectic fashion statement would have looked city-slicker ridiculous on anyone but the man standing before her.

"I was inspecting the area around the construction site and decided to stretch this lady's long legs a bit. We'd just finished a good run when we topped the ridge." He glanced at the camera in her right hand. "Working?"

"Uh, yes." She twisted the camera back into its normal position and looped the strap over her shoulder. "Some, uh, promotion shots. You know, breathtaking panorama and all that." *And speaking of breathtaking.*

He turned his head, lifting it slightly in the direction of the ridge behind him, and Jordan had to restrain a gasp of pure pleasure. Sunlight streamed across his profile, accentuating his rugged jawline, the strength of his face. "Perfect view."

"Yes." At the sound of her voice, soft, husky and drop-a-man-at-twenty-paces sexy, Cole's head snapped around.

He must be dreaming. He had to be... because the only time she looked at him, *looked* the way she did now, was in his dreams. Her skin was flushed to a delicate tawny, her lips slightly parted and moist, and her eyes. Lord, her eyes were so green, so vibrant and compelling, gazing at him as if he were the only man in the world, the only man for her. As he had that night on the porch of the old hotel, Cole struggled with an almost unconquerable urge to touch her. Seeing her here was the last thing on earth he had expected, but if Fate, or whatever passed for it, had decided to lend a hand, he'd be damned if he would question his luck.

Jordan blinked, realizing she was staring a hole through him. She shifted her weight slightly to adjust the camera dangling from her shoulder. "Did... uh, did you say you were inspecting the site?"

With his last milligrams of restraint Cole slipped his hands, palms out, into his back pockets. "Yeah."

"The vandalism you told me about yesterday?"

"Yeah."

"Is everything... all right?"

He shrugged. No need to upset her over the incident he now doubted was minor, or the similar one last night. "It will be."

"I'm glad."

He nodded.

Now what do we talk about, Jordan worried. *The weather? The stock market? The flutter in the pit of my stomach that feels like no less than a thousand butterflies?* Her thumb and index finger nervously worried the thin leather camera strap. "Nice horse," she said inanely.

Holding the reins in one hand, with the other Cole patted the mare's neck, absently stroking the smooth jugular groove. "She's a beauty, isn't she? Belongs to a friend of Sheridan's that owns a spread west of Alma."

"She's lovely."

"Strong, too. Surefooted as a mountain goat, aren't you, beauty?" The soothing, affirming quality in his voice had a predictable effect on the mare. She whinnied softly and nuzzled the owner of the tranquil voice. Cole turned his gaze from the horse to the empty road behind Jordan. His eyes narrowed. "Where's your car?" He dropped the reins and the bay immediately lowered her head and started to nibble the meadow grass.

"My Jeep is down the road." She pointed southward. "Just around that bend."

"Out of sight?"

"Yes, but—"

He stepped closer. "Don't you know you shouldn't go off so far from your transportation?"

"It's not that—"

"This is rough country, and that highway—" he pointed to the empty road "—is hardly bulging with traffic. What if you fell and sprained an ankle, or worse? You might be out here hours before anyone came looking for you." The soothing quality in Cole's voice had vanished completely. Even the mare reacted nervously to the controlled anger barely under the surface of his words.

"It's all right, Cole. I do this sort of thing all the time."

"You shouldn't. Not alone." He took a step closer, then another, his dark eyes burning into Jordan.

In less than the time between heartbeats, her senses were inundated with Cole; the piercing blackness in his eyes, the sheer power of his physical presence, the scent of his subtly enticing cologne mingled with the smell of sunshine, outdoors . . . and danger.

"The world isn't all sun-kissed meadows and cloudless blue skies. It's riddled with decay, and scum who thrive on the worst kind of human degradation." His voice was now cold, flat and frightening. "There are men who would take you from this place and by nightfall you'd be the centerpiece of a white-slavery auction known only to players who use money like you use water. And before sunrise your soft, delectable body would know more about erotic torture than your mind could handle." He inhaled deeply. "My God, you don't have any idea . . ."

Cole stopped himself. More accurately, the look in Jordan's eyes stopped him. Fear. He saw it reflected in her eyes. And something else. He saw himself reflected in those emerald depths. The man he used to be. The man he hated. The man who had betrayed him, left him whimpering in a cold cell, save for the sweet memory of the woman he loved more than life. The man who had so much ugliness locked deep inside his soul, at times it possessed him with the ferocity of the vilest demon from the darkest regions of hell.

The agony in his eyes went through Jordan in one swift, shattering instant, wiping away her fear, obliterating everything but the need to ease his pain. The leather strap slipped unnoticed from her shoulder, down her arm, allowing the camera to settle to the ground. Without realizing her intent, she reached out and touched his cheek, whispering his name.

He caught her hand and held it against his face. Her touch was hot clear to his soul, searing, sealing old wounds, healing. At one point in his life he would gladly have died for just one second of the exquisite joy now flashing through him. He couldn't believe she was real. Here. Now.

But she was real, as real as his need. And from the same netherworld that housed his private demons came the unreasoning, unrelenting, insatiable urge to know, just one more time before he died, the taste, the feel, the hunger of her mouth beneath his. Cole tried to speak, tried to warn her, but the words got tangled with a myriad of emotions past and present, good and bad.

"Need . . . Jordan," he whispered brokenly a split second before his mouth came down on hers. Hard.

He took unqualified possession, demanding unconditional surrender. His tongue invaded her mouth, forcing her to accept his possession, forcing her to capitulate to the desperation that flowed through his body like quicksilver. His arms closed around her, crushing any resistance, bringing her body full against his.

Jordan couldn't have resisted if she wanted to. And she didn't want to. Nor was she afraid. Opening her lips, welcoming his raid on her mind and body, she felt a shudder of desire go through him, felt more than heard the groan that started deep in his chest, felt and responded to the flame that had never been extinguished. Not by time, not by pain.

Like a rainstorm in the desert, the kiss was violent and thunderous...awesome in its intensity. And it went on. And on. And on. Until anger and desperation spent itself, dissolving, sliding, slowly transforming into a hunger that was softer, deeper and in its way more demanding than the intensity could ever be.

Cole's arms shifted subtly, giving her just enough freedom to pull away if she wanted to. She didn't. What she wanted was more. More of him. More of them, together. As their tongues caressed, she made soft little sounds of pleasure.

Those tiny cries brought Cole crashing back to reality when nothing else on earth could have. With more strength of will than he thought humanly possible, he curled his fingers around her upper arms and gently but firmly pushed her away.

The raggedness of their breathing testified to how close Cole had come to losing complete control. How close he had come to breaking his promise. That he could have subjected her to the blackness inside him was more than he could bear. He backed away from her.

"Cole?" The sound of his name on her lips, the confusion in her eyes almost ripped him apart. God, what had he done?

"I'm . . . I'm sorry. I had no right to do that."

Rocked to her foundation by the kiss and by her own response to the raging, almost violent and barely contained need, Jordan didn't have a chance to do more than reply honestly. "You did once."

"That was a long time ago."

"It didn't feel like a long time ago," she said, displaying a courage she might otherwise have questioned. "It felt more like moments ago instead of years."

"Too many moments." He shook his head. "A lifetime ago."

"You weren't always so—"

He cut her off. "I'm not the same man you knew four years ago."

Jordan saw the change in Cole, saw the anger and coldness. She heard the change in his voice from soft to harsh determination.

For a fleeting moment she thought his attitude might have something to do with his accident. Maybe he didn't feel his body was as agile, or even as attractive as it once had been. But the thought was quickly dismissed. The man she had known would never allow a physical disability to alter his self-confidence, would never wallow in self-pity. No, he wasn't the same man. The man she had known was more centered, less cynical. This man who was a stranger, yet achingly familiar, had been wounded in some way that transcended the mere physical. He was adept at hiding the change, but then she suspected he was good at hiding a lot about himself, particularly his past and his pain.

"Things...happen," Jordan said, thinking of the changes in her own life, specifically Fancy. "People change."

When Cole looked at her, some of the darkly haunted shadows had faded from his eyes. "You haven't. Except that you're more beautiful."

Heat flushed her body and she glanced away. "I wasn't fishing for a compliment."

"I never thought you were. You're not the kind of woman who plays word games."

Jordan's gaze met his. "What...what kind of woman am I?"

"Honest. You're the only woman I've ever felt I could trust."

His words hit Jordan like a hammer blow to her heart. She almost stopped breathing. If only he knew just how *dishonest* she had been. If only he knew how much her lie could affect his life.

"Don't pin any medals on me," she insisted. "I worked in a newsroom too long to believe in fairy tales or white hats."

"But you never allowed it to impugn your integrity."

"In the news business you live or die by charisma, not integrity."

"All the more reason to discard it as excess baggage. You didn't."

This talk of honesty and integrity was grating on her nerves and gnawing on her conscience. "How can you be so sure *I'm* the same woman you knew before?"

He wanted to say her body, her lips, everything that deemed her woman to his man told more in one kiss than a million words ever could. He wanted to say if they both lived to be one hundred that *telling* would never change, no matter what. He wanted to say all the words she would like to hear and deserved to hear, but he couldn't. Instead he simply replied, "Instinct."

Every ounce of Jordan's conscience was practically screaming for her to tell him the truth, but how did she explain that she lacked enough guts to face raising the child of a man she supposedly loved more than life, without the self-serving facade of a make-believe husband and father? Where was all the honesty and courage he admired so much when she discovered she was pregnant with his child? Even if he had vanished from her life, did that justify her lie? Her mind spun crazily. Tell him. Don't tell him. Was she right or wrong? All she knew for certain was, that even though she might have lost his love, she couldn't live with his hate. And hate her he would if he ever learned the truth.

Nervously Jordan retrieved the camera, slung the strap onto her shoulder and took a step back. "Sometimes instinct can be misleading," she said flatly, needing desperately to leave.

"Sometimes." Every instinct Cole had was telling him she had made some kind of decision in the past few seconds and that the decision was not in his favor.

"I'm, uh, late for an appointment." She turned to leave.

"Jordan."

She stopped, glanced back. "Yes."

"Don't take any more unnecessary risks."

"I won't," she assured him.

"Promise me."

"I...I promise." She turned and walked off in the direction of her Jeep before he could see the tears sliding unchecked down her cheeks.

Cole watched her walk away and wondered if he would be able to take his own advice. Don't take any unnecessary risks, he had told Jordan. *Then what do you call what just happened? A necessary risk?* For a man who had lived most of his adult years playing in a high-stakes game of life and death, how could a little kiss be so dangerous? But it was. Dangerous and addictive. Dangerous because that one kiss could be the key to unlocking the shackles of his promise, and addictive because a little of Jordan had never satisfied Cole. That addiction was one of the facets of their past relationship that kept the memory of her burning with such fire.

One touch, one kiss had never been enough for either of them. Cole remembered how one brief, delicious brush of his lips over hers was all that was required to stoke a constantly smoldering ember into an out-of-control blaze of passion. It had been so from the first time they kissed, and obviously time had done little toward smothering the flame. The kiss a few moments earlier confirmed what Cole had known in his heart all along and tried to deny, confirmed what he knew was the greatest threat to his promise, yet he was powerless to change.

In his mind, in his heart, Jordan was a fire he couldn't put out.

* * *

For the remainder of the day Jordan existed on a tight wire, balanced between the rebirth of feelings for Cole and the knowledge that those feelings meant certain and abundant pain, if pursued.

At the shop she did her job, or at least gave a good impersonation of being in charge. *What are you doing?* she asked herself, all the while trying to concentrate on work. *You're playing a dangerous game with stakes too high to even contemplate losing.* What if he found out about Fancy and decided to take legal action? A judge might think long and hard about her elaborate story of a fictitious father and her obvious disregard of the child's real father. But she hadn't disregarded Cole; he simply hadn't been there.

If her two other employees, a secretary named Susan and a stringer named Robert, noticed the tension in their boss, they tactfully ignored it. Thankfully a couple of outside assignments kept Barry busy most of the day so she wasn't forced to evade his perceptive gaze. When he finally did return to the shop around five-thirty, she quickly prepared to go home.

"Hey, sugar. What's shakin'?"

"Not much," she replied, placing a completed video onto the shelf marked Delivery.

"You get that promo stuff shot this morning?"

A reminder of her encounter with Cole was the last thing she needed. "Uh, yeah. It's already in process."

"Anything smashing?"

"You know." She shrugged. "Same old blue skies and sun-kissed meadows." Same old broken heart, she could have added.

Barry grinned. "Tough job, but somebody's gotta do it."

"Yeah, well—" Jordan tried not to meet his inquiring gaze "—I promised Fancy we would watch the new Disney video tonight, so I guess I better get a move on."

"Hey, sugar." Barry placed a hand on her arm as she turned to leave. "You okay?"

"I'm fine."

Gently he pulled her around to face him. "Uh-huh, pull my other leg, it's got bells on it."

Jordan's smile was as smooth as she could make it considering it was ninety-percent fake. "You're as big a worry-wart as my grandmother used to be. Why don't you get yourself a girlfriend and exercise your protective tendencies on her?"

"Because most of the women in my life are either former Roller Derby queens or lady wrestlers. Why waste my time? You, on the other hand, underneath all that sharp talk and sassiness, are about as tough as wet tissue paper."

"What are your rates, Doctor?"

"No charge."

"Which only goes to prove advice is worth what you pay for it."

"All right, all right." Barry held up his hands in a feigned gesture of surrender. "I get the message. By the way," he added as she stacked the last of the completed videos on the shelf. "You checked up on the construction?"

Jordan shot him an I-thought-we-agreed-to-let-this-alone look. "No, I haven't." *Nor have I checked up on my feelings about the man who does the checking up.* She almost groaned out loud then. Such convoluted thoughts seemed to be the rule lately rather than the exception, and definitely representative of her state of mind. *What mind?* a tiny voice asked. *You can't stop thinking about Cole Forrester long enough to process Hey Diddle Diddle, much less a higher brain function.* "Give it a rest," she said under her breath.

"Pardon me?"

She glanced up at Barry watching her curiously. "Uh, nothing."

"So then I guess you haven't heard about what's been happening at the construction site?"

"You mean the opened crates and stuff. Just vandals I thought."

His gaze narrowed. "Who told you about the crates?"

"Uh, Mr. Forrester mentioned it in passing."

Barry's eyebrow raised inquiringly. Obviously Forrester wasn't so hung up on his work that he didn't appreciate an attractive woman when he met one. "Getting chummy with the enemy?"

She shot him another warning look. "A few rowdy teenagers does not a destruction force make."

"I hardly think a few rowdy teenagers have the expertise to spike trees or disassemble generators."

Stunned at such disturbing news, she looked at him in disbelief. "Was anyone hurt?"

"Fortunately, no."

"When did it happen?"

He shrugged. "I'm not certain. Yesterday, last night."

No wonder Cole was personally inspecting the site, she thought. And the tension she had noticed was undoubtedly a direct result of the incident.

"Barry, this is terrible. I honestly thought once the project began, the hard-core dissenters would reconcile themselves to the inevitable."

"Hey, they may all look like a handful of lambs, but they're roaring like lions."

"Barry, you aren't..." Jordan danced around the serious question uppermost in her mind, trying not to sound accusatory. "You're not a lamb, are you?"

He grinned. "Don't sorry, sugar. A black sheep maybe, but definitely not a lamb."

Jordan sighed in relief.

"As a matter of fact," he added, "after learning about the sabotage, I've decided you were right."

"Decided to be a lover, not a fighter, huh?"

"Sounds good to me."

"I'm glad. You wouldn't look good in prison stripes."

He screwed up his face in an exaggerated expression of disdain. "Passé, my dear. Black and white is definitely out this year."

Smiling, Jordan propped both hands on her hips. "I'll tell you what's not passé." She pointed to several tapes strewn across the editing table. "Paying the bills."

"Oh, you're so middle-class."

"Hey, at least I've got some."

"Cute, real cute. Now why don't you take your sassy little mouth and your even sassier little butt out of here so I can make more filthy lucre to pay those bills."

"Capital idea."

"Elementary, Lockridge."

Satisfied Barry was back on track as far as his views regarding the outlaw environmentalists were concerned, Jordan collected her handbag and left via the back door.

She had no sooner stepped through the back door of Video Images than Cole stepped through the front.

Strolling in as though gathering information any more dangerous than the time of day was the farthest thing from his mind, Cole walked straight to where Barry stood behind a counter. "Is Jordan in?"

"She's gone for the day, Mr. Forrester. Can I help you?" Barry asked coolly.

"No. Thanks." Cole eyed the other man. "Have we met?"

"Barry Clark. I'm a personal friend of Jordan's." The emphasis on the word *personal* grated on Cole's nerves. The two men did not exchange handshakes.

Cole glanced around the shop. "And an employee?"

"Associate." After a pause, Barry added, "Would you like to leave a message?"

Having already discovered Jordan's phone number was unlisted, Cole said, "I suppose you wouldn't consider giving me her home number, would you?"

"You suppose right." Determined the big man could turn to stone before he allowed him to make a play for Jordan, Barry said, "We don't give out our employees' numbers. Company policy, you understand."

"Completely." Regardless of what Jordan had said, Cole wasn't sure Clark considered her "only a friend." He was as protective as a she-bear, and the thought sent another bolt of jealousy flashing through Cole.

Barry leaned his hip against the counter separating them. "By the way, sorry to hear you're having problems out at the site."

"You're well informed."

"I try to be. Spiking trees is nasty business. A chain saw blade hits one of those babies, and you can kiss your butt goodbye."

"Know much about lumberjacking, Mr. Clark?"

Barry's gaze narrowed. "I know a little about a lot of things."

Cole nodded, his smile smooth, affable...deceptive. "I'm sure you do."

"So." Barry crossed his arms over his chest. "Have you caught the guy responsible?"

"What makes you think only one person is involved? Or for that matter, male?"

Barry's shoulders raised in an ever-so-slight shrug. "Figure of speech. But you have to admit it seems unlikely a woman would have the kind of strength hammering spikes requires."

Obviously Clark was fishing, but Cole wasn't about to rise to the bait. "I've learned never to underestimate the so-called weaker sex, Mr. Clark."

"Yeah. I guess with your background you've probably learned not to trust anyone."

Cole's smile never wavered. "You do know a little, don't you?"

"Hey, you know what they say about knowledge—"

"Yes. A little is a dangerous thing," Cole finished for him.

Barry smiled back. "Yeah."

The two men fell silent, staring, the level of thinly veiled animosity almost palpable. Finally Cole broke eye contact, deliberately taking a half step back. Otherwise he made no move to leave. Instead he casually gazed around the shop. The ploy was an old but effective one, giving his opponent the impression he had backed away from the pseudo-confrontation while he prepared a counterattack. In this case, allowing Clark to think he had won a round, then asking a quick question he might have otherwise answered guardedly.

"So, how long have you been involved with saving the planet?"

"Not long enough."

"About the same amount of time you've known Jordan?"

"A little less."

"But no less adamantly."

"I put my money where my mouth is, if that's what you're asking."

Irritated that Clark had more or less evaded his little snare, Cole decided the game had lost its charm. "Speaking of money, Jordan appears to be doing very well."

Barry, too, must have grown weary of the verbal sparring because he looked Cole in the eye and said, "Look, Mr. Forrester, I appreciate the fact that you've got a job to do, but if you want information about Jordan, politically or personally, you'll just have to go to the source."

"You think I'm interested in Jordan because of her connection with the ecology group?"

"Partly."

"And otherwise?"

"You're not blind or stupid as far as I can tell."

"Does that bother you . . . my being *interested* in Jordan?"

"Let's just say she's been through a lot and I'd hate to see her hurt any more."

Cole wondered how much Jordan had revealed about their past relationship. "You must have known her for quite some time."

"We knew each other causally when we worked at the same TV station in Louisiana. When she started Video Images I saw a good opportunity and came looking for a job."

"Lucky for her."

"Hey, the luck swings both ways," Barry said sincerely. "I needed a change in my life. Some clean, fresh air and a new perspective."

"And what did Jordan get in the bargain?"

Barry straightened, his gaze boring into Cole. "A shoulder to lean on. And nothing more. She'd just lost her husband and the last thing she needed was—"

"Husband?"

Barry's smile was several degrees past smug at seeing the stunned expression on Cole's face. "Well, it appears you're not as well informed as you thought, Forrester. Your back-

ground check on Jordan obviously has a gaping hole in it.''
Barry leaned across the counter, targeting his words. "Her
husband died right before she moved to Colorado. And a
short time later her daughter was born.''

Chapter 5

"She...she has a daughter?"

"A pint-size version of her mother."

For long moments Cole stared at Barry Clark as if he had just announced the world was coming to an end. Which, in fact, from Cole's suddenly unsteady perspective, was a distinct possibility. The end of the world. His world. A world he had lived in since the first time they made love. A world where Jordan burned like a fire, not only in his memory but in his every thought, conscious or not.

A husband. A child.

No matter how many times he had told himself Jordan had gone on with her life and rightfully so, deep in his secret heart lurked the hope that she had clung to his memory as he had hers. Obviously he had hoped in vain. She had married, carried another man's child and...Cole closed his eyes to combat the wave of gut-wrenching pain surging over him at the thought of Jordan in the arms of someone else, Jordan holding another man's baby to her breast.

"How long?"

"Look, Forrester—"

"How long has she been a widow?"

Something in Cole's voice, some resonance of emotion Barry couldn't quite label but recognized as much more serious than idle curiosity, urged him to answer. "Three or so years, I don't keep track of dates. All I know for certain is that the guy was already dead by the time I showed up. She was hurt, scared and very pregnant. She needed a friend and I needed a job."

A suspicion at the back of Cole's mind worked its way into a series of nagging questions and suppositions. Time was the key. How long did it take Jordan to go from his arms straight into her new lover's bed and bear him a child? Or had she lied when she said there was no other man in her life? And if she hadn't lied, why would she marry someone else almost as soon as he left on assignment? Cole racked his brain. Why would she tell him she loved him, then turn to someone else? Either she lied or...

Something kept tapping at his memory. Something Jordan said. What was it? *I looked for you.* Why would she look for Cole if she had another man on the string? An idea, faint and scarcely believable, formed at the back of Cole's mind. Had she searched in order to tell him something? Something extremely important? What if... Was it even possible? Dear God, what if the child was his!

Cole swallowed hard trying to withstand the anticipation creeping into his consciousness. His heart was beating so fast he knew a second or two of genuine concern that it might drum right through his skin. "How old is the child?"

"Barely three, I think."

Against all reason Cole's heart sank. First-grade math could have told him the child wasn't, couldn't be his. Their time together had been four years ago.

Regardless of how hard he tried to convince himself the events of the past must remain in the past, the present was awash with an unbearable sense of loss. Recriminations swamped him. If only there had been enough time to say goodbye. If only he had told her enough of the truth for her to understand and wait. He had vowed to stay out of her life, and that vow wasn't in jeopardy. He should be relieved. There could be nothing to tie her to him. He should be glad.

Then why did he feel as though Fate had just kicked him in the teeth?

"Like I said, Forrester, if you want to know about Jordan, ask her. She doesn't lie and she wouldn't know subterfuge if it walked up and smacked her in the face. But she does believe in dealing with people and situations head-on, so don't be surprised if she tells you it's none of your business and to go to hell." His warning delivered, Barry ended the conversation by leaving a stunned Cole standing at the counter by himself.

Cole didn't remember leaving Video Images. He didn't even remember getting in his car and heading toward Fairplay. The only thing he remembered was the pain, hot and deep, scoring his heart. And the rage. Mirroring his thunderous mood the summer sky grew dark and angry in preparation for a storm.

The pain stayed with him past the outskirts of Breckenridge, almost to the top of Hoosier Pass. The rage overruled the pain, sending Cole dangerously close to the outer edge of control.

She lied to him.

And he had lain in her soft, willing arms and believed every deceitful word. He could almost hear her whispering to him in the heat of passion. *No one's ever made me feel*

this way, Cole. There'll never be another man for me. Ever.
God, what a fool he'd been.

Unmindful of the impending thunderstorm as he drove,
he yanked up his car-phone receiver, punched in a number
and asked, no demanded, that his secretary access the pro-
files on all members of the Park County Ecological Society, one member in particular. He wanted Jordan's address
and he wasn't above using his resources to get it.

Any armchair psychologist could have calmly informed
Cole that the flip side of his fear and pain was anger, and
given enough time he would be able to view the situation
rationally. But he wasn't in the mood for calmly offered
advice or, for that matter, for rational viewpoints. His or
anyone else's. What he wanted was an old-fashioned, one-
on-one, nose-to-nose confrontation, and nothing less would
satisfy him. What he wanted was revenge.

Fortunately the half-hour drive forced him to cool his
temper, plus his secretary didn't retrieve Jordan's home address and phone number until he drove into the little
mountain town. Even though the wait had taken some of the
edge off his anger, Cole never even considered calling before heading for Jordan's house.

Finished with their evening meal, Jordan left the dishes
in favor of some playtime with her daughter. The preschool
Fancy attended three days out of the week had escorted all
of the students on a trip to the Denver Zoo that morning,
and if Fancy was any example, there were a bunch of happily tired youngsters tonight. She had been treated with an
almost nonstop account of every animal, every sound they
made and everything they did since the minute she walked
through the door, not once but twice. Now Fancy, her
tummy full, bathed, dressed for bed and cuddled next to

Jordan on the sofa, yawned in the middle of her favorite bedtime story.

"That's it, young lady, Sandman time for you."

"Pleeeaase, Mommy, just—" another yawn "—one more story."

Jordan laughed softly, kissed the top of Fancy's head and said, "You wouldn't last long enough to make it past 'Once upon a time.' Tell you what." She hugged the sweet-smelling holder of her heartstrings. "You carry Winky and I'll carry you upstairs."

"Okee, dokee." Fancy collected her clown and tumbled into her mother's arms.

After the nightly brushing of teeth and last potty stop came prayers. Kneeling together, heads bowed, Jordan listened as Fancy recited her memorized bedtime prayer, then went into her "Blessings."

"God bless Mommy. And Jill. And Barry. God bless all the sick peoples and all the am-menuls in the zoo. And all the kids in my school."

"And," Jordan urged.

"All the plants and flowers. And..." Fancy paused when a roll of thunder filled the night. "God bless kitties and keep them from getting wet." The last was said as she scrambled into bed and pulled the covers up to her chin.

Looking down at the wide-eyed, well-you-can't-blame-me-for-trying innocence on her daughter's face, it took all of Jordan's willpower not to laugh. "Good night, my little manipulator."

"What's a nipa...gater?"

Jordan gave up and smiled broadly. "A little girl with red curls and a softhearted mother. Now go to sleep." Several kisses and "sleep tights" later, Jordan was making her way downstairs, wondering how she was going to be able to hold out against Fancy's sneak attacks in the kitten-or-not-to-kitten war, when a knock sounded at her front door. When she glanced through one of the curtainless, floor-to-ceiling sidelights flanking the door, her heart almost skipped a beat. Her visitor was the last person she expected to see standing on her porch, and the look on his face was as threatening as the storm-black sky.

Jordan opened the door. "Cole?" she said, more than a little apprehensive after their encounter that morning.

"May I come in?" Without waiting for a response, he stormed past her, making her polite reply unnecessary.

Cole came to a halt in the middle of the living room, his back to her, and for a second he thought he must be reliving another memory. The comfortably rustic and South-west-flavored interior of the cabin was almost exactly as she had once described her dream house. A picture flashed across his mind of the two of them sharing their dreams just as they had shared their bodies. His hands momentarily knotted into fists at his sides, then he forced himself to relax.

Nervously, she glanced at the stairway. *Thank God Fancy was fast asleep.* "Would you like some coffee or perhaps a soft drink?"

"Nothing, thank you."

His voice could have been chipped to serve in the soft drink she had offered, and the only appropriate label for his body language was hostile, the essence of coldness.

"Is there a particular reason for this visit?" Jordan asked, feeling a bit frosty herself. He had been running hot and cold ever since the moment their paths had crossed again, and she was sick and tired of the seesaw ride. Tempted to tell him to hit the road, she hesitated only because, despite the expensively tailored suit and designer tie, he had the look of a man who had just rolled up his sleeves in preparation for a dirty job.

"Yes." He turned to face her and felt as if the rug had been jerked from beneath his feet. As he stared at her, some of his anger and the last vestiges of his self-designed protection, slipped from his grasp like steam from a tea kettle.

Dressed in hunter-green leggings and a matching oversize sweatshirt that had slipped precariously off one smooth, bare shoulder, her hair loosely piled atop her head and secured with a wide tortoiseshell barrette, she looked forest cool and serene, almost regal despite the casualness of her outfit. And more beautiful than any mere mortal woman had a right to be.

Suddenly Cole knew he had made a fatal mistake. *What the hell do you think you're doing here? So she met someone else and moved on. So through all those months of torture her memory kept you going. So what? The world doesn't stop for one battered ex-agent. You didn't want revenge. You wanted another chance.*

"Cole?"

Regardless of his real reason for showing up on her doorstep, now he had to know if she had been happy. Maybe then he could walk away from her the way he should have from the first. Maybe. Besides, after what he had done, who was he to point the finger at Jordan?

"I...I dropped by your shop this afternoon, but you had already gone."

Jordan couldn't believe he had stomped into her home and was now making small talk. "I had some errands to run and I wanted to be here—" She stopped herself before she could say, *when Fancy got home.* "For a delivery I was expecting."

"I met one of your employees. Barry Clark."

"Yes."

"He, uh, seems to know you pretty well."

A frown marred her otherwise smooth forehead. What had Barry told him? What kind of information had Cole and his undoubtedly expert techniques managed to wheedle out of Barry?

"I told you. We're good friends. Barry and I—"

"He said you were a widow."

Jordan froze.

"Is it true?"

Jordan opened her mouth to speak, but no sound came out. She simply stared at Cole, all the while racking her brain trying to figure out what damaging information, no matter how scant, Barry might have given Cole.

"Is it?" he demanded more sharply than he intended.

Here's your chance to wipe the slate clean. What are you waiting for? Stop living a lie.

"Yes," she finally whispered, courage failing her.

Cole clenched and unclenched his fists, the anger he so easily relinquished moments earlier now coiling in the pit of his stomach like a rattlesnake preparing to strike. *Let go of the past,* he told himself, at the same time wondering how he would accomplish that feat since it appeared the past was all he had left.

"And you had . . . have a child?"

Jordan's heart nearly shot out of her body. *Oh, please, no.* She tried to swallow her fear but couldn't. Unable to trust her voice, she nodded.

"Did he make you happy, Jordan?"

The question was so totally unexpected she almost cried out her astonishment. He believed her story just like everyone else had! Part of her was giddy with relief, while another part was shocked and angry that he believed she could move so easily from one man's bed to another. And if he believed her now, did he think she had lied to him before?

"Not in the way you think," she said, skirting the truth.

Cole's expression darkened.

"He, uh, gave me something I desperately needed. Something I could trust."

"Security. Love," he said, his voice ragged with emotion. All the things he hadn't be able to give her.

"A baby." Every word she spoke was the truth, yet twisted. In the back of her mind, the shadowy form of her make-believe husband had always been Cole, regardless of whether or not she recognized him. And Cole *had* given her the one thing she needed above all else. Part of himself. "I made him a part of my life for all the wrong reasons." *My pain. My loneliness,* she silently added. "But it turned out right."

"I'd be the biggest hypocrite that ever lived if I said I was glad." *Hypocrite is right. Standing here asking for answers you know cut deeper than sin while what you really want is to shake her until her teeth rattle in her head for lying to you.*

"Why are you doing this, Cole?" Jordan finally found enough gumption to ask. "Why are you dredging up things that serve no purpose—"

"I don't know," he said, his expression tight, strained.

"Then maybe you should just go." Feeling battered and bruised, Jordan moved toward the door.

Her words hit Cole like kerosene splashed on smoldering embers. Maybe it was the pain of learning she had been with another man. Maybe it was remembering all the days and nights of holding on to a memory that now wasn't even his exclusive property. Whatever the reason, Cole ignited. Rage poured out of him like the rain pouring out of the lightning-streaked sky outside.

"You'd like that wouldn't you? Then you wouldn't have to face your conscience, face the fact that you went from one man's bed straight into another's."

Jordan turned and frowned at him, the venom in his words lighting the fuse to her own temper. The irony, the absolute ridiculousness of the situation, made her want to scream in frustration. He bought the lie about her and another lover and in doing so automatically assumed she had lied before. In some weird, crazy way, she supposed it all made sense, but for the life of her she couldn't get far enough past her own resentment to see the logic. Fear or no fear, as far as she was concerned he was the last person on earth entitled to righteous indignation.

Head-to-head, lie to lie, memory to memory, this was the confrontation they had danced around from day one. This was the showdown they should have had four years ago, and it had all the makings of a real doozy. To her credit, Jordan took one last shot at avoiding the inevitable.

"I think you should leave before we both say things we might regret."

"No regrets. Wasn't that what you told me the first night we made love?"

Low blow, Jordan thought. She reeled from the impact of his words, but was prepared to give as good as she got. "That was before I knew who you were instead of who I thought you were."

"There were reasons—"

"The reason was you didn't trust me. My God," she said, her voice almost breaking. "You didn't even trust me enough to tell me your real name."

"So you fell into bed with the first guy who came along?"

All of the color drained from Jordan's face. Outside, lightning slashed across the night sky like a rapier cutting through black velvet, ripping through the darkness the same way his words ripped through her heart.

"Go to hell," she said.

"I've been there."

"Too bad it was a round trip."

"Who said it was?"

She jerked her head toward the door. "Get out."

The weight of the past, present and future, focused on this one moment in time, bore down on Cole, driving him relentlessly toward either a peace of mind that had so far eluded him or a total madness. And somehow the passion to find that end got all mixed up with his passion for Jordan and an overwhelming need for her to understand why he couldn't deal with the lies, why he couldn't deal with losing her. He wanted everything he'd lost. He wanted her.

"Not until you understand." His words were serrated, edged in pain.

"I understand you've decided to sit in judgment. The honorable Judge Cole, handing down verdicts based on the law according to Forrester. Well, thanks but no thanks, Your Honor, if it's all the same to you, I'll take hard labor, or better still, thirty days solitary confinement."

"You wouldn't last thirty minutes," Cole said tersely. He turned away, but not before Jordan saw the raw, undisguised agony etched across his face as he added, "And you have no concept of what *solitary* means."

"Oh, and I suppose you do. I suppose you're the expert on facing the world alone. Then tell me what it feels like to wake up one morning and discover the person you've given your heart to has vanished," Jordan said, her voice resonating with anger. "Tell me what it's like to search for that person until you think you'll go insane or drop dead from exhaustion, then to be told he doesn't even exist. Tell me, Cole, what it's like to ask yourself if living is worth the pain."

"You'd be surprised what some people will endure just to go on living. You'd be surprised what *you* might do to stay alive."

"This morning you told me that you weren't the same man I knew four years ago. Well, you're right. The man I knew had joy and compassion. The man I knew lived life on his own terms."

Cole whirled around to face her. Two strides brought him to within inches of where she stood, the look in his eyes more violent than the storm raging outside. "The man you knew spent twenty-one months in hell while they shredded his mind, one...thin...strip at a time." As they had that morning, his fingers curled around her upper arms, only now he almost lifted her off the floor. "The man you knew sold his soul. Yes," he said, his voice hoarse, his words puffs of anger-tinged air against her face, "I know what it's like to be totally, completely, irrevocably *alone*. And you know what kept me going, Jordan?" he asked, giving her slender body a shake. "I could deal with the solitude, the pain, as long as I could hold on to your memory. To the most honest, *untainted* thing in my life. And now..." He shook her again, harder this time. "And now, and now—" Cole stopped, halted by the single tear sliding down her pale cheek. He stared into her eyes, and as he had that very morning, saw his own reflection in those tear-filled emerald depths. Not the man he had been, but the man he had become. Lost. Utterly, hopelessly lost. Blind to the only road out of the darkness and back into the light.

But he wasn't alone in this sightless self-imposed dungeon. Jordan was there, too. They had lied to each other, and worse, they had lied to themselves.

"Oh, God, what have we done to each other?" His voice raspy with emotion, Cole crushed her against him, holding her, needing her. "What have we done?"

"Don't," she sobbed against his shirtfront, her arms instinctively encircling his waist. What they had done to each other was unfair and unreasonable but not unforgivable.

Even as the thought was born in Jordan's mind, she knew it was true. For so long she had blamed Cole for lying, leaving and never coming back. And now to realize he hadn't been able to come back was a jolt of harsh reality. And thinking of him holding her memory close while he suffered, shattered her heart.

Slowly she raised on tiptoe and placed her tear-dampened lips, ever so softly, ever so gently on his, all the anger she had hoarded like a miser now spent without any concern for emotional bankruptcy. She didn't want it anymore. She had closed her account the instant her lips touched his.

"Jordan...Jordan," Cole whispered into her mouth, his moments-ago savagery now erased by her simple act of understanding. He kissed her mouth softly, delicately demanding. Then his tongue touched hers, filling her mouth as he wanted to fill her body. More, he wanted more.

Jordan felt as if she were aflame, and she made a small sound of frustration and hunger at the back of her throat, wondering how much more she could take. Wondering how far her hunger would take her. She forgot about the lies, the anger. She forgot about the missing years and the pain—his and hers. All she remembered was that no other man had ever, would ever touch her soul the way Cole did.

With a low moan she pressed her body closer to his, and still she wasn't close enough. She needed to feel his skin next to her, flame to flame, need to need.

Oh God, how he needed her. How he wanted her in all the ways he remembered and more. "Please don't let this be another dream," he pleaded. "Tell me I'm not dreaming." His hands stroked her body from her collarbone to her hips, then slipped beneath the hem of the sweatshirt, stayed, caressed and pressed her against the hot, hard length of his arousal. "Tell me."

"You're not dreaming," she said breathlessly, eagerly accepting the tiny flashes of fire as his tongue licked her lips.

"Thank God," he whispered, kissing the softness of her ear, the satin skin of her neck. "Thank God." He returned to explore again the silky heat of her mouth, stroking, coaxing, demanding in a thousand ways to make up for the thousands of moments like this that they had missed. When his fingers closed around the fullness of her breasts Jordan sighed against his mouth.

"Cole . . . Cole . . ."

"Mommy?"

Jordan and Cole shot apart instantly.

"Mommy?" said a sleepy-eyed Fancy from the bottom of the stairs. "I heard mad voices."

Jordan hurried to the stairs and gathered the child into her arms. "Oh, sweetheart, I'm sorry we woke you up. Here," she said, scooping the little girl up in her arms. "Mommy will carry you back to bed. Then I'll tuck you and Winky in all nice and snug, and I promise no more mad voices, okay?"

"Okee, dokee." The last word was smothered against her mother's shoulder. Little eyelids drooped, then closed as the two disappeared from sight.

"I . . . I'm sorry," Jordan said a few minutes later, returning to the living room.

Hands thrust deep into his pants pockets, Cole stood in front of the clear doors that opened onto the very spot on the deck where occasionally Jordan moon-watched. He turned at the sound of her voice.

"Is she all right?"

"Fine. She was asleep again before her head hit the pillow." A hundred times more nervous than she had been at her first on-camera interview, Jordan fidgeted with the hem of her sweatshirt. "I, uh, I love this cabin, but one of its major flaws is that sound travels up those stairs like a direct hookup from Mountain Bell.''

Cole longed to tell her how much he had wanted to ask to see the child. And how much he didn't. The brief glimpse of dark red curls and an angelic face pressed against her mother's shoulder hadn't been enough and yet almost too much. How was he going to react the first time he came face-to-face with the child of a man who had touched Jordan as he had, made love to her as he had?

No, Cole thought. *The child notwithstanding, no man has ever loved her the way I have, just as no woman has ever touched my soul the way she has.*

"I hope she wasn't frightened."

Jordan shook her head. "I can't say the same for her mother."

"Or me," he smiled crookedly, striving for balance after the turmoil of the past half hour. "Jordan, what just happened—"

"Needed to happen." She had blamed Cole for too long. It wasn't his fault, not completely. Like an immature child, she had loaded him down with all her dreams and all her expectations, along with her love. And he had taken what she so *freely* offered. No strings, no regrets.

He glanced away briefly. "You're right. I just never thought it would. And I sure as hell never expected it to end the way it did."

Her slow, sweet sigh told him she, too, had been caught unsuspecting.

"Where do we go from here?" he asked softly.

"I don't know. I'm almost afraid to think beyond this moment."

He nodded. "But I don't think we can avoid the future the way we have the past."

"No, we can't," she said, thinking about Fancy.

Lacing his fingers with hers, he led her to the front door. Warm, strong hands framed her face. "I only know one thing. I've been living in a prison of my own making and tonight I felt free for the first time in almost four years." He brushed her lips ever so lightly, then left.

Jordan stared at the closed door, knowing in her heart she would never know complete freedom until Cole knew the truth about Fancy. The question was, did she have enough strength to set them all free?

Hours later Jordan tossed and turned, the sleep she so desperately needed evading her like an elusive wisp of smoke. Outside, the night was black, wet and dismal. Inside, she was equally depressed. A part of her wished Cole would go away and never come back, and a part of her wanted to run to him and beg him not to leave, ever.

Cole was right. They couldn't avoid the future the way they had the past. But what did the future hold? *Age-old question. Too bad you don't know a reliable psychic. Or maybe you could get your own crystal ball.* What she needed was to be honest with Cole and end this tension, but that meant confessing he was Fancy's father, and she couldn't quite bring herself to do that yet . . . *You're going around in circles. Vicious circles.*

The word *vicious* brought to mind the depth of Cole's anger. Jordan had honestly been stunned by the tightly leashed, awesome power of the man who had held her tonight. And by the tortured soul she had seen so closely linked to that power. It was as if Cole were two men, one enraged at the hand life had dealt him, and the other too wounded to defend himself. The angry Cole provided perfect protection for the wounded Cole. And which Cole was the man she had loved? Both? Neither?

She knew only one certainty. When he kissed her, touched her, it didn't matter which Cole he was. All that mattered was the way he made her feel. Alive. More alive than she had been in four long years.

Chapter 6

"Got a minute, sugar?"

Jordan glanced up from the monthly balance sheets as Barry, fresh from a late-afternoon assignment, sauntered into her office and helped himself to a seat. "You can have five."

"Big spender. But, hey, when do I ever walk away from a freebie."

She smiled, pushed her chair back, clasped her hands together over her head and stretched. "I sleep so good at night knowing I've surrounded myself with first-class professionals." The comment about sleeping well was a bold-faced lie, but she didn't want to tell Barry she had spent most of the night tossing and turning, thinking about Cole. Rolling her shoulders, she worked tension from her upper body.

"Speaking of first-class, how's about you, me and the red-headed Munchkin grab a bite, then catch a flick? We haven't done that in weeks."

"Thanks, Barry, but not tonight. I've got two clients scheduled back-to-back in the morning. I don't want to show up looking like the ragged end of nowhere. Need my beauty sleep."

"Never knew anybody who needed it less, but if you feel you can't make it, then hey, we'll do it another time."

"Thanks."

Barry eyed her critically. "Say, sugar, you okay?"

One day and two kisses ago Jordan could have honestly answered yes, but not today. She should have known Barry would see through her pretense of normalcy like reading giant print through tissue paper. To be honest, she was relieved to have someone to talk to other than herself.

"That depends," she said on a sigh.

"On?"

"On whether or not you think getting . . . *involved* the second time around with the same person is dangerous."

"Depends."

"On?" she said, bouncing his words back.

"On how good it was the first time around and why it didn't last."

The sixty-four-thousand-dollar question, Jordan thought.

"I hesitate to ask your definition of involved." Barry arched his eyebrow questioningly. "Are we talking consenting adults, here?"

Jordan had the good grace to blush. "Yes."

"I see," he said, absently toying with a pencil on her desk. "And this guy is somebody you used to know?"

"Yes."

Barry discarded the pencil, walked over to a small table set up with a freshly brewed pot of coffee and the necessary accompaniments, poured himself a cup, then turned to face her. "And I take it you had it pretty bad for this guy the first time around?" he asked.

She nodded, rubbing the back of her neck, worriedly.

"Do I know him?"

Jordan's fingers stilled, her gaze darted away briefly. She had to talk to someone about Cole, and Fancy... and the whole mess her life was in. She glanced at her friend waiting, obviously concerned. "Barry, what would you say if I told you Fancy's father was still alive?"

When he simply stared at her, she hurried to explain. "What would you say if I told you I concocted a fictitious husband for myself and father for Fancy, then sort of conveniently buried him when I decided to grow up and face reality?"

"I'd say this sounds like an old Alfred Hitchcock plot."

"I'm serious, Barry."

Her tone of voice more than the straightforward words convinced him she was indeed serious.

"Then, I guess my first question would be *why?* Were you so afraid the old double standard was still so alive and well, you needed a shotgun wedding even if it was only make-believe?"

"That was part of it. It was also to protect Fancy and... revenge."

"Revenge?"

"Yeah," she admitted, slightly ashamed of herself. Now that she had actually voiced the truth, it sounded so petty and embarrassing. "It's no wonder the Bible says, 'Vengeance is mine, saith the Lord.' He's the only one who can pull it off without it coming back to bite him in the rear."

"You lost me."

"Fancy's father left without a word, and I assumed the worst of course—that he didn't love me and never had. I could have gone through the pregnancy as a single woman, but I wanted to punish him for lying to me and for leaving. So I replaced him with a fictional man, and in some way I thought the punishment fitting. Just wiped him out of my life and put a wonderful fabrication in his place. Sounds crazy, doesn't it?''

"Not if this guy hurt you."

"We hurt each other," Jordan said.

"Then why the hell are you even considering a second ride on the merry-go-round?"

"Because I believe he lied to me all those years ago because he *couldn't* tell me who he was or where he was going. He didn't even have a choice of whether he could go or stay. He had to go. He didn't leave me because he wanted to, but because he *had* to."

"And now this guy has walked back into your life and decided he wants to be a husband and a daddy?"

"Not exactly."

"Don't tell me, let me guess. He doesn't want kids. He can't commit—"

"I don't know. I mean, the subject hasn't come up."

"Hasn't come up? You mean you haven't told him he's her father?"

"No."

"Why, for God's sake?"

"It's . . . complicated. And there are other considerations."

"Such as?"

Jordan gnawed her bottom lip. "Such as who he is."

"Who is he?"

"Cole Forrester."

Barry's coffee cup halted halfway to his mouth. Carefully he lowered the cup, steadying it with both hands. "You got anything stronger than coffee stashed away in one of those drawers?" he asked, motioning to the bank of file cabinets along the opposite wall.

Jordan had to smile. "Sorry. No liquor license."

"Damn shame," Barry mumbled. Then he walked to the chair he had vacated earlier and plopped onto the thinly padded seat.

"I know you're shocked."

"Who, me? Shocked? Whatever gave you such a ridiculous idea? Hey, in all the time I've known you, you've never dated anybody except at an occasional business-related function when you couldn't sucker me into a tux. You pretend you had a husband, then you kill him off. When Forrester shows up, you never even *mention* the fact that he just happens to be the father of your child, to me or to him, for that matter. Shocked? How can you even ask?"

"I told you it was complicated."

"Complicated? Sugar, alongside this situation, war in the Middle East looks like a bunch of Scouts playing Capture The Flag." Barry took a sip of his coffee, then shook his head. "To top it all off, your ex-lover—he is ex, isn't he? You said, involved, I mean, you aren't..."

"No, we aren't."

"To top it all off, your ex-lover is the enemy."

"Cole is not the enemy. And I wish you'd stop thinking of him as such."

"Well, you can't expect me to think of him as my bosom buddy," Barry retorted. "He's thinking sabotage, and my name is probably at the top of his list."

Jordan had no sooner walked into the shop that morning when her second in command had begun to relate the details of his encounter with Cole. Despite Barry's agitation, she had been convinced the questions were not singularly directed at him, and she said so now.

"Cole was only doing his job."

"Great! Now you're defending him."

"No, I just . . ." she raked back a wayward curl that had drooped low on her forehead. "Oh, God, this is such a mess."

"So, are you going to tell him?"

"I don't know. I want to but—"

"But you're afraid he'll hurt you again."

"Yes. Only this time the pain would be ten times worse. And then there's Fancy to consider. What if I tell Cole and he can't forgive me? What if he decides to fight me for Fancy?"

"Hey, sugar, don't get yourself all worked up. Let's take this one step at a time. To begin with, you obviously still care about the guy, right?"

"Yes. I wish I didn't, but yes."

"Typical female response," he teased, trying to lighten the heaviness of the conversation. "How does he feel about you?"

"I'm not sure," she said, hesitant to read too much into their kiss.

"Great." Barry threw his hands up in the air. "We're back to square one."

"No, we're not," she insisted. "At least I feel better after talking to you. Only a true friend would put up with a crazy woman." She reached over and touched his hand. "Thanks."

"Anytime, sugar." He paused, then asked, "So where do you go from here?"

"I think I'll take your advice and take it one step at a time."

"First step," Barry said, pointing to the telephone sitting on the corner of Jordan's desk. "Call Jill and tell her to make Fancy a grilled cheese sandwich, 'cause I'm taking you to dinner."

"Barry, I don't—"

"That's right, you don't argue with me. Now, you've been doing paperwork most of the day. Jill is perfectly capable of holding down the fort. You have to eat, and it might as well be with me. One other thing. I promise no more discussion about Forrester. You need some downtime, so get up off your rear and let's go."

Deciding it was not only futile to argue but that Barry's plan did sound like just what she needed, Jordan smiled and surrendered. "Don't shoot, I'll go quietly."

On the other side of Breckenridge, Cole slammed the phone down, reminding himself he shouldn't shoot the messenger. Make that messengers. The girl answering the phone at Video Images had politely informed him Ms. Lockridge was gone for the day, then the baby-sitter had just as politely told him Ms. Lockridge was at the office. Cole wondered just where the hell *Ms.* Lockridge could be. He was halfway out the door to look for her when it dawned on him that both of the "messengers" had referred to Jordan as Ms. Lockridge.

Lockridge?

But that was Jordan's maiden name. Why not her married name? Following closely on the heels of that question came several others that were suddenly extremely important to have answered. Who was Jordan's husband? What was his name? Where did he come from and what did he do for a living? Questions Cole could easily acquire the answers to by using the high-tech resources of his company. In fact, at Great Northern, extensive security checks had been done on several of the ecological society's members, so it would be easy to add Jordan's name. If a security check was run, he wouldn't have to deal with the nagging suspicion that something wasn't right about this mysterious husband. Even knowing he could pick up a phone and have his questions answered within hours, Cole hesitated, unable to justify his reason as anything other than personal. Intensely personal. No, there was only one source of the information he desired. Jordan.

But after last night, would she even talk to him? He had acted like a madman, and he wouldn't blame her if she told him to get lost. But he had been so filled with rage at the thought of her marrying another man that he couldn't think straight. Then to learn about the child had almost been too much. His anger had spun out of control. But he had to see her again to apologize, and to get some answers.

The Whale's Tail on Main Street proved to be pleasantly quiet and exactly what Jordan needed. She and Barry talked about the following day's assignments and work in progress. They discussed the possibility of hiring an assistant to help Barry and take up some of the slack since their current work load was so heavy. True to his word, Barry steered the conversation clear of any mention of her concerns about Cole and Fancy.

"I'm glad I let you talk me into coming," she said, finishing a delicious seafood salad.

Barry grinned. "Stick with me, sweetheart," he said, in a very poor Bogart imitation. Abruptly his grin faded, replaced by a decidedly dour expression as he stared over Jordan's shoulder. "I may have to break my promise."

"What promise?"

"The one I made about mentioning your ex-lover." With a nod, he motioned in the direction of his stare. "Looks like it's unavoidable."

Jordan turned and found Cole watching them from across the restaurant. She turned back to Barry, who was staring a hole through Cole. "Ignore him. I doubt he has an interest in us."

"In your dreams. He's heading straight for us."

"Oh, Lord." She waited, hoping Cole's appearance was simply a coincidence, hoping he would pass them by.

"Good evening." The soft, deep timbre of his voice flowed over Jordan like hot fudge sliding over French vanilla ice cream, and a tiny shiver raced up her spine.

"Forrester," Barry acknowledged, curtly.

Jordan didn't need to look up to know he was standing close, at her left shoulder. Very close. "Hello, Cole."

"Enjoy your meal?"

Nor did she need to look up to know Cole wasn't thrilled to find her with Barry; she could hear it in his politely asked question. She could also feel the tension radiating from his body.

"Yeah." Barry's gaze never wavered from Cole's. "We'd ask you to join us, but as you see, we've just finished."

"Good, then you won't mind if I talk to Jordan. Privately."

Barry was halfway out of his seat, before her hand on his arm stopped him. "It's all right."

"You sure?" When she nodded, he said, "I'll wait for you up front."

"No need. I'll be happy to drive Jordan home."

Straightening to his full height, which was considerably less than Cole's, Barry wadded his dinner napkin into a ball and tossed it onto the table. "I'll just bet you would."

The sudden tension in Barry's body told Jordan she had better intercede fast or they might wind up paying for the dinnerware and glasses.

"I have my own car," she stated pointedly.

Barry looked down at her. "You want me to wait, I'll wait." An unspoken but understood addition to the message was clear: And if Forrester doesn't like it, he can take a flying leap.

"Thanks, Barry, but there's no need for you to wait. I'll be fine."

Barry shot Cole a scathing look as he left the table.

"That's some watchdog."

"I told you—"

"He's a good friend," Cole finished, taking the chair Barry had vacated.

"He's my best friend, and I don't appreciate the way you treat my friends."

"Sorry, but I needed to talk to you."

Suddenly an unsettling thought crossed her mind. Perhaps coincidence had nothing to do with Cole's appearance at the restaurant. "Have you been following us?"

"I couldn't care less what Clark does." *Except of course, when he does anything with you.*

The coldness in his voice was unexpected, and Jordan found herself automatically responding in kind. "So you've been following *me.*"

"In a town with less than a thousand people and only a handful of restaurants, it wasn't difficult to find you."

"Particularly for a man with your background."

After last night, she had not expected their next meeting to be moonlight and roses, but neither did she expect the encounter would hold traces of Cole's previous coldness.

"I need to ask you some questions."

Feeling the need to regain some of the ground they had won last night, Jordan added softly, "You know me better than anyone. What could you possibly need to ask?"

"Why you're still using your maiden name."

Jordan's heartbeat shot into overtime. "My business," she answered, her voice considerably calmer than she felt. "My reputation as a news journalist goes hand in hand with the work I do now. Starting a new career, a new business, I felt I needed all the help I could get, so I use Lockridge as sort of a professional name." Thank the Lord, this was not the first time this situation had come up, or she might have been blindsided by Cole's question.

A logical answer, but he still wasn't completely satisfied. "So—" Cole smiled, remembering the tough make-it-on-my-own woman that had won his heart. "You'd rather be known as Ms. Lockridge than Mrs..." He waited for her to fill in the blank.

"I'd rather be just exactly who I am. A hardworking businesswoman with a child to raise."

Her response was so straightforward, so like the Jordan he had fallen in love with, Cole's heart turned over. Obviously she had sailed over an emotional hurdle he had never been able to clear. She was, at least for the most part, able to put her past behind her.

"Your husband must have been one of those liberated, understanding men."

"He was." She smiled. *As liberated and understanding as my vivid imagination could make him.*

"And one lucky man."

Suddenly the fragile intimacy they had achieved last night was reestablished, making Cole wish they were someplace less public. They stared at each other for long moments, until finally Jordan spoke.

"Was that all?"

"What?"

"Your questions."

"I have a confession to make. I could have simply called, but I...wanted to see you."

"Then I have a confession, too," Jordan said softly. "I'm glad you came looking for me. And Cole..."

"Yes?"

"Someday I'll tell you all about my husband. I'll answer all your questions, but for now let's give the past a rest and ourselves a break.'' She reached across to gently touch his hand, and a second later their fingers intertwined.

Cole had never appreciated her honesty as much as he did at that very moment, and he was grateful he had not included her in the list recommending security checks. Perhaps it was better not to know so much about the man he envied beyond imagining. Perhaps it *was* time to give the past a rest.

"Last night I asked you where do we go—"

"Go," Jordan said, suddenly glancing at her watch. "Oh, good grief. Cole, I'm so sorry, but I've got to go home. Jill will be wondering what on earth has happened to me."

"Your daughter?"

"No, Jill Dobson, my sitter," she explained, collecting her purse and pushing back her chair at the same time. "She's the ninth wonder of the world as far as I'm concerned, but she'll have my head for not calling."

"I'd like to meet her."

"Who, Jill?"

"No, your daughter."

His request stopped Jordan dead in her tracks. "I thought we just agreed to give the past a rest."

"Your little girl is definitely your future, isn't she?"

"Definitely."

"Then I *definitely* want to meet her."

An hour later Jordan had decided she had lost what good sense God had given her when she agreed to let Cole meet Fancy. What was she doing, shaking her finger at Fate? Sticking her head in the lion's mouth? Did she honestly believe she could pull off this little test of fire? *What if he takes one look at Fancy and knows that she is his?*

Even though the odds were in her favor, Jordan was terrified. Her only hope lay in the fact that Fancy didn't actually resemble Cole except around the eyes. In fact, except

for those big beautiful brown eyes, Fancy was a tiny dupli-
cate of her mother, right down to the delicate nose and high
cheekbones. And the personality was certainly shades of
Jordan. So, maybe she could pull this off. *Yeah, right. When
pigs fly.*

Trying to subdue the knot of fear in the pit of her stomach, she was a split second away from reaching for the
phone to call off the meeting when the doorbell rang.
"Damn! Too late."

"Hi."

"Hi," she said, attempting an effortless smile that didn't
quite make it. Not so much because of the stubborn knot of
fear, but simply because Cole was standing in her doorway,
his lean, well-built body clothed in a snugly tailored navy
Polo shirt topped with a camel-colored sport jacket and the
softest-looking, most-form-fitting, what-he-did-to-denim-
was-almost-sinful jeans she had ever seen. Moonlight
splintered through the aspen trees glinting off his dark-as-
midnight hair and casting intriguing shadows across his
handsome face.

"Come . . . come in," she managed to stammer.

"Thanks."

Closing the door behind her, Jordan took a deep breath
to steady herself and got hit with another whammy—traces
of Cole's after-shave. The clean, fresh scent made her think
of balmy tropical nights and breezes off white-capped ocean
waves, made her remember other nights, other *sensations*
she was better off forgetting.

"I like this room," Cole said, standing in the middle of
her living room. "I liked it the other night, but I wasn't quite
in the mood to appreciate its ambiance."

Her back against the front door, her hand still on the
knob, Jordan stared at him, savoring the way his presence

seemed to fill up the room, fill up her life. *Dangerous thoughts,* she reminded herself. *You can't dwell on the past, but you can't just wipe it away, either. You need time to adjust, time to learn about each other all over again.*

"Thank you." *Relax. Stop acting so . . . so stiff.* "Please, have a seat."

"Thanks," he said, but made no move to sit. Instead he stared at her like a tiger kept on short rations far too long. *Take it easy,* he cautioned himself. *Stop staring at her as if you intend to ravish her right here on the rug.* Not that the thought hadn't crossed his mind the moment he saw her standing in the doorway. His breath had jammed in his throat at the sight of her slender hips and long legs sheathed in pale denim and a long-sleeved, darker denim shirt, knotted at her narrow waist with the top two buttons undone. It was all he could do to mouth some prattle about how he liked her living room.

"I'll, uh, I'll go upstairs and . . . we'll just be a minute."

"Fine," Cole said, hoping his smile didn't appear strained.

When Jordan disappeared up the stairs he released a sigh and sat down on the sofa. *God, this is going to be tougher than I expected.* Had he actually thought he could spend any amount of time with Jordan and not want her as much as he always had? Had he actually believed he could weave in and out of her life for a few days, perhaps a week, then walk away?

Last night after he returned to his hotel, and again on the drive here, Cole had convinced himself he could do precisely that. Keeping his promise in mind, he would see Jordan while he set up the bobsled security, then leave. Clean, uncomplicated and necessary. Sure, that was the plan. But as plans went, this one had holes big enough to drive a Mack truck through. Like the hole in his heart that grew every

time he thought about leaving her again. The first time he
had had no choice, and as much as he tried to convince
himself that this second time was just as predetermined,
every moment he saw her his conviction grew weaker and
weaker. Now, here he was waiting to meet her daughter
when he should get the hell out of her life.

"Cole?"

His head snapped up and he looked straight into the
softest little pair of brown eyes he had ever seen.

"Cole, I'd like you to meet my daughter, Francesca."

He rose from the sofa, stepped forward and held out his
hand. "Very nice to meet you, Francesca."

"Uh-uh," Fancy said.

Perplexed, Cole looked at Jordan.

"It's the name," she explained. "We rarely use her given
name. She's always been such a little clotheshorse and so
particular about her appearance, I nicknamed her...Fancy."
Jordan held her breath, waiting for a flash of recognition in
Cole's eyes, a glimpse of memory that might bring her deception crashing down around her head and heart.

"Then, very nice to meet you, Fancy."

"Fancy, say hello to Mr. Forrester."

"Hello."

Jordan's heart almost hammered out of her chest when
Cole stooped to the child's level. "I can see why they call
you Fancy. You're very pretty." The smile he received was
as sparkling as the string of *faux* gemstones scattered over
Fancy's kelly green, knee-length knit top that matched her
green-and-blue paisley leggings.

Seeing them together, so close yet so far apart, Jordan
wanted to cry. She wanted to break down and sob the truth
to Cole, then beg him not to want their daughter in his life.
That's why letting him come here tonight was nothing short
of insanity. It was inconceivable to Jordan that he could see

Fancy, spend even a teacup full of time with her and *not* want her, love her.

Never one to be shy, Fancy offered a bright thank-you.

"You're welcome."

"You take pictures?" the little girl asked. "My mommy takes pictures."

"No, sweetheart, Mr. Forrester..." Jordan looked to Cole for a simple explanation of what he did for a living.

"I, uh—" Cole thought for a moment then said, "I do take pictures, in a way."

"Up, up in balloons?"

Cole grinned. "Not exactly. Inside buildings, mostly."

The child gave him a curious look as though she didn't see why anyone would be interested in pictures of the inside of a building. "Can I see the pictures?"

Cole's grin widened. "I don't have any with me, but maybe next time, okay?"

"Okee, dokee."

"Now, little Miss Question Box," Jordan said, pointing her daughter in the direction of the stairs, "I think you better get ready for bed."

"But I not sleepy," Fancy protested.

"You never are. Hurry up and put on your pajamas and I'll come up and tuck you in."

Accustomed to showering good-night kisses on Jill and Barry, the precocious three-year-old quite naturally decided her new friend was entitled to the same. In a flash, Fancy dashed back to where Cole still balanced himself on the balls of his feet and stopped directly in front of him. "Night, night," she said sweetly, then leaned over and kissed him on the cheek. Before Cole could recover his power of speech, she dashed back across the room and up the stairs.

"She can be the sweetest *and* the most unpredictable child in the world. I'm sorry if she embarrassed you," Jordan said, poised at the foot of the stairs.

Straightening to his full height, Cole gently touched the spot on his cheek so recently kissed. "Don't be."

"I hope you don't mind a few minutes alone. We have to do the bedtime thing, you know, brushing her teeth, then we say prayers—"

"Don't worry about me."

Jordan smiled and started up the stairs.

"And Jordan..."

"Yes."

"Tell Fancy that I said 'sweet dreams.'"

The entire time Jordan hurried to dress Fancy and complete their bedtime ritual, she was wondering just how sweet her own dreams would be that night. The thought that Cole was downstairs in her living room, waiting for her was enough to guarantee several sleepless nights. What would she say when she went back down? How should she act? It wasn't as though they were old friends renewing an old acquaintance. They hadn't known each other long enough to become friends, only the most tender of lovers. So, they couldn't very well sit around and talk about old times. Old times were too hot, too sensual and too emotionally revealing to discuss over coffee and cake. Besides, if the two kisses they had exchanged were any indication, talking about the old times was dangerous in the extreme.

"All tucked in?" Cole asked when Jordan rejoined him.

"Safe and snug."

"She's quite a beauty."

"Thank you."

"Like her mother."

"Th-thanks. Would you—" she cleared her throat "—would you like some coffee and a slice of chocolate cake?"

"Coffee would be fine, but I'll pass on the cake."

He lightly patted his middle as if to indicate he didn't need the calories, and Jordan's eyes were drawn to his lean, flat stomach. She couldn't imagine where one ounce of fat could hide on his toned and tanned, hard-muscled frame. And the fact that she vividly remembered kissing and touching every inch of that body did nothing to slow her heart rate or the rush of other memories that threatened to pull her under waves of remembered pleasure so sweet, so hot—

"Jordan?"

"Yes." She almost jumped at the sound of his voice. "Yes?"

"Don't go to any trouble."

"Oh, no…no trouble," she insisted, heading toward the kitchen. The only trouble was in her mind. The only trouble was she couldn't look at Cole and not think about all the ways they had pleasured each other.

"Black, right?" she said moments later as she handed him a mug of streaming coffee.

"You remembered."

Jordan swallowed hard and licked her lips. "Uh, you sure I can't tempt you with the chocolate cake?"

"No. Not the cake." *But you can, you do, tempt me with your sweet-as-wild-honey mouth. Just watching your tongue glide across your lips almost drove me crazy.*

She took a step back, then walked to the sofa and seated herself at one end. Standing close to Cole was like standing at the edge of a precipice looking down into a yawning darkness that promised excitement and danger. "I hope my daughter didn't make too big a pest of herself with all her questions about your work."

He took a seat at the opposite end of the sofa. "She could never be a pest."

"Oh, you have no idea. She redefines the word."

"She's curious, like all kids."

"I must admit, until Fancy brought it up, I'd never given much thought to exactly what the security business is all about."

"About keeping people and things secure. Only in my case, mostly on a commercial basis. We don't do home security systems unless, of course, the home is a thirty-thousand-square-foot mansion owned by the third-richest man in the country."

Grateful to find a safe topic of discussion, Jordan said, "You use a lot of high-tech equipment, don't you."

"State of the art. Cameras, monitors, whatever the client requires."

"And the bobsled site requires stuff like that?"

Cole grinned. "Yeah, lots of *stuff* like that. We have a control center with a bank of monitors continuously checking all camera sites. Plus the fenced-in equipment area, and of course, dogs."

"You mean like watchdogs?"

"For sentry duty. A necessity when you're trying to keep an eye on hundreds of thousands of dollars' worth of equipment and supplies."

Jordan was stunned. "I never thought that security would be so...elaborate."

"Believe me, what we have on site now is nothing compared to what we could have. And probably will."

"Because of the sabotage."

"Yes. As a matter of fact, I'm supposed to meet with Sheridan tomorrow morning in Vancouver to discuss additional manpower and surveillance equipment."

Jordan glanced down at the cup of cooling coffee in her hand. "So you're leaving?"

"For a day, maybe two." *Does that bother you, Jordan? Will you think about me when I'm gone? I'll damn sure think of you. Constantly.* He set his cup on the coffee table in front of the sofa and leaned closer to her. "Are we through talking about my job?"

"Well, I—"

"Because if we are, I'd like to talk about last night."

The knot was back in her stomach. "Cole—"

"I've been thinking about something you said. About my not trusting you all those years ago. About—"

An electronic beeping sound cut him short, and Cole released a sigh of frustration. "Excuse me," he said, flipping back one side of his sport jacket in order to access the button on the beeper obviously clipped to the back of his jeans. "Could I use your phone?"

"Of... of course. In the kitchen."

While Cole walked the few steps to the kitchen and dialed a number, Jordan was experiencing some frustration of her own. *When you play with fire...* She understood the risk she was taking every time Cole was near, yet she continued to dart in and out of the flame like some demented moth with a death wish.

"I'm sorry but I've got to go," he announced a moment later, heading straight for the door.

"Is there a problem?"

At the door, Cole stopped and turned to her. "Yes. There's been an explosion at the construction site."

Chapter 7

A few more sleepless nights, and Jordan thought she would need a week in a health spa to repair the damage. Between worrying about Cole and worrying about the problems at the site, the circles under her eyes stood a good chance of becoming permanent. As had been the case for the past several mornings, she had awakened long before the alarm went off and decided she might as well get on with her day rather than lie in bed and dwell on her problems.

She had just slipped into a cotton knit short-sleeved dress and applied the finishing touches to her makeup, including a little extra concealer, when her doorbell rang. Barefoot, she hurried downstairs, peeked through the sidelight and found Cole on her front porch.

"Good morning."

"Good morning. Can I come in?"

"Please," she said, surprised to see him. "Coffee?"

"Thanks, I could use a cup."

And a shave and probably eight hours of sleep, she thought, noticing his stubble-darkened face and the fact that he was still wearing the same clothes he had worn last night. "Cole, what happened?"

"Someone planted explosives in the compound where the graters and heavy-duty bulldozers are kept at night. Two of our most-often-used machines will be down for at least a week."

Jordan handed him a cup of coffee and they both took seats on the sofa. "Was anyone hurt?"

"Fortunately, no. But it's only a matter of time before someone is."

"What do you mean, a matter of time?"

He took a swig of the steaming brew, set the cup on the coffee table and said, "Escalation."

"I don't understand."

"Jordan, these incidents started out as minor nuisances—survey stakes moved, materials missing. Then they moved on up to the bigger stuff—tree spiking, junk added to the oil cases in the bulldozers, and now the explosion. Whoever is behind this is serious. They're out to stop the construction, or at the very least, slow progress to a crawl. And Great Northern is going to pay dearly in man-hours and equipment, the least of which is my additional costs."

"Yours?"

"I'll have to bring in expensive surveillance cameras, laser devices, sound equipment and more men. If I don't get to whoever is behind the sabotage, Great Northern will be lucky to break even on this deal."

"Is it . . . dangerous?"

"Very. These people mean business, and before it's over someone could get hurt."

Jordan's heartbeat double-timed. Cole was in charge and he would most certainly be a target. "What...what are you going to do?"

"My job," he said calmly. Too calmly to suit her. The tone of his voice was ice-cold.

"But how are you going to stop them?"

"I have to find them first." He pulled a folded piece of paper from the inside pocket of his jacket. "Jordan..." Cole's gaze locked with hers, and she read an apology in the dark depths. "I hate like hell to put you on the spot, but I have to ask you some questions."

"What kind of questions?"

"About some of the members of the ecological society."

Stunned, Jordan stared at him. "You can't possibly think they had anything to do with what happened at the construction site."

"I have to check *every* lead, and you know all of these people. You can tell me which ones might have a tendency toward a more militant form of protest. You understand? This isn't personal."

"The hell it isn't," she said, realizing that he wanted her to help him implicate her friends. "You want me to rat on people I care about."

"I thought you cared about the planet, particularly the Rockies."

"I do," she protested.

"Then help me stop these people, because as long as they insist on playing hardball, your organization and all the other environmental groups get a bad rap. Then the more difficult it becomes to get funds and public support. Don't you see? Whoever is behind this is as detrimental to your cause as they are to the project."

Jordan couldn't deny that his argument made sense. Still, the idea of implicating her friends was repugnant. "If I help, can you be certain no one will be hurt?"

"If you don't, I'm certain they will."

She gnawed at her bottom lip. "What do you want to know?"

Cole hadn't realized until that very moment he had been holding his breath, praying she would understand his position and be willing to help. "Just tell me what you know about each of these people as I call off their names. Are they real barn burners or just hot air?" He reached and gently touched her hand. "Ready?"

She nodded.

For the next half hour Cole read names and Jordan did her best to provide honest information and hopefully exonerate each individual. When the last name had been read and dismissed, Cole looked at her, and his heart almost broke to assess the courage she had exhibited. Her answers had been honest to a fault. Not once did she try to hide any flaws or gloss over negative personality traits. Instead she had included in each description those traits and comments she felt would cancel out any of the negatives. Even Barry Clark had come out clean as this week's laundry, and Cole had his doubts about Jordan's second in command. Cole admired her loyalty, but then he had expected nothing less. Strange, he thought, when it came to their personal history he had believed she lied, but today, no such thoughts crossed his mind. In his heart he knew she had been totally honest and forthcoming.

"Thanks," he said finally. "You were a big help."

"To do what? Send some of my friends to jail?"

"No. If it makes you feel any better, I don't think our saboteur is in this bunch."

Instantly her spirts lifted and she smiled. "Really? You mean it?"

Cole couldn't help but smile back. "I mean it. None of the names on this list have enough malice between them to confront a traffic cop."

"Oh, thank God," Jordan breathed, raising a slender hand to her throat.

"Feel better?"

"Much."

Now that the hateful business he had come to conduct was over, Cole allowed himself the luxury of simply gazing at her. Lord, but she was beautiful, more beautiful than even his most vivid memories.

"You look exhausted," she said. "Did you manage to get any sleep last night?"

He grinned. "If you can call dozing for fifteen minutes in a straight-backed chair, sleeping. Besides, I could have had ten hours of rest and I'd still look like a scruffy old hobo standing next to you."

"Boy, you do need sleep." Jordan smiled, trying to make light of his remark, while secretly thrilled at the compliment.

I need you. The thought, sure and swift as an arrow scored a direct hit, dead center of Cole's heart. Yes, he needed her. But fulfilling that need was out of the question. Unable to do more, he took the edge off his need by giving in to the urge to touch her.

Slowly he reached out and brushed back the wisp of a curl lying against her cheek. His thumb stroked her velvet-soft skin, then lightly touched her ear. "Today you look sunshine-sweet and fresh as morning dew."

She fought the urge to grasp his hand and hold it against her cheek. He was doing it again, filling up her senses, filling up her mind and her heart with just a touch. Filling her to overflowing with memories and longing and an aching need to be with him. A need she could surrender to so easily.

"You—" she swallowed hard "—you shouldn't say things like that."

"Why not?"

"I might believe you," she said, trying to keep her voice light, trying to keep him at arm's length and failing miserably at both.

He closed his eyes briefly, wondering if they would ever be able to conquer the past. "You don't trust me even to give you a compliment."

Jordan shook her head. "I don't trust myself to accept it. You . . . you make me feel so . . ."

Oh, God, don't let her say sad. Don't let her turn away and into the past.

"Beautiful. You always did." She finally managed a faint smile. "Even after a twelve- or fourteen-hour day struggling with a tough story, my hair a mess and dog-tired, you could always make me feel beautiful."

"You were." He stepped closer. Close enough for his jacket to brush against the front of her dress. Close enough to feel the heat of her body radiating toward his. "You are," he whispered, wanting to match her honesty. "The most—" he leaned closer "—beautiful woman—" So close their lips were almost touching, he finished with, "In the world."

And then their lips touched.

When they had become lovers before, the excitement and tension were almost overpowering. Their desire for each other knew no bounds, no limits. Their kisses were fiery, passionate beyond belief. And this kiss was nothing less than all of that, but it was more. It was the same, yet different. Sweeter, deeper. And that's when she knew.

She was falling in love all over again.

Cole sealed her mouth with his and knew a deep sense of longing, red-hot desire and...comfort, all mingled together, swirling pleasure through him in a rush. Comfort was the last label he would use to describe their kiss, yet that's exactly what he felt, a soul-deep contentment that stoked a hunger for more.

"Cole...oh, Cole—"

"Don't talk. We've talked too much. Just kiss me, kiss me."

She kissed him, moving closer, fitting her body to his, wanting, needing, at the same time wanting to give, needing to give all that she was. All that he wanted. When his tongue withdrew slightly then teased the corner of her mouth, she moaned, slipped her hand to the back of his neck and with gentle but determined pressure, urged him to return.

He gladly complied, deepening the kiss, stroking the silky texture of her mouth with his tongue. He crushed her to him as if to meld their bodies together for always.

Jordan wanted the kiss to last for always. She wanted it to go on until they lost track of time and lost themselves in each other. And when it ended, albeit reluctantly, she wanted to cry. For all the pain of the past and for the pain that most certainly lay ahead unless Cole could forgive what he considered to be treason of the heart.

"Cole, I...have to know if the wanting is enough," she whispered, still dizzy from the kiss.

He kissed her cheek, her temple. "Enough for what?"

"For forgiveness."

Cole's lips stilled at her temple. When he looked into her eyes, Jordan read her answer. She slipped out of his embrace.

NO RISK, NO OBLIGATION TO BUY ... NOW OR EVER!

CASINO JUBILEE
"Scratch'n Match" Game

Here's how to play:

1. Peel off label from front cover. Place it in space provided at right. With a coin, carefully scratch off the silver box. This makes you eligible to receive two or more free books, and possibly other gifts, depending upon what is revealed beneath the scratch-off area.

2. You'll receive brand-new Silhouette Intimate Moments® novels. When you return this card, we'll rush you the books and gifts you qualify for ABSOLUTELY FREE!

3. If we don't hear from you, every month we'll send you 6 additional novels to read and enjoy months before they are available in bookstores. You can return them and owe nothing but if you decide to keep them, you'll pay only $2.96* per book, a saving of 43¢ each off the cover price. There is **no** extra charge for postage and handling. There are **no** hidden extras.

4. When you join the Silhouette Reader Service™, you'll get our subscribers-only newsletter, as well as additional free gifts from time to time just for being a subscriber!

5. You must be completely satisfied. You may cancel at any time simply by sending us a note or a shipping statement marked ''cancel'' or by returning any shipment to us at our cost.

YOURS FREE!

This lovely heart-shaped box is richly detailed with cut-glass decorations, perfect for holding a precious memento or keepsake—and it's yours absolutely free when you accept our no-risk offer.

CASINO JUBILEE
"Scratch'n Match" Game

**CHECK CLAIM CHART BELOW
FOR YOUR FREE GIFTS!**

YES! I have placed my label from the front cover in the space provided above and scratched off the silver box. Please send me all the gifts for which I qualify. I understand I am under no obligation to purchase any books, as explained on the opposite page.

(U-SIL-IM-11/92) 245 CIS AGNG

Name _____

Address _____ Apt. _____

City _____ State _____ Zip _____

▼ DETACH AND MAIL CARD TODAY! ▼

SILHOUETTE ''NO RISK'' GUARANTEE

"The one thing you and I always had plenty of was passion." Turning away from him, she rubbed her hands over her bare arms as if to ward off a sudden chill. "But passion isn't a substitute for trust, is it, Cole?"

"Jordan—"

"And you're right. We would both be liars to deny my kisses affect you every bit as much as yours do me, but without trust those kisses are meaningless. For two other people, that might be fine, but not for—" Jordan turned and suddenly her eyes widened in surprise.

Cole whipped around to find Fancy standing at the bottom of the stairs, listening intently to every word.

"Good morning, sunshine." Jordan pasted a smile on her face. "I, uh, didn't know you were awake."

Even though she and Cole were separated by several feet and hardly in any semblance of intimacy, Jordan knew her perceptive little daughter wasn't fooled for a minute. The child glanced from Cole to her mother, then back to Cole, curiosity clearly evident in her soft brown eyes.

"Aren't you going to say good-morning to Mr. Forrester?" Jordan urged.

"Morning," Fancy said, still dressed in her gown, clutching some clothes in one hand and her ragged clown in the other. "I wear my new shorts?" She rubbed her eyes with the back of the hand holding Winky, and he flopped back and forth like a flag in the breeze.

"May I—" Jordan started to correct her daughter's grammar.

"May I wear new shorts? I be careful, Mommy."

"I, uh, thought you were saving those for the picnic."

"Uh-uh. Please, please," the child begged.

Deciding her permission was a small price to pay to distract her little eavesdropper, Jordan smiled and said, "Okee, dokee."

"Yippee!" Fancy jumped up and down, her mop of red curls flouncing around her shoulders, then turned and raced up the stairs and out of sight.

"That's twice now my timing has been incredibly bad. I'm sorry," Cole said.

"For the kiss or Fancy seeing us?"

His gaze met hers. "I wouldn't upset your daughter for the world."

"Thank you." A small sigh of relief whispered through Jordan. At least he wasn't going to deny their still-dangerous attraction to each other. "As for Fancy, believe me, if she was upset, we'd know it. She doesn't know what the word *restraint* means."

The object of their discussion suddenly reappeared, appropriately dressed in her new purple walking shorts and lavender camp shirt. "Hungry now," she announced. "Winky, too."

"See what I mean?"

Cole scrubbed his face with both hands. Lack of sleep and Jordan's kiss had taken their toll, his body felt knotted with tension. "I, uh, I guess I better get some sleep before I crash and burn."

Fancy walked over to Cole. "You take a nap?"

He grinned. "I could sure use one, beauty."

The little girl looked up at the man who towered over her and said without hesitation, "I get my snuggle. You have it."

Puzzled, he glanced at Jordan and she mouthed, "Her blanket."

Realizing what Fancy had just offered, Cole looked down into her sweet face, so open, so innocent. His chest tightened and he had an overwhelming urge to scoop the child into his arms and hug her to him. Instead he lowered his powerful frame until they were at eye level. "Oh, beauty, that's the nicest offer I've had in years. But I have to take a nap at my hotel, and I wouldn't want to take your snuggle so far from home.''

Fancy considered his words for a moment, then offered what she obviously felt was the solution. ''You too big for my bed. You sleep in Mommy's.''

''Fancy—''

''I, uh, I'd probably be too big for Mommy's bed, too,'' Cole said, trying to hide a smile. ''But thank you.'' He straightened and turned to Jordan, the last traces of the smile lingering at the corners of his mouth. ''And thank you for the coffee.''

So much had happened in such a short time, Jordan felt as if that simple courtesy had taken place hours ago. ''You're welcome.''

Their gazes met and held. Unable to say in words what either of them wanted to because of Fancy, their eyes spoke volumes about old hurts and fresh desires, of need and loneliness.

Cole wanted to take her in his arms again and kiss away the pain and doubt he saw in her eyes, but he knew that was only a temporary answer. She was right. Without trust, they had nothing.

More than anything Jordan wanted him to take her in his arms and kiss away her fears, prove her wrong, but she knew he couldn't. At least not yet. And maybe, she sadly admitted, not ever.

''Well,'' Cole said at last, drawing the word out as if that act alone could prolong his stay. ''I guess I'd better go and—'' His sentence cut short by a determined tug of his pant leg, he glanced down at Fancy.

''Wanna see my kitty?''

''Well, I'm not much on cats, but—''

Jordan groaned. ''Oh, sweetheart, not now.''

"I can spare a couple more minutes," Cole offered.

"Not for this you can't. We don't *have* a cat. What we have is a picture book containing every breed known to man and—" she gave her daughter a pointed look "—a streak of plain old-fashioned hardheadedness a mile wide. What we have here is a buy-me-a-kitten campaign."

"I get the book?" Fancy asked, ignoring her mother's forbidding but not yet dangerous expression.

"No, you don't, young lady. Mr. Forrester has been up all night and he's very tired. You can show him your cats some other time."

The child looked up at Cole. "Please, please?"

"Fancy," Jordan warned, the calm, no-nonsense tone of her voice dispelling any doubt as to her seriousness. "I said, some other time. Now tell Mr. Forrester goodbye."

"Good try, but I think we've been outvoted." Cole winked.

With the well-honed instincts of any other three-year-old master at the game of manipulation, Fancy knew when it was time to retreat. "Bye, Mr. Forest-der."

"So long, beauty."

When she had gone, Cole looked at Jordan. "You've got your hands full."

"Tell me something I don't know," she sighed. "But you were very good with her. In fact, I don't believe I've seen her take to someone so quickly." The flash of genuine pleasure in his dark eyes made Jordan's heart simultaneously soar, then crash. Instinctively Cole had responded to his own daughter, but he didn't know that, couldn't know that.

"For, uh, all of her look-out-world-here-I-come attitude, she's very discerning when it comes to adults."

"Particularly men?"

Cautioning herself against the flare of hope that his question might be prompted by jealousy, she replied, "Her opportunities are limited to Barry and the fathers of her playmates.''

"I'm ... surprised. I mean, it's only natural for you to want ... companionship, even a father for Fancy.''

"I'm not looking for ... companionship. And Fancy has—" she glanced away "—*had,* a father. For her sake, I would never bring a strange man into the house.''

"I was a stranger.''

Jordan's head snapped around. "I just meant, some ... someone I didn't know. When it comes to my child," *God, how I want to say "our" child,* "I don't take risks.''

Cole glanced across the living room and into the spacious kitchen where Fancy was busy pouring cereal into a bowl. "I don't blame you. If I were a parent, I'd move heaven and earth to make sure my child was protected from everything dark and ugly in the world.''

Jordan watched him, saw the pained expression in his eyes and wondered at his similar references about the world's character or lack thereof. Something had happened to him. Something dark and terrible, she thought, recalling his words of last night. *Twenty-one months in hell while they shredded his mind.*

"There's a fine line between protection and smothering, concern and isolation. We all want what's best for the people we love.''

"Yeah," he said on a ragged, weary sigh. "I guess so. Uh, I need to head out." He walked to the door.

"Cole?''

"Yeah.''

"Be careful. You haven't had much sleep and the road over the pass can surprise you if you're not completely alert.''

Her genuine concern swept through him like a gust of warm spring air on an icy January day. Not since he had withstood the unsolicited and difficult-to-accept pampering of his family when he had been released had he felt so comforted, so... He almost added the word *loved,* but didn't. "Thanks," he said and quietly closed the door behind him.

That same night, long after Fancy's prayers and long after the house had settled into late-night quiet, Jordan lay awake thinking about Cole. No, she corrected herself, staring up at the ceiling, she wasn't thinking about Cole so much as she was thinking about her reaction to him. Make that attraction. Ever since the realization that she was falling for him again, she hadn't been able to think about much else.

Twice a fool and only yourself to blame. Hadn't she promised herself she would never let anyone hurt her that way again? Hadn't she learned anything about life, about herself, in four years? Wasn't she foolish to contemplate renewing a relationship that was fragile at best? Yes, yes, and yes. She *had* made promises to herself. She *had* learned a lot. And she was probably the biggest fool in the state of Colorado. All of that was true. And it didn't change one very significant fact.

She had fallen in love again with Cole Forrester aka Jason Cole, aka the father of her child, aka the man who had broken her heart. There. She admitted it. It was out in the open. No more lying to herself. And it was a relief to have everything so clear in her mind.

Then why didn't she feel better?

Because it wasn't the complete truth. Because she hadn't fallen in love with Cole *again*.

She had never stopped loving him.

The admission afforded her the first real peace she had known in four years. And the first real unclouded look at herself.

She didn't like what she saw.

When she first met Cole, she had been full of fire and fury, out to make her mark on the world. Out to prove she could make it to the top on her own. Alone. Always alone. She had worked hard to perfect an image of polished self-assurance. Jordan Lockridge, smart, beautiful, classy, a woman for all seasons. A woman who faced the world without all the neurotic fantasies about a man taking care of her. So she had been abandoned as a child. So what? She overcame that little glitch in her life. So people might think she had overcompensated. So what? What did she care for other people's opinions?

Then along came a man who called himself Jason Cole, and her carefully polished veneer melted right down to the bare truth, right down to the frightened little girl buried beneath all those layers of gloss. He had loved that frightened child *and* the woman who had worked so hard to pretend she didn't exist. Both of them were part of Jordan. From one she drew courage, from the other she drew strength. And Cole had loved and accepted all of her. With him she had been wonderfully, gloriously, marvelously whole.

With startling clarity, she suddenly realized that the bitterness and need for revenge she had experienced when Cole left had little to do with his leaving. And everything to do with the fact that, while they were together, she had begun to learn who the real Jordan Lockridge was. His love had opened a door and turned on the light to a whole new world, a world where she could be everything she wanted without having to balance herself on a tightrope stretched between fear and protection, need and being self-sufficient. When he left, the light went out, the door was closed.

She couldn't find her way in the dark.

Oh, she had made a good show of finding her way. But she had resented every minute of trying, no matter how easy she had made it look. The immaturity of her behavior, her absolutely relentless grudge was appalling, and she decided only time and a little dumb luck had prevented her from passing any of that on to Fancy. Thank God, her daughter had inherited her father's ability to see beyond the obvious. Now Fate had dropped a second chance right in her lap, and she had almost turned around and walked right back into the darkness. Away from Cole.

So, twice a fool?

Suspended between the lies of the past and the truth of the present, Jordan's only course was the truth. No, she wouldn't be a fool again. Strange, she thought, love was the most powerful force in the universe, strong enough to bond a man and woman together for an eternity, yet so fragile it could be fatally wounded by a careless word spoken in anger. Anyone would be crazy to pass up something so rare and wonderful once, much less twice.

I may be a fool, but I'm not crazy.

But recognizing love and living happily ever after were two different things. She and Cole had changed. Circumstances had changed. By Cole's own words, he was not the man she knew four years ago. There was a restraint, a reticence about him now that hadn't been there before, as though he desperately needed to keep a secret inside himself. A secret he kept confined, not because the world would be horrified, but because he was. Whatever had happened, had changed Cole in a way Jordan couldn't understand. But she wanted to understand, and she instinctively knew that without that understanding there was no hope for a future together. And she wanted a future with Cole, and she wanted Fancy to have her real father.

But maybe he's changed so much he doesn't want me. No, she assured herself. He couldn't kiss her, hold her the way he did, and not care. *But are you mistaking desire for caring?* Yes, he wanted her, but she also sensed he needed her in a way he never had before. *God knows Fancy and I need him.* She knew she had to tell him about his daughter, but how and when? And time was short. Cole had stated up front that he didn't expect to stay in Fairplay long. Would it be long enough to fan into flame a long-burning ember? And if it wasn't? What if her future, their future, was limited to days, minutes?

Then she would just have to live a lifetime in every minute.

That same night, long after necessary paperwork and long after the quiet of his room had settled into late-night loneliness, Cole lay awake thinking about Jordan. And Fancy.

He had never spent much time around children, and admittedly felt uncomfortable with them, so his reaction to Fancy had surprised him. Far from feeling uncomfortable, he had experienced a connection he couldn't explain. Perhaps the feeling stemmed from the fact that she was Jordan's child, but it was more than that. The beautiful little girl had touched a cold place he thought hidden so deep no warmth could ever penetrate, but Fancy had. That sunshine-in-the-morning smile and unconditional acceptance he knew whenever he was in her presence stayed with him long afterward.

Never in a million years would I have thought I could be so thoroughly charmed by a child who wasn't mine. And how could he feel so tender toward Fancy and exclude her mother?

Answer that one.

Despite the lies of the past, Cole knew Jordan had been totally honest with him about the ecological society members and about her own participation in the fight to stop the bobsled project. And about her feelings?

Her kisses don't lie. No one could fake the passion I feel shimmering through her body when we touch. True, as Jordan had said, lack of passion had never been a problem, but they were different people now. Would she still respond so lovingly if she knew his shame? After his imprisonment he had learned to live with the new Cole Forrester, the man who looked at himself and his weaknesses with a realistic and unforgiving eye. Could he even *think* of exposing anyone else to his jaded point of view?

While he told himself the answer was no, a tiny flame of hope glowed deep inside him, a flicker of faith. Maybe Fate had given him the second chance he didn't deserve.

Chapter 8

"Forrester," Cole answered, cradling the mobile phone between his chin and shoulder while he worked.

"Hello, Cole."

"Jordan?"

"Uh, yes, I, uh, that is, Fancy and I would like for you to join us for dinner tonight, if you can. I know it's short notice, but—"

"Dinner? I . . . well, yes. I'd love to," Cole said, wondering if Fate had decided to kick into high gear.

"You can?"

"Yes."

"Wonderful. That's . . . wonderful."

"What time?"

"Do you mind early, say, five-thirty? I need to get Fancy into bed by eight or so. And I can guarantee you she will talk your ear off and drag the visit out as long as she can."

"Early is fine. As a matter of fact, I've been so busy the past couple of days I've skipped lunch. And since it's almost noon, looks like today won't break the record, so an early dinner will be great.''

"Well, then . . . great.''

A long pause followed before Jordan said, "Oh, by the way, we don't dress for dinner. I mean we do dress . . . I mean, we wear clothes—''

"That's a relief.''

"But we don't . . . oh you know what I mean.''

At the other end of the line Cole chuckled. "Casual.''

"Yes. Casual and comfortable.''

"Sounds . . . nice. Thanks for the invitation.''

"You're welcome.''

Another stretch of silence. Neither seemed eager to end the conversation.

"So, you're really busy?'' Jordan finally asked.

"Yeah. We're installing additional equipment, and speed is premium if we want to catch the perpetrators.''

"I see.'' Actually she had only a vague idea of what comprised Cole's business, but what she knew was intriguing.

"And speaking of speed . . .'' He hated to end the conversation, but he was already so far behind, the men would probably have to go to twenty-four-hour shifts.

"Oh, of course. I'm sorry, Cole.''

"No problem.''

"See you tonight.''

"Tonight.''

For several seconds after she hung up the phone, Jordan simply stared at the receiver, wondering if she was moving too fast, wondering if Cole would read more into the invitation than she wanted, wondering if—

The phone rang again. "Hello.''

"I forgot to ask you something important.''

"Oh?'' Was that her voice sounding so breathy?

"Are you really dead set against a cat?"

"A cat?" she asked, surprised by the question.

"Yeah, you know, one of those furry little things with the long tails that go meow."

She laughed. "Actually, no. It's just that summer is my busiest season and I simply haven't had the time to look around, find a good kitten and a good deal. She's crazy to have one with spots, so that's another criterion. Why do you ask?"

"Oh . . . just curious."

"Well, don't tell my daughter I'm even *thinking* about a cat, or my life will be on your head."

"My lips are sealed."

A moment later, Jordan again stared at the phone, only this time she wasn't wondering, she was remembering. Actually savoring was a more accurate description as she played and replayed the mental picture of Cole's lips sealed over hers in a to-die-for kiss.

Miles away at the construction site Cole stared at the mobile phone, remembering his last words. The image of his lips sealed by Jordan's sweetly seductive mouth was enough to make him squirm in the seat of his truck. Heat filled his sex. *If all it takes to make you hard is thinking about kissing her, how in hell are you going to make it through an entire dinner?* He wasn't sure, but one thing was for certain. Whether or not they were willing to admit it, he and Jordan wanted each other like hell on fire. No matter what lies had been told or how lives had changed, the same kind of burn-down-the-night desire they had known the first time they touched each other was still there and hotter than ever. And Cole wasn't at all sure how long he could continue to fight the fire. Or if he even wanted to anymore.

* * *

"He's here. He's here." Fancy squealed and made a mad dash for the door when the bell rang.

"No, Fancy, wait. It's too early for—" Sure enough, a peek out the sidelight confirmed their visitor was indeed Cole.

"Hi," Fancy said, fully expecting a greeting.

"I know I'm early," he said as soon as she opened the door. "But I came straight from the construction site, and..." The sentence was never completed because once Cole got a good look at Jordan, he almost forgot how to speak.

If the denim short shorts she was wearing, frayed at the hem and cupping her bottom like a man's hand, weren't illegal, they should have been. And if the shorts weren't guaranteed to give a man sweaty palms and cotton mouth, the skimpy turquoise tank top was. To compound his already heightened senses, she smelled fresh-from-the-shower clean, and her dewy skin looked soft enough for a man to sink into and never want to leave.

"Hi," Fancy tried again.

"You're early," Jordan repeated his words, unable to take her eyes off the way his T-shirt outlined his muscular shoulders, accentuated his biceps and emphasized his narrow waist. Or the way his dusty work jeans hugged his flat stomach, breathtakingly defined his...

Jordan's gaze flew to Cole's and stayed...and stayed. He swallowed hard. "I, uh, I thought maybe I could..." Trying not to lose himself in her bewitching green eyes, he dropped his gaze...to her breasts. "Borrow your shower and save some time."

"S-sure."

"Hi," Fancy tried a third time, now perturbed that she couldn't get Cole's attention. Finally she wedged herself between the two adults and demanded to be heard. "Mr. Forest-der!"

"What?" Jordan and Cole said in unison.

"I say, 'hi.'"

"Oh, I'm sorry." Reluctantly Cole forced his gaze away from Jordan's breasts to his younger hostess. "Hello, Fancy." Unfortunately, glancing down only drew his eyes to Jordan's long, slender, bare legs. He swallowed hard again and directed his gaze to a safe zone—the top of Jordan's head.

"I can come in?"

"Oh!" she said, embarrassed that she had been staring. "Of course. The stairs are right over...well, you can see the stairs. Uh, there's a bathroom at the top and to your right. A tub. A tub and a shower."

"Thanks."

For the first time Jordan became aware of her appearance. "I just showered myself and I didn't want to wear my good clothes while I cooked so..."

"What's for dinner?" Cole asked, looking as if he might take a bite out of her.

"Grilled chicken, but I haven't even—"

"Good. Then that will give me time to cool off, uh, shower off."

"I'll get you a towel."

"I do it, I do it," Fancy insisted, once again stepping between Cole and her mother.

"Why, thank you," he said, finally able to focus his attention somewhere other than Jordan's delectable body. "You're a gracious hostess."

"C'mon," the preschooler said, leading the way.

"You're in good hands," Jordan assured him, and was rewarded with a melt-right-down-to-your-toes smile. She waited until she heard the sound of running water, then dashed up the stairs, glanced in Fancy's room to find her bent over a coloring book and hurried to her own room.

By the time Cole joined his hostesses in the kitchen, Jordan had changed into a pair of softly pleated cream-colored slacks and a blouse of deep teal. Personally he would not have been disappointed to find her still dressed in the shorts and tank top. Particularly since the tank top had prohibited a bra, and the blouse, though softly seductive, didn't do justice to her figure.

Clean jeans, clean shirt and clean-shaved, Cole walked toward her, and Jordan thought how right he looked, in her home, in her life.

"That's quite a window you've got."

"Window?"

With his thumb, he motioned toward the ceiling. "Your bathroom."

Jordan had forgotten about the ceiling-to-tub-rim picture window in her bathroom. The six-foot-by-six-foot, wood-framed, curtainless clear glass window had been her only structural indulgence when she had the cabin built. Well aware of its decadent appeal, she usually tried to warn first-time visitors, but with the shock of Cole's early arrival, she had forgotten to mention her naughty little secret.

"Oh, yes, well . . ."

"Good thing your neighbors live half a mile away and there are a lot of trees in between."

"I . . . it's very relaxing to, uh, soak and enjoy the view."

"Undoubtedly." Only relaxing was the last thing that had crossed Cole's mind when he saw the tub. How relaxed could he be when all he could think about was Jordan in a tub of warm water, wearing nothing but an inviting smile and a come-to-me look in her eyes?

"Mommy, Mommy, I get'em now?" Fancy asked her mother.

"Since we're running behind, we thought you might like some hors d'oeuvres to tide you over until dinner."

"Fantastic."

Jordan turned to Fancy. "All right, you can bring the plate to the serving island, now."

"Okee, dokee." The eager child picked up a small plastic tray, previously placed on a table she could reach, and brought it to where Cole sat perched on one of the bar stools. "For you," she said, grinning happily.

"Thank you. Did you make these?"

"Mommy did it. I helped."

Cole made a production out of selecting the perfect pimento-stuffed celery stick. "Delicious," he said, popping one in his mouth.

At that moment the phone rang, and it was for Cole.

"Yeah," he said into the receiver. "You've got one, for sure? How many? Well, that's probably okay. What color? Great. And tonight is okay with your wife? Outstanding. I'll call you right back."

Her curiosity piqued, Jordan tried not to eavesdrop, but she couldn't help herself. How many what? And whose wife was he talking about?

"You know," he said as soon as he hung up the phone, "I believe I forgot to turn off the bathroom light. Fancy, would you mind checking for me?" Jordan gave him a quizzical look, but told Fancy to go ahead. "We need to talk," he said as soon as they were alone. "One of the construction workers has a litter of kittens he wants to unload. They're about five weeks old, had their preliminary vaccinations and..." He grinned, quite pleased with himself. "One has spots. Whaddaya say?"

What she said was "possibly," then five minutes and more discussion later she said, "maybe," and before she knew it, dinner was put on hold and the three of them were on their way to select a kitten.

Until the moment Fancy picked out the small ball of black-and-white fur she had decided wanted to live at her house, Cole could not have said exactly what had prompted him to pursue the "cat caper," as Jordan had dubbed their adventure. Yesterday one of the project workers had innocently mentioned his mother cat's recent litter, and the idea took root. But the instant Fancy gathered the wide-eyed kitten in her arms and looked up at him, Cole knew precisely why he had gotten involved. The sheer joy and unconditional love shining in her eyes was the greatest reward any mere mortal could ever hope to have.

Jordan watched Cole gazing down at his daughter and thought her heart would surely burst into a million fragments. When he went down on one knee and spoke to her softly while stroking the kitten, it was all she could do not to break down and sob. Although she couldn't hear his words, she could see Fancy's face. The phrase "hanging on every word," didn't begin to describe the intense concentration on her child's face. Big brown eyes wide, her sweet mouth slightly parted, Fancy was gazing at Cole with a look in her eyes that could only be described as worshipful. With their heads close together, locked in a brief, intimate world, each completely focused on the other, they were unmistakably father and daughter. Torn between the importance of keeping that fact secret, at least for now, and wanting the whole world to know, in that instant, she would have sold her soul for a camera. On second thought, she decided no photograph and certainly not her meager skill, could ever do justice to the exquisitely tender moment. Besides, what her eyes had captured was already indelibly engraved on her heart.

Cole stood, reaching for Fancy's free hand as he turned to Jordan. "We've made our decision. Even without a spot to her name, and no tail, this is definitely the one."

"She wasn't bornded with a tail."

"That's because she's a Manx," Cole explained.

"She's so soft, Mommy. You wanna feel?"

"Jordan?" Seeing tears glistening in her eyes, he stepped closer.

"Don't . . . don't mind me." She sniffed. "We mothers have a tendency to get a little weepy at firsts. You know, first pet, first day of school, first date." *First real time spent with her father. Oh, Lord, help me do the right thing. Help me to find the right time to tell him.*

"You're entitled." He smiled. "I should have known something was up when you didn't correct 'bornded.'"

"I think she's hungry," Fancy announced, drawing the attention of both adults.

Jordan swiped at a tear. "Well, then, we'll have to stop at the grocery store and buy some cat food, won't we?"

"Kitty food."

"I stand corrected, kitty food, it is." Since they were in Cole's rented truck, Jordan asked, "Do you mind stopping?"

He smiled. "It's on me."

Not only did Cole foot the bill for the food, but for a plastic litter box as well, along with the litter, bowls for food and water and a wicker-basket bed with a blue plaid pillow. All purchased with Fancy's direction, over Jordan's resistance and at Cole's delight. By the time the three arrived back at the cabin, it was dark and dinner had been completely forgotten.

"Okay, young lady, it's way past yours and kitty's bedtime, so while I'm fixing a peanut butter and jelly sandwich and a glass of milk, hurry upstairs and get yourself dressed for bed.''

"Okee, dokee." The kitten tucked in the crook of her arm in the same manner she carried her clown, Fancy started for her room.

"Whoa," Jordan ordered, catching a glimpse of the kitten's bulging eyes. "Sunshine, you can't carry kitty like you do Winky. Winky doesn't need air, and the kitty does. By the way," she said, rescuing the dazed cat, "what are you going to call her?"

"Spot," the little girl replied without hesitation.

"Spot?" Cole and Jordan said in unison.

Fancy smiled proudly. "I found one," she announced, reclaiming her pet.

Sure enough, upon closer inspection they discovered one tiny spot of white fur on the kitten's almost completely jet-black body.

"You know, beauty, Spot is a name usually reserved for dogs."

"But she gots one."

"Has one," her mother corrected.

"Yes, she does," Cole agreed. "But she's also got four white feet that look like she's wearing boots. Wouldn't you rather call her Boots?"

Fancy shook her head and hugged the animal to her tiny body.

"And look at all the fluffy white fur under her chin. We could call her—"

"Uh-uh," Fancy insisted, shaking her head adamantly. "Spot."

Cole looked at Jordan. "I'm ready to wave the white flag, how about you?"

"Might as well." The kitten meowed softly as she lifted it from Fancy's arms and raised it to eye level. "I officially dub thee, Spot."

Fancy clapped her hands and jumped up and down.

"Now." Holding the cat to her chest with one hand, Jordan pointed upstairs with the other. "Scoot."

With Fancy occupied, she turned her attention to Cole. "You must be starving."

"I'll live." Gently he rubbed the kitten's ear and in the process his knuckles grazed the swell of her breast.

Jordan almost gasped, the contact was so immediate, so electric, so... thrilling. Her nipples hardened instantly and she was grateful the kitten shielded her from his eyes. "If, uh—" she swallowed and licked her lips "—if peanut butter and jelly doesn't tempt you, what about an open-faced roast beef sandwich?"

You tempt me, Cole thought, watching her dainty tongue make another pass across her full lower lip. "Don't go to any trouble."

"Would you like a glass of wine?"

"Sounds good."

While she prepared his sandwich, Cole set up Spot's bed in a corner of the kitchen and tried to corral Spot at the same time. "Any bets on how long this cat sleeps downstairs?" he asked as a pajama-clad Fancy bounded into the kitchen, raced across the floor and picked up her new pet.

Jordan placed a plate on the counter in front of him. The delicious aroma of roast beef heaped on two thick slices of sourdough bread and covered in gravy pointedly reminded him of the hours since his last meal. "This looks great."

"Fancy, leave Spot in her box and come eat your sandwich."

"I pet her a little? Please, Mommy?"

Jordan looked over at her daughter cuddling the tiny animal and didn't have the heart to separate them just yet. "Okay, but just for a minute." From the opposite side of the narrow serving counter she set a glass of wine beside Cole's plate. "I don't think I'll take that bet about where the cat sleeps."

Cole grinned and set about devouring the sandwich. "Smart lady."

Smart enough not to try and hold you when you want to go? she wondered. *Smart enough to know that if you never spoke of love the first time, my chances the second time are even slimmer?* "At least I've got someone fooled," she said almost to herself.

Cole had an uneasy feeling she wasn't referring to bets or sleeping arrangements for Spot. "Who are you trying to fool?"

Jordan blinked, as if just realizing what she had said. "Only myself," she whispered. "Only myself."

"You're too honest for that."

"I like to think so."

"You are."

"But isn't that a form of self-deception? Don't we all *think* of ourselves as honest until something forces us to face reality?"

Cole pushed his now-empty plate aside. "Reality is its own form of self-deception. You can live your life based on certain values you consider to be reality, then one day be forced to trade one reality for another. Which one is real? How do you make that kind of judgment? What criteria do you use?"

Instinctively Jordan knew he was speaking of himself and that it was all tied up with the twenty-one months in hell he had mentioned.

Reaching across the counter, she touched his hand. Their fingers intertwined. Then, ever so slowly, he pulled her to him around the corner of the serving counter and drew her between his legs.

Cole hadn't planned to kiss her; even told himself he shouldn't. But one touch, one long look into those bewitching green eyes, and his good intentions vanished as fast as a gambler's luck. He lifted her hand to his lips and kissed each fingertip. "You're the only reality I'm interested in right now." His teeth gently nipped the pad of her thumb. "The only reality that matters." Desire burned in his eyes like meteors aflame in the night sky and left little doubt about the veracity of his intent.

Jordan caught herself a split second away from begging him to kiss her. "Fancy..."

Cole stopped and they both glanced toward the area of the kitchen designated as Spot's bedroom. The bright blue plaid pillow mattress intended for the wicker bed had been placed beside the basket on the floor and now cushioned a head of tousled russet curls. Her breathing deep and even, the kitten curled contentedly against her little body, Fancy was sound asleep.

Acting purely on instinct, Cole walked across the kitchen, scooped the sleeping child, kitten and all, into his arms and headed for her bedroom. "Poor beauty," he whispered, "she gave it her best shot."

Following Cole, when they reached the top of the stairs, Jordan directed him into Fancy's softly lighted bedroom. He laid her on the bed as if he were placing spun glass on a velvet pillow, then pulled the covers over her. The cat poked its head from beneath the embroidered comforter, meowed, blinked sleepily, and settled down again.

Cole leaned over, placed a soft kiss on the even softer little cheek, then stepped to the end of the bed to make room for Jordan. For a minute she simply looked at her daughter, her eyes filled with such love and gratitude for the joyous miracle she beheld that he almost looked away, not wanting to intrude on such a private moment. Instead an unnamed need compelled him to watch, and in doing so, for one brief instant was a part of the joy, a part of them. Finally Jordan bent low over her sleeping child and whispered, "Good night, my dearest heart. Sweet dreams and God's blessing." Then she kissed almost the exact same spot on the soft little cheek that Cole's lips had touched.

"It's been quite a day," Jordan said when they were back in the kitchen.

"Yeah." He stretched his lean hard body, feeling better than he had in a long, long time. "Need help cleaning up?"

"No...no, thanks."

"Then, let's relax for a moment." He took her hand and led her into the living room.

As they settled side by side onto the comfortable sofa, Jordan was suddenly swamped with conflicting emotions. While a part of her was outrageously thrilled to be seated so intimately next to the man who still had the ability to melt her bones with just a kiss, another part of her was scared half to death about where the intimacy might lead. Not because she feared her own emotions, but because she still wasn't certain of Cole's feelings.

"I want to thank you for one of the best days of my life."

"Some day," Jordan said. "You get an invitation to dinner, and wind up footing the bill for my daughter's cat obsession. On top of that, we almost starve you to death."

"Do you hear me complaining?"

She gazed into his velvety brown eyes, hoping for some sign, some indication of how he felt about her. "No. As a matter of fact, you've been an absolute angel."

"Don't look for any halos."

"Halos never held much interest for me," she said honestly.

Still holding her hand, he lifted it to his cheek very much as he had that morning in the meadow, then slowly turned his head and kissed the center of her palm. "Besides, I'm right where I want to be."

Jordan's emotions no longer warred. Outrageously thrilled won hands down. And he was sending her as clear a message as she could want.

"Unless..."

"Unless what?" she whispered.

"Unless you need me to leave?"

Leaving wasn't what she needed. What she needed was Cole. What she needed was the two of them together, and that need was fast becoming a living, breathing, *wanting* presence in her mind and body. So much so, the thought of touching him, having him touch her, stroke her, made her tremble.

"No," she said, her voice barely above a whisper. "I don't want you to—"

Cole didn't wait for her to finish because the time spent on one more word was time spent not kissing her. In a single fluid motion his mouth came down on hers, and he pulled her hard against his body.

Jordan couldn't, wouldn't deny him, or herself. Instead she gave free rein to all the delicious sensations sweeping over her. She reveled in the taste and texture of him as heat bloomed inside her, sending the intoxicating nectar of desire singing through her veins.

Cole's fingers speared into the thick mass of her hair, holding her prisoner for his kiss. But Jordan needed no bonds; she gladly surrendered to his lips, his tongue, to the rings of fiery need expanding through her body until she thought she would be consumed in a blaze of white-hot pleasure.

He seduced her mouth, taking his own sweet time, exploring, measuring, delving into the heated moistness time and time again. While his mouth did wonderful, wicked things, his hands settled on her collarbone, his fingers slowly kneading her shoulders. Instinctively she swayed toward him, her body gently rocking to the rhythm set by his fingers and thrusting tongue. The motion repeatedly caused her breasts to brush against his chest. Her nipples hardened instantly and she made a tiny gasp.

Cole took the kiss deeper, deeper, stealing her breath with repeated sensual forays of his questing tongue.

Jordan's body moved restlessly, the slow sensual teasing drawing her on a rack of pleasure and pain so strong she wanted to cry out for him never to stop. The fire licking through her body only sent her racing madly toward the source of the flame. Cole. His mouth, his hands. Cole touching her in ways that melted her memories into puddles of nothingness. Cole wanting her as much as she wanted him.

When he finally drew back, his eyes hungry and wild with need, she tried to tell him how long she had waited for her memories to live again, how long she had waited to be with him, but she couldn't form the words.

"You feel better, taste better than any memory," he said, his breathing rough. "Remember how it was for us? So hot. So perfect. I want that again." His hands cupped her breasts, gently kneading them through the silky fabric of her blouse. Shuddering with passion, she arched her back, offering him greater access. He took full advantage of her offer, rubbing his hard palms over her softness until her nipples were as hard as his erection pressed against her thigh.

Jordan moaned, still unable to voice her need, but now fearing she might somehow disappoint him. Reality usually didn't fare well against memories. Would she be all he remembered? She tried again to speak, express her fears, if only to hear him dismiss them. If only to have him prove nothing in the past could ever be as good as here, now.

"Please," she whispered, finally finding her voice. "Cole, please. I need..."

"Yes, baby. Tell me what you need. Tell me what you want."

"So long... it's been so long."

"I know, baby. I know. So long, and I've dreamed of you."

"Cole... Cole, I'm afraid."

"Don't be. Remember. Remember how good we were. How perfect we fit."

"I haven't... Cole, please..."

Finally her words penetrated his sensual fog, and he looked into her eyes that glittered with a mixture of desire and anxiety. "Jordan?"

"I want...I want you, but I haven't...haven't been with anyone since..." She wanted to say, "since you," but she couldn't. Then as suddenly as desire had flared in his eyes only moments earlier, it died.

"Since your husband," he finished for her.

"Cole... wait," she begged, as he pulled away from her, leaving her emotionally as well as physically.

His breathing ragged, Cole stared at her. "For a few seconds I forgot there was someone else after me." The pain in his eyes scored her heart. "For a few seconds the past didn't exist. Only you. Only us. I wanted you so bad," he grated, as though he had just described the unforgivable sin.

"I wanted—want you just as much."

"But you stopped."

"Because I was afraid I wouldn't be as good as you remembered," she said, her voice shaking. "I was afraid, after all this time, that the reality would come in a poor second to your memories. And mine."

"So," he sighed heavily. "That's it? We shake hands and part friends."

"Not likely." *Not while either of us draws breath,* she wanted to add.

"Maybe it happened too fast."

"I don't know if it can happen any other way for us," she said honestly.

"But you want to try?" The frustration so evident in his tense body almost made her tell him no. Almost made her tell him to take her the way he wanted to.

"I...yes. I didn't realize it until a moment ago, but yes."

"All right." He rose from the sofa.

"Cole—"

"No. Maybe you're right," he said, knowing she was. "For us the physical was always first. Maybe we need to think with our hearts this time instead of our bodies." He leaned over, kissed her lightly on the cheek and let himself out.

Long after he had gone, Jordan stayed on the sofa, feeling empty, and wondering if insanity ran in her family.

"This is probably the worst idea I've ever had," Jordan mumbled as her Jeep bounced along the dirt road leading up to the construction site.

Strapped into the bucket seat on the front passenger side was a fully loaded picnic hamper containing fried chicken, roast beef sandwiches, deviled eggs, three kinds of fruit, a loaf of sourdough bread, a thermos of iced tea and even half of a chocolate layer cake, not to mention the necessary picnicking accoutrements. On the floorboard sat a cooler containing soft drinks and even a bottle of wine. Jordan was prepared for all contingencies.

Except Cole turning her down flat.

You're going to have an awful lot of food to eat if he does.

To be honest, after last night she wasn't sure how he would react when she showed up toting an apology and a lunch basket, but she was determined to talk to him. She was equally determined that he would listen.

Jordan braked the Jeep to a stop in front of a newly constructed, closet-size wood structure resembling a turnpike tollbooth that she supposed was a security checkpoint. A khaki-uniformed guard carrying a clipboard stepped out of the booth and walked toward her.

"Good afternoon," he said, respectfully touching the bill of his cap. "May I see your identification, miss?"

"Of course." Jordan showed him her driver's license.

He examined the license. "Yes, ma'am, could I also see your company ID?"

"I'm afraid I don't have one. I'm not an employee of Great Northern."

"Yes, ma'am. Well, then, I'm sorry, but I can't allow any unauthorized visitors in this area."

"If I could just speak with Mr. Forrester, I could clear up—"

"Yes, ma'am, but you see, we have explicit instructions—from Mr. Forrester himself—that absolutely no one is allowed on site without a security check and an authorized pass."

"Officer, I understand, but if you would be so kind as to contact Mr. Forrester, I'm sure he can vouch for me." Jordan's frustration level was rising by the minute. If this guy called her "ma'am" one more time she was going to scream.

"Yes, ma'am, but—"

"What's the problem, Sanders?"

"Oh, Mr. Forrester," the guard said as Cole approached the Jeep. "This lady says she knows you and—"

"It's all right, Sanders. I'll vouch for Mrs. Lockridge."

The guard touched his hat again. "Have a nice day, ma'am."

Jordan gnawed her bottom lip and pulled through the gate, then over to the side of the road and waited for Cole. Even though she couldn't clearly make out his eyes from beneath the brim of his hard hat, the set of his jaw told her he was not particularly thrilled to see her.

"Why the hell didn't you let me know you were coming?" he practically shouted. "I would have made a point to have you cleared ahead of time and be here when you arrived."

"Cole, I—"

"Do you have any idea how dangerous it is for you to be driving around up here with a bunch of kooks running about, cooking up God knows what?"

"I'm sorry."

"You should be." He jerked off the hard hat and wiped his forehead with the back of his forearm. "I ought to yank you out of that Jeep and paddle your butt until you can't sit down—"

"No. I'm not sorry I came. I'm sorry about last night."

His forearm halted in the middle of a second pass across his forehead. "What?" Slowly he lowered his hand.

"I said I came up here to tell you I'm sorry about what happened last night."

"Nothing happened last night."

"I know."

Their gazes locked, exchanged a silent message of understanding.

In a heartbeat her words had wiped away all of the leftover frustration. She was the last person in the world Cole expected to find waiting outside the security gate, but he wasn't crazy enough to interpret her apology as socially polite. Without stating what had been on both their minds last night, she was telling him as clearly as possible how much she regretted the way the evening had ended. She was telling him how much she had wanted him, still wanted him.

Cole sighed. "Get out of the Jeep."

"Cole, I thought—"

"Jordan." He put his hands on his hips. "Shut up and get out of the damned Jeep."

She did as he commanded, and the instant the driver's door slammed shut, he grabbed her by the upper arm and led her into a thick clump of trees. As soon as the trees obscured them from the curious eyes of the guard, he turned her in his arms and kissed her. Thoroughly.

Jordan forgot all about her apology. She forgot about the picnic. For a moment she almost forgot who she was. The only thing worth remembering was how much she loved being kissed by Cole. How much she adored being kissed by Cole. When they came up for air, she took a deep breath and said, "Remind me to apologize more often."

"You didn't have to come." He nibbled on her lower lip.

"I know."

"I would have called you sooner or later. Probably sooner."

"I was afraid it might be later." She wrapped her arms around his waist and urged him closer, but it wasn't close enough to suit her.

"You still deserve to have your butt paddled for roaming around alone."

"I wasn't roaming." She kissed his cheek. "I knew exactly where I was going." Unerringly her tongue found his earlobe and investigated its texture, its curve.

She was right on target, and the hard ridge of his arousal behind the fly of his jeans testified to her accuracy. Cole groaned. "As much as I'm enjoying this, I think we better stop."

She pulled back just far enough to look into his eyes before asking, "Are you hungry?"

"Dammit, Jordan—"

"I brought lunch."

With his body pressed hotly against hers and with several places, one in particular, getting hotter by the minute, he leaned forward until their foreheads touched, and he breathed, "We better eat it in a public place."

Before they could find a suitable location, Cole had to check on the installation of cameras and asked Jordan to come along. After fifteen minutes of trailing behind, watching him direct his crew and seeing the vast amount of ingenious equipment being installed, Jordan developed a new respect for what she had erroneously thought comprised a security system.

Cole pointed out the cameras being installed throughout the site, explaining they would be connected to the central monitoring system inside the blockhouse called the Security Shack, manned around the clock. The guard inside would have radio contact with the other security officers who walked the perimeters, reporting back periodically. He also showed her ground devices, photoelectric cells that, if disturbed, would trigger an alarm.

The scope of technology was mind-boggling, and Jordan was awed to observe just how precise the equipment was, despite its size. For example, the cameras, called Sensorvision, that were being installed in the trees along the intended path of the bobsled run were hardly bigger than a pencil eraser. Yet, mounted on poles, these cameras could tilt, zoom in and out, picking up anything that moved within a predetermined area. Inside the Security Shack a bank of multiscreen monitors continuously switching from camera to camera, enabled the guard to police the areas viewed by dozens of cameras.

"And if all of this doesn't get the job done," he said, ending the highly informative tour, "then we move on to infrared devices."

"What do they do?"

"Send out vectors or a series of rays. Then when a heat source passes, say like a bird or small animal, the first vector is disturbed. Like the cameras, they're monitored in the Security Shack and will indicate a disturbance, but no alarm is sounded. But if the second and third vectors are disrupted, an alarm is tripped, signaling something larger has penetrated. The cameras zero in, and we get a picture on the monitors."

At the awed expression in the depths of her green eyes, Cole smiled. "Everything you always wanted to know about security, but were too bored to ask, right?"

"Quite the contrary. I'm impressed right out of my socks."

"Don't be. This is all standard stuff. If you really want to be impressed, you should see some of the items in our government's little bag of top-secret goodies."

"The kind of goodies you know all about, right?"

At her innocent question, Cole abruptly went cold. "That was in another lifetime."

Sensing she had inadvertently crossed a forbidden boundary, she also sensed this taboo subject was connected to the darkness she sometimes saw in his eyes. "Was it so bad?" she asked, daring to risk his turning back into that darkness again.

"Yes."

She touched his arm, and he lifted his gaze to hers. "Can you tell me about it?"

"No. At least . . . not yet."

By tacit agreement they changed the subject back to cameras, monitors and other aspects of the security operation, but the bloom had faded from what had promised to be a special picnic. And try as she might, Jordan was unable to forget the look in Cole's eyes or the stabbing pain in her heart. The unknown "something" from his past that she had sensed from the very beginning had very definitely intruded on the present.

Chapter 9

Jordan spent the rest of the afternoon in the edit bay, slaving over a not-so-hot video. Because the balloon ride she had filmed the day after the charity show had not satisfied the client, she had offered them a reedit. The task was proving more difficult than usual, and she couldn't figure out why.

Because you're distracted, obviously. And the name of that distraction is Cole Forrester.

Jordan propped her chin in her hand. True, she hadn't been able to string two consecutive thoughts together without one of them being about Cole, but her lack of concentration didn't necessarily stem from the fact that she was dewy-eyed or love-struck. She was curious and worried and unable to put out of her mind the way he had withdrawn at the mention of anything connected to his former life.

Was it so bad?

Yes.

But he wasn't prepared to talk about it.

At least, not yet.

Whatever *it* was, Jordan knew instinctively that sooner or later Cole would have to tell her, because *it* was eating away at his insides like a malignancy. She saw the pain in his eyes, felt it in his body every time the subject was mentioned. Maybe he was waiting for the right time to tell her.

Where had she heard that before?

She sighed, rubbing the bridge of her nose between her thumb and index finger. Once more she tried to focus her attention on the video.

A few seconds later Barry strolled in. "Hey, sugar. What's doin'?" he asked, dragging up a chair beside her and taking a seat.

"A make-good," she answered. "Do me a favor and take a look at this one. I'm not sure it's any better now than it was the first time." Jordan rolled her chair aside to give him room at the editing controller.

"So, what's the problem?"

"The client loves the 'sweeping-over-the-water bit,'" she quoted using a nasal tone, "but wants the two fishermen bleeped."

"So far, so good."

"Oh, yeah? The two guys are smack-dab in the middle of the swoop."

"Not so good."

"You're telling me."

"Okay," Barry said, scanning the section of tape in question, "let's have a look."

Sure enough, right in the middle of the segment as the balloon drifted over the breathtaking lake, two men dressed in waders and fly-fisherman's vests and standing in front of a parked pickup truck appeared to be in deep conversation. Probably discussing the merits of flies over bait, Jordan thought. But then something snagged her attention.

"That's funny," she said, eyeing the tape closely.

"What?"

"Neither one of those guys had a fishing rod. For that matter I don't see a tackle box, or even a beer cooler. Nothing."

Barry pivoted his chair and in doing so, completely blocked her view of the screen. "Well," he shrugged, "maybe they're just scouting a new spot."

"The conversation looked pretty intense."

"Hey, these fishermen take their trout seriously. Uh, listen, you've been at this for a while. Why not let me have a crack at it? Go grab yourself a cup of coffee. Better still, get out of here for a few minutes. Get some fresh air."

She shook her head. "Thanks, but I want to get this finished and mailed to the clients." When she started to roll her chair back into the editing bay, he didn't make room by moving aside. Jordan hiked her thumb. "Move it, buster," she said teasingly.

"Make me," he said, folding his arms across his chest. Jordan was on the verge of delivering a playful slug to his shoulder when she saw the look in his eyes. Regardless of the lightness in his tone of voice, there was a steely hardness in his eyes. He wasn't teasing.

"C'mon, Barry. I've got to get back to work." The situation had suddenly taken on a uneasy quality she didn't care for.

"You work too hard, *and* I'm offering to pinch-hit for a while."

"Barry—"

"I insist."

She raised her hands in mock surrender. "Fine. Be a glutton for punishment. I'm going for lemonade. You want some?"

"Naw. Now, go on, scram."

She did as he requested, but not before she noticed that he didn't turn back to the viewing until she picked up her purse and headed out the door.

Once outside in the sunshine and fresh mountain air, Barry's strange behavior didn't stay with her for long. She left Georgian Square, walking up Main Street, then over to Lincoln and the Lincoln West Mall. Twenty-five minutes later she breezed back into Video Images, feeling refreshed and ready to tackle the make-do, if Barry hadn't succeeded in her absence.

"Hey, sugar," he said, with a much more agreeable disposition than when she left. "How was the lemonade?"

She glanced at the first editing bay and noticed the screen was blank. "Cold. Where's my tape?"

"Done. *Finito,*" he said with an exaggerated flourish of his hand.

"So quickly?"

"Hey, what can I say? I'm good."

"I'll say. Where's the tape?"

"Uh," he glanced around. "I had it right here a minute ago. Oh, well, no big hurry, you can see it in the morning."

"No, I'd rather make sure it's ready— There it is," Jordan said, pulling the tape from beneath a stack of invoices. "Let's have a look at this masterpiece."

Barry snapped his fingers. "I almost forgot, you have a message."

"Who from?"

"Your daughter. Something about a collar?"

"Oh." Jordan couldn't prevent the trace of disappointment in her voice. She had hoped Cole would call. "Fancy means a cat collar, more specifically a collar for her new kitten."

"So, she finally wore you down, huh?" Barry said, flashing his broad grin.

"With an assist from Cole."

"Cole Forrester?"

At the mention of Cole's name, Jordan noticed an immediate change in Barry's attitude, even in his body language. She tried to credit the defensive tone of voice and stance to the protectiveness of a good friend, but somehow she sensed that wasn't all there was to it.

"Yes. One of the construction workers had a litter of kittens, and last night Cole, Fancy and I drove over and picked out the cutest little black-and-white—Manx, I think Cole called it—you ever saw."

"And baby makes three," he said under his breath.

"What?"

"Sounds like a nice little family outing. So, tell me, what does friend Forrester think about becoming a father overnight?"

Jordan couldn't believe the venom in his voice. If she didn't know better, she would think Barry was jealous.

"I thought you weren't going to tell Forrester about Fancy," he said sharply, "and the next thing I hear, the three of you are picking out pets. What's next? Playing house?"

Jordan's sudden intake of breath warned Barry he had gone too far. "Sorry," he muttered. "That was uncalled for and I apologize."

"For your information, I haven't told him. But I don't understand your antagonism. Cole has a job to do like everybody else."

"Yeah, well. His job sucks."

She blinked, shocked at her friend's vehemence. "What's gotten into you, Barry?"

"Me? What's gotten into *you?* I thought you cared about me. I thought we shared the same values, the same concerns about the earth and about right and wrong. Now you're sleeping with the enemy."

If Jordan hadn't been holding the video in both hands, she would have slapped his face. For a second she entertained the idea of tossing the tape aside in favor of doing just that. Instead she took several deep, cleansing breaths and said, "Obviously this isn't a subject you and I can discuss rationally. But just to set the record straight. Cole Forrester is *not* yours or anyone else's enemy in this town. And you may be my best friend, but that does not give you the right to appraise my private life. I'll sleep with whoever I damn well please, and it's none of your business."

"If you've got a problem with that, Clark, talk to *me.*"

Jordan's head snapped around. Cole stood on the other side of the customer counter. She had no idea how long he had been standing there or how much of their conversation he had overheard. From the murderous look in his eyes, obviously he had heard enough to know Barry was trespassing on very personal ground.

Had Cole also heard Barry ask if she had told him about Fancy?

"Back off," Cole told Barry succinctly.

The ice in Cole's voice made Jordan go dead still inside. Never had she heard him speak with such chilling, threatening intent in his voice, and it frightened her. For perhaps the first time, she caught a glimpse of the man who had lived on the edge all those years. A man who had probably faced death or even worse in his line of work and had survived. She wondered at what cost. The fact that the same man could whisper tender endearments to her and cut Barry cold with merely a look made her wonder if she knew Cole as well as she thought.

The two men glared at each other for so long, their bodies taut with anger, that she was afraid they might come to physical blows. But finally Barry did as Cole recommended and backed away.

"I'll see you tomorrow," he said and left the store.

Cole stepped around the counter and put his hand on Jordan's shoulder. "Are you all right?"

"Yes. Cole, Barry didn't mean any harm. He only wants the best for me—"

"Like hell. He wants you."

"You're wrong. Barry and I are friends. Period." Jordan held her breath, waiting to see any indication that he had overheard Barry's question about Fancy. When none was forthcoming, she added on a shaky breath, "But I'll admit he has a tendency to be overprotective. It's my fault. I'm afraid I've depended on him far too many times. Until today I didn't realize just how symbiotic our relationship had become."

"Good thing I showed up when I did."

Jordan sighed, releasing some of the tension. "Why did you come by?"

"To ask you out to dinner."

Her spirits lightened instantly, then fell just as quickly. "I'd love to, but I don't have a sitter, and on such late notice..." Her shoulders lifted in a hopeless shrug.

"Then we'll take Fancy with us."

Jordan picked up her purse and dropped the videotape inside. "You may regret your invitation after sitting across the table from a three-year-old with questionable table manners."

"I doubt that very much. Besides—" He put his arm around her shoulder and drew her to his side. "I'll have the pleasure of spending the evening with two beauties instead of one."

As Cole walked Jordan to her car, his gaze scanned the area, checking for any sign of Barry Clark. A sixth sense he had depended on to save his life more than once told him Clark was less of a friend than Jordan realized. Even though Cole's suspicions were as yet unproved, he had no intention of giving Clark the benefit of the doubt. The thought that Jordan might be in even the slightest danger doubled his intent to keep an eye on her friend.

"What time shall I pick up my dates?" he asked, looking at Jordan, but still attuned to all the movement in his peripheral vision.

She checked her watch. "An hour from now?"

"An hour it is. And Jordan . . ."

"Yes."

"Be careful."

"I'm always careful."

"Then be extra careful."

On the drive home, Jordan thought about her confrontation with Barry, and Cole's insistence that Barry wanted more than friendship from her. Was there any truth to Cole's admittedly prejudiced point of view? she wondered, recalling Barry's words. *I thought you cared about me. Sleeping with the enemy.* Was it possible Barry had crossed over the line of their friendship into something more and she hadn't seen it, hadn't even realized it could happen? And had she ever said or done anything to encourage him to cross over that line? After searching her conscience, she could honestly answer no, but that knowledge did little to squelch the idea that hers and Barry's relationship would never be the same again.

Cole was right on time, and she and Fancy were ready and waiting. Delighted to be part of the "date," Fancy jabbered nonstop over Hoosier Pass, on into Breckenridge and right up until the moment Cole parked his truck in front of her favorite fast-food restaurant.

Jordan eyed the fast-food chain's famous Golden Arches. "You're kidding."

Cole reached over and unbuckled Fancy from the child's safety seat they had transferred from Jordan's Jeep to his truck. "What do you think?"

"I think," she said softly, "that you're terrific."

His gaze swung to hers and stayed, warmed her, in fact, grew warmer and warmer until her body was flushed with heat, tight with longing. Finally Fancy's rambunctious insistence that they get going forced them to disengage the lingering look. Jordan made a mental note to make sure she had a reliable sitter at the ready from now on.

And how long is, from now on? she wondered. How long would Cole be in her life? A week? Two? Maybe it would take four weeks to establish security at the construction site. How ironic if that were the case, since the first time they were together lasted only four weeks. Maybe she was doomed to have him only four weeks every four years.

Oh, stop this witch hunt for reasons not to enjoy the moment. Don't ruin today thinking about yesterday or tomorrow. This is reality. Make the best of it.

Dinner, at least for Fancy, was a rousing success. For Cole and Jordan, the food was received less enthusiastically but the company was highly appreciated. While Fancy scampered up ladders and slid down slides, they watched, waved and, in between, talked. No heavy topics, just comfortable conversation, the kind a married couple might have while they enjoyed seeing their child at play. Jordan knew she was courting trouble by entertaining such thoughts, but oh, how wonderful to dream.

One Happy Meal, an ice-cream cone and one and one half hours of playtime later, they were on their way back to Fairplay, a drowsy Fancy nodding in her seat. Carefully Jordan tried to position her purse as a pillow for Fancy's head, only to discover she had forgotten to remove the videotape of the make-good she and Barry had worked on. Without thinking she removed the hard plastic case containing the tape and laid it on the seat beside her.

Ten minutes later, Cole's truck rolled onto Jordan's gravel driveway and braked at the foot of the rock stairs leading to the cabin's front door. As he had the night before, Cole carried the sleeping Fancy while her mother led the way. No light glowed from inside the cabin except for the barely perceptible glow of a constantly burning night-light in the kitchen, and Jordan berated herself for forgetting to switch on the outside lights. When they reached the porch, she took out her key and started to unlock the front door.

Before the key touched the lock, the door swung open.

Instantly Cole handed Fancy into Jordan's arms and whispered, "Stay here. Don't move. Don't make a sound until I come back for you." Those instructions delivered, he slipped soundlessly into the inky darkness surrounding the cabin.

Jordan's first instinct was to turn around, race back to the truck and lock herself and Fancy inside. Instead she fought the age-old fight-or-flight urge, hugged Fancy to her chest and prayed. While her body trembled and her heart hammered, she listened for any sound she could identify as being made by Cole and not some masked intruder. She understood why he had left them outside the house in order to protect them from anyone who might still be inside, but understanding did little to calm her frayed nerves. She held her child tighter and thanked God that Fancy had been too played-out to stay awake.

Standing in the darkness, waiting for Cole, the night closed in around her, black and forbidding, far from the soothing velvety summer nights she so enjoyed. A breeze, the kind she would have labeled gentle only moments ago, whistled through the aspens, singing a mournful night song. Even the moon offered her no comfort, its pale, tree-shrouded light more ghostly than gossamer. The only person she could depend on to conquer the night was inside her home, possibly about to come face-to-face with thieves or worse.

Dear God, please protect him, she prayed. *Please bring him back safe to me.*

She waited in the dark. And waited. For the sound of a struggle, a gunshot. For the sound of Cole's footsteps, his voice. Fear gnawed at her insides like a ravenous wild animal. She waited until she thought her fear would unravel her mind like loose yarn, snatched by the wind and blown away into the darkness. Just when she thought she couldn't take one more second of waiting, the living room lights came on and Cole reappeared.

"You all right?" he asked, stepping through the open doorway.

"Y-yes."

"I've searched the house, and if there was an intruder, he, or they, have gone." Carefully, so as not to waken Fancy, he lifted her from Jordan's trembling arms.

"You're...s-sure?"

"Positive. Trust me, baby. If I thought for one split second this house wasn't empty, I'd get you and Fancy so far away so quick you'd think you were jet propelled."

She sighed, knowing in her heart that she had nothing to fear as long as Cole protected her. She may have resented the kind of life that had once taken him from her, but she also respected the fact that such a life bred survivors, men who knew how to deal with danger and dangerous situations.

Upstairs, Cole supported Fancy's limp-with-sleep body while Jordan stripped off play clothes, then slipped a gown over the mop of red curls and down her little body. Now, safely tucked into her own bed, the child dozed, unaware of the brush with danger.

"We'll check in on her in a few minutes," Cole said as Jordan kissed Fancy's cheek and smoothed back a wayward curl. She followed him out of the room.

"Shouldn't we call the police?" Jordan asked.

"From out here, your emergency calls go to the sheriff's department, don't they?"

"Yes. Usually one of the volunteer deputies responds, unless it's serious. Why?"

"Because I can probably accomplish as much as they can and with a whole lot less hassle." He paused for a moment, then added, "We'll call them later. Right now, I want you to walk through every room in the house and tell me if anything is missing or disturbed in any way. If you do, point, don't touch, or we could screw up a decent set of prints."

Jordan hesitated, staring up at him, more than a little awed by the Cole Forrester who was the survivor of that lifestyle she had found so comforting only a few moments ago. His gaze was so intense, his brown eyes had darkened almost to black. His voice was deadly calm and tempered-steel cold. This was the Cole Forrester of the past, and Jordan wasn't sure how to deal with him.

As if sensing the reason for her hesitation, he raised his hand and gently stroked her cheek. When he spoke, his voice was soft, reassuring. "Don't worry, baby. I'm with you every step of the way. And I won't let anything happen to you or the little beauty. Not ever."

She turned her head, leaning into his caress and whispered, "Thank you."

He took her by the hand and motioned to the guest bedroom. "C'mon, let's start in here."

They searched the upstairs room by room, finding everything just as Jordan had left it. Then they moved on to the downstairs, again finding nothing taken or disturbed until they came to the knotty-pine armoire that housed her television, stereo equipment, VCR, audio- and videotapes. Both sides of the double-door cabinet stood open, and videotapes were strewn everywhere. Forgetting Cole's warning, Jordan stretched out her hand to retrieve the copy of Fancy's favorite Disney video sticking halfway out of the VCR. Cole grabbed her arm.

"I know your instinct is to put everything back the way you had it, but don't."

"So they can...check for fingerprints," she said, almost as if she were reminding herself.

Cole nodded. "And my guess is, it will be tomorrow at the earliest before the sheriff's department can do that."

"Tomorrow." Jordan stood there, staring at the jumbled mess that used to be her entertainment center, and considered the number of times she would have to walk past the armoire before the police could dust for fingerprints. She thought about having to repeatedly look at the blatant reminder that her home had been violated. She shivered.

Cole put his hands on her shoulders, gently kneading them for a moment, then led her to the sofa. Like a puppet whose strings had just been cut, she plopped down onto a cushion.

"I'll be right back," he said, and disappeared into the kitchen. He returned a moment later carrying a glass of wine. "Here, take a sip of this. You'll feel better."

She took the glass, but didn't drink. "Why, Cole?" she whispered. "Why would anyone break into my house? For a television, a VCR and a few measly tapes? That's crazy."

Cole glanced around the room. "Looks that way, doesn't it?"

"What do you mean, 'looks that way'? It *is* that way." She gestured toward the armoire.

"Maybe."

Jordan shivered again and set the untouched glass of wine on the coffee table. "I need to check on Fancy," she said, and headed for the stairs. At the bottom, she glanced back at Cole as if to make sure he was still there.

"You go on up. I'm going to call the authorities."

She smiled, satisfied, at least temporarily, that she wouldn't be alone. When she came back downstairs the floodlights strategically placed around the cabin had been turned on, the front door was locked and chained, and Cole was standing in the middle of her living room, his head bent, his concentration centered on a . . .

Jordan gasped. "Is that a gun?"

His head snapped up. "Jordan—"

She pointed a trembling finger at the pistol in his hand. "I don't want it in my house."

"They might come back."

"I don't care."

"You will if they come back."

"Then we'll leave. I'll take Fancy and go to a motel."

"This is your home, Jordan. You have a right to protect it."

"Don't preach the constitution to me, Cole. The only thing worth knowing about guns is that they kill. Please," she begged, her eyes never leaving the pistol, "please...take it out of my house."

The fear mixed with determination sparking from the emerald depths of her eyes was a force he couldn't combat. "All right." He fished his keys from his pocket and left, returning moments later wearing a lightweight jacket. He was deliberately giving her the impression that he had locked the gun in his truck. Cole saw no reason to upset her by correcting her assumption with the truth, particularly since she had no concept of the malicious people she might be up against.

"Thank you," she said on a ragged sigh.

"You're welcome." The weapon, riding snugly between the small of his back and the waistband of his jeans and concealed by the jacket, felt oddly comfortable. Even though it had been a long time since he had had occasion to use a gun, his years of training came back as easily as though he had turned in his weapon and credentials yesterday. The realization called forth memories long buried and too painful to remember. He shoved such thoughts to the back of his mind and concentrated on the problem at hand. Making sure Jordan and Fancy were safe. He took some comfort in the fact that he was protecting them, even if he was going against Jordan's express wishes regarding the gun. In this case, better prepared than sorry.

"Well, I…" She didn't want him to leave, but wasn't sure she had the courage to ask him to stay. "What did the police say when you called?"

"About what I expected. An officer will be out tomorrow to investigate. I asked them to call before they showed up and gave them Video Images' number."

"Thanks. I don't know what I would have done if you hadn't been here. And I don't even want to *think* about how I would have reacted if Fancy and I had been by ourselves."

"You would have done the smart thing. The brave thing. Turned around, jumped in your car and driven like hell on fire for the first available help."

She managed a weak smile, thrilled that her initial instincts had been good ones. "I hope I never have the opportunity to find out for sure. Right now I don't feel very brave, and something tells me I'm going to need all the courage I can get to face the rest of the night alone."

"You won't."

"Won't what, need courage? Oh yes—"

"You won't be alone. I'll be here."

"Cole, I—"

"No arguments."

"But I'm—"

"If you're uncomfortable with the idea of our spending the night under the same roof, tough. Get comfortable, because I'm not going anywhere. I'm staying right here and that's final."

"Good," she finally managed to say.

"What?"

"I said 'good.' And if you had let me finish, I would have added a very heartfelt thank-you."

"Oh."

She crossed the room to where he stood and looked up at him, her eyes shining with unshed tears. "Thank you, Cole. For being here, for protecting us, for...for..." Her voice wavered, and she shuddered as the events and emotional turmoil of the past hour finally took their toll, rolling over her in a single engulfing wave, threatening to suck her under, drown her.

Cole saw the backlash coming, saw the tears she had probably been holding back since the moment they stepped onto her porch, slide down her smooth pale cheeks.

"Everything..." she said on a broken sob.

"Oh, God, baby." Cole took her in his arms. "Don't cry. Don't you know..." He captured her tear-streaked face between his hands, and whispered, "Don't you know I'd die before I'd let anyone hurt you?"

She raised up on tiptoe. "Kiss me, Cole. Kiss me."

He was a heartbeat away from accepting her invitation when he felt her hands move to his waist. Fearing she would discover the gun, he reached down, caught both her hands in his, brought them up to his chest, then quickly wrapped his arms around her. Trapped in Cole's bear hug, her head on his wide chest, Jordan released a deep sigh of satisfaction. She couldn't remember the last time, if ever, when she had felt so secure, so loved. Cole's strong, steady heartbeat beneath her ear was the music of her dreams, the powerfully eloquent rhythm of life. Her dreams, her life. Her man.

Cole had seen this whiplash of trauma too many times not to recognize how fragile Jordan's emotions were. A scrape with danger was guaranteed to send the lucky survivor wild with a heady rush of grateful-to-be-alive adrenaline. She was in the throes of the first rolling wave, and to take what she so sweetly offered would not only be unfair to her, but to him as well. When they made love again, he wanted it to be for all the right reasons and at the right time.

"Jordan, listen to me." His breath fanned the top of her ear. "You've had a bad scare. You're wound tight, tighter than you realize. You need rest, baby." He kissed her temple and said softly, "Go to bed."

She blinked, gazing up at him. "But, Cole—"

"Trust me?"

She nodded.

"Then go to bed. I'll be right here all night."

Sensing further protests would be met with equal stubbornness, Jordan gave up and went to bed.

After three restless hours of tossing and turning on the sofa, Cole had decided he must have been out of his mind to send the most beautiful, intelligent, sensual woman in the world to lie alone. While his saner, more chivalrous self applauded his actions, his baser self writhed with frustration. *Bucking for sainthood, Forrester?* Cole almost laughed. If there was a less likely candidate for that honor, he didn't know one. No gold stars here. Just a mortal man who had the good sense to know when not to cross the line.

But God in heaven, how he wanted to cross that line! Wanted it more than he wanted his next breath. The only thing stopping him was the certain knowledge that the time was not yet right. Instinctively he knew that no matter how moved Jordan had been or how much she wanted and needed the physical affirmation of life, if she had awakened tomorrow morning beside him with her daughter a room away, she would have felt guilty.

Hell, what was he thinking? He would feel just as guilty, maybe more so. No, he did the right thing by sending Jordan to bed. Alone. *Then why the bloody hell did it feel so wrong?*

He wished she was here now so he could hold her, just hold her, so she could feel how much he needed her, how much he had always needed her, but hadn't realized until it was too late.

"Cole?"

He sat bolt upright on the couch. "Are you all right? Is Fancy—"

"Fine. Everything is fine. I just couldn't get to sleep."

Cole scrubbed his stubbled face with both hands and swung his stockinged feet onto the floor. "Yeah. I know what you mean."

He heard the whisper of air moving over silky fabric an instant before he felt the weight of her body beside him on the sofa. "You want to talk?" he asked.

"No."

Oh, please, don't let her ask me again to kiss her. No man is that strong.

"I want . . . can you just hold me?"

Cole smiled in the darkness. "Yes," he murmured and gathered her into his arms.

Chapter 10

When Jordan opened her eyes the next morning, she was alone on the couch and someone had covered her with a quilt. Still muzzy from lack of sleep, she had a vague recollection of asking Cole to hold her, then falling asleep in his strong arms. At first, she decided it must have been a dream. But then she sat up, and her hand touched a piece of paper lying on the arm of the sofa. A note, hastily scribbled in bold script read "Left at sunrise. Coffee's on. Everything secure. Call me, Cole."

The memory wasn't a dream. She *had* slept in Cole's arms. Following closely on the heels of that revelation came the reminder of why Cole had spent the night at her house in the first place.

The break-in!

She threw back the quilt, dashed up the stairs and into Fancy's room, only to find she, too, had been neatly covered. Knowing her daughter was prone to toss and tunnel through the bed covers like a mole, Jordan deduced that

Cole had not only made sure she was snugly tucked in, but had done the same for Fancy.

Thank God for Cole. Last night's harrowing experience would have been considerably worse had it not been for his quick thinking and total disregard for danger. Jordan shuddered to think what might have happened if he hadn't been there. Such bravery deserved a reward.

How about the truth?

Yes, the truth. After last night she owed Cole that much. But his bravery notwithstanding, it was past time for her to tell him about Fancy. The fact that he considered her honest to a fault didn't make for a happy scenario when she told him, but tell him she must. And maybe Fate had provided an opportunity she couldn't ignore.

Weeks ago, Jill had invited her and Fancy to her family's annual reunion, and even though business prohibited Jordan's attendance, she had decided to let Fancy go. Since the reunion was to be held in Denver, a two-hour drive from Fairplay, Jill's parents had persuaded Jordan to allow Fancy to stay overnight and return the following afternoon. As of noon today, Jordan would be, if not footloose, then Fancy-free. Mixed in with all of the usual parental anxiety over being separated from her child, she felt an additional dread that tonight would be the prime opportunity to confess her lie.

She was glad Fancy would be gone when she told Cole the truth. Why, she wasn't sure, but it had something to do with her gut instinct that his reaction would not be gentle or happy, at least not a first. No, that was a lie, or at least a justification. One she had used from the beginning to keep from telling him the truth. The fact of the matter was she didn't know for sure how he would react to her news. He cared about Fancy, of that much she was certain. Partly because she was her child, but also because he genuinely cared.

Jordan saw it in the depths of his beautiful coffee-brown eyes when he looked at Fancy, saw it in his smile when she was near.

And when she told him the truth, after the smoke cleared, regardless of how he would feel about her mother, he would still care deeply about Fancy. But, she admitted honestly, his first reaction might not be an expression of how deeply Cole did care about Fancy, and for that reason, it was better that Fancy wasn't around. With her inquisitive and perceptive little mind, she would intuitively know something was wrong between her mother and the man she had grown so fond of. Jordan was concerned that undercurrent of tension alone might be enough to inhibit the fragile bond between father and daughter. So...

She had to tell him tonight. No more putting it off. No more justifications. Before the sun rose tomorrow morning Cole would know that he was Fancy's real father.

Tired and a bit bleary-eyed, Cole sat in his truck, the driver's door wide open, one booted foot propped on the hinge. His left wrist was draped over the steering wheel, and he held a cup of steaming coffee in his other hand. With the construction site behind him, he stared out the truck's windshield into the wooded landscape yet to be touched, thinking about the events of the past twenty-four hours.

Last night had been one of the best and worst nights of his life. Best because he had spent it holding Jordan in his arms, and worst because sometime before dawn he had realized what he had almost lost. Jordan. And Fancy.

Even the thought made him sick to his stomach. Every time he remembered the fear in Jordan's eyes or the sweet weight of Fancy snuggled in his arms, he felt physically ill. If anything had happened to them... He couldn't finish the thought. The *if* was too big and the possibilities too horrific to contemplate.

I'd kill anyone who touched either one of them. And I guarantee the death would be slow and excruciatingly painful.

The problem was, they had already been touched. Not physically, of course, but emotionally, and as much as Cole wanted to wrap his fingers around the culprit's throat, he didn't have a name. But he had an idea whose name he could paste into place when the time came, and it would break Jordan's heart when he did.

Barry Clark.

Cole sipped the strong, hot brew and thought about the people in the past he had known and liked, on both sides, who had, for one reason or another, slipped into greed or carelessness as the years went by. Each time he had been disappointed but not devastated, choosing to believe it went with the territory, so to speak. Not many could hold up to the prolonged exposure of living on the edge without experiencing some corrosive effects. Over the past few hours, thinking about his suspicions of Barry and realizing what those suspicions would do to Jordan, Cole had also reached a profound realization about himself and why none of those past falls from grace had affected him deeply.

As much as he had liked those people, even called some of them friends, he had never been close to any of them. Not close enough to hurt for them or to be hurt by them. The admission cut into old emotional scar tissue Cole had long since thought tough as boot leather, and he discovered the wounds beneath were still tender. He might not like the nasty little bit of self-discovery, but he could deal with it. Because those times were in the past.

Jordan wouldn't have that luxury.

Cole glanced at the file folder lying on the seat beside him and thought about the information it contained. Not solid proof, but certainly strong suspicion. When Jordan learned of Barry's probable involvement with an extremely militant environmental organization that specialized in hard-line action, the news would hit her hard. Because whether she would admit it or not, she still believed in all the things Cole had learned were expendable. Dreams, faith, even honor. Whether she realized it or not, she still believed in fairy tales.

And he was going to have to be the one to tell her there were no shining knights on white horses or frog princes. Sadder still was the fact that for a few days, during these few bright hours since finding Jordan again, *he* had caught a glimpse of that fairy tale and almost . . . almost believed it himself.

Thankfully the chirping of the mobile phone cut into his thoughts.

"Forrester here," he barked.

"Lockridge here."

Cole smiled, his voice softening. "Good morning."

"Good morning. Thanks for the coffee."

"Figured you might need a quick boost."

He heard her yawn. "I'm not sure rocket fuel would have helped, but thanks."

"Jordan, I need to talk to you."

"If it concerns last night, I'd rather not. At least, not now. I've got a difficult shoot this afternoon and I've got to pack for Fancy—"

"Pack? What for?"

"Jill is taking her to Denver this afternoon for the Dobson family annual blowout reunion. They won't be back until tomorrow afternoon."

"And that's all right with you?"

"Of course, why wouldn't it be?"

"She's just a baby. And how well do you know these people?"

"Very well. Jill has been Fancy's only sitter, practically since she was born."

"How old is this Jill person?"

"Nineteen."

"Nineteen? Isn't that a bit young for you to let her cart your daughter off to another city?"

Jordan smiled to herself. If it wasn't for the genuine concern in his voice, she might be upset with his questioning. "She's not carting—"

"You know, there's no such thing as 'too careful' where kids are concerned."

"Cole—"

"What do you know about this girl's family, anyway?"

"Cole."

"What?"

"I've known Tanya and Ed Dobson for as long as I've been in Fairplay. I even lived at the Dobsons' home while my cabin was under construction. They're generous, hard-working *family* people. Jill is the oldest of their eight children and so responsible that occasionally she makes me look like a juvenile."

When he didn't respond, she said, "Feel better now?"

"I'm sorry. I didn't mean to sound like the Grand Inquisitor. It's just after what happened last night, I'm...concerned."

You have every right, she wanted to say but couldn't. "And I'm...very grateful for your concern, but actually, what happened last night convinced me even more that Fancy should go with Jill. Not only has she been looking forward to the trip for weeks, but maybe it's better that she's not around when the police investigate. I don't want her frightened to stay in her own room."

"Yeah," Cole agreed. "The world is scary enough. No point looking for bogeymen where there aren't any. Would you . . . do me a favor?"

"Sure."

"Kiss her goodbye for me."

"O-of . . . course." Fortunately he couldn't see the tears in her eyes or the tortured expression on her face. She wanted to tell him then, wanted to pour out her heart and beg him to forgive her lie. But that wasn't the kind of confession you made over the telephone. Instead she simply added, "Thanks, Cole."

"For what?"

"For caring."

"Couldn't help myself," he said. "I'm a sucker for red-heads."

The silence that followed was long and filled with unspo-ken dialogue.

All redheads?

Just one in particular. A tall gorgeous woman I can't seem to forget.

You want to?

Not anymore.

Because . . .

Because she's a fire I can't put out.

Finally Cole cleared his throat. "Did you say something about a difficult shoot?"

"Uh, yes. I, uh . . . a client wants to go over Mosquito Pass."

"In a hot-air balloon?"

She laughed. "No, in a Jeep. As a matter of fact two Jeeps."

"I don't understand."

"Four-wheeling," she replied. "This guy has rented a couple of Jeep CJs and had a mount for my camera fitted inside one so I can record his nerve-racking trek."

"Have you ever done any four-wheeling?"

"Only once, over Black Bear Pass near Telluride. I'll admit it's not my cup of tea, but my driver is an expert and so is the client. Actually Barry is the four-wheel daredevil, but he was booked solid or he would have jumped at the chance. It's a sport for him. As a matter of fact he's got a two-room cabin east of Breckenridge that's only accessible by four-wheel drive."

"How long will you be gone?"

"We're leaving around one, so I'd say we'll be back around three or four o'clock."

Cole was glad she couldn't see the frown on his face. He didn't like the idea worth a damn of her careening over narrow mountain roads. He started to tell her so, but decided she probably wouldn't appreciate his sticking his nose into her business. "Can we have dinner together?" he asked instead.

"I'd love to."

"Call me when you make it back over the pass and we'll decide where."

"Great."

"And Jordan?"

"Yes."

"Be careful."

Several hours later as she stood watching the client and her driver check and recheck the vehicles, Jordan was reminded of Cole's words. Both Jeeps sported V-8 engines with four-to-one gear ratios and were fitted with lift kits so that the body and springs of each vehicle had been raised at least four inches above factory specifications. Each vehicle had heavy-duty shocks, full roll cages and wide tires specifically designed for the sport of four-wheeling. Parked on the east side of the pass, Jordan shielded her eyes against the blinding sun and appraised the narrow ribbon of dirt road that wound around, up and over the area that experienced four-wheelers referred to as "a bitch of a ride" for more than eleven thousand feet. Judging from the number of switchbacks she could see from where she stood, Jordan could understand why. Thank goodness her driver, Jake Evans, had spent enough time on most of the hazardous mountain passes in this part of Colorado to file for a homestead exemption.

"Ready?" Jake called from his side of the Jeep.

"As I'll ever be," she said, and climbed inside.

She was almost two and a half hours late, and Cole was climbing the walls.

Where the hell can she be? And why the hell hasn't she called me?

He had waited a full half hour past the time she was supposed to return before he made the first call to Video Images. The employee who answered the phone hadn't seemed concerned at all and promised to have Jordan call the moment she came in.

That had been over two hours ago.

The second time Cole called, he talked to a woman named Susan, who told him she didn't really know any more than the first time he had called but took his number promising faithfully she would have Jordan call, the very instant she walked through the door. Then Susan reassured Cole that there was probably no cause for concern. He had the feeling she wasn't telling everything she knew, but when he tried to push her, she ended the conversation, saying she had a customer.

Probably no cause for concern. Probably no cause for concern. The phrase bounced around inside Cole's head, clattering like a warning signal from hell. Something was wrong. He could feel it in his gut. He punched in the number of Video Images for the third time, then abruptly hung up the mobile phone, started the truck and headed for Breckenridge. In Cole's mind, *probably* was too damned close to *possibly.*

By the time he parked at the rear entrance of Jordan's business, Cole's nerves were tied in more knots than a macramé potholder. He stormed into the store, stalked up to the counter and aimed his words at the man behind the counter like a marksman at a turkey shoot. "My name is Cole Forrester. I want to know where your boss is, and I want to know now."

"M-Mr. F-Forrester," the young man stammered. "I was just about to dial your—"

"Where is she?" Cole demanded.

"There was a slight problem during the shoot. One of the Jeeps tried to make it over a rock slide in the road and—"

"What? What happened?"

"The Jeep slid pretty bad. Then they tried a 'come-along,' but it didn't work. Then it started to rain and the Jeep just . . ." He shrugged, helplessly. "Fell off the mountain."

"Jordan," Cole said, his voice hoarse with emotion. "Where's Jordan?"

"They took her to the hospital, but—"

Cole never heard the rest because he was already gone.

He didn't remember actually driving to the hospital, only that it seemed to take hours instead of minutes. And the parking lot seemed to be miles from the emergency entrance instead of a few feet. And the nurse behind the admittance desk seemed to be ignoring his demand to know where Ms. Lockridge was, rather than calmly directing him to one of the treatment cubicles.

Heedless of the fact that he could be interrupting crucial treatment, Cole yanked the curtain aside, totally unprepared for the sight that met his eyes.

Jordan, in a hospital gown, sitting cross-legged in the middle of the bed, looking untouched and gloriously alive.

"Cole!" Her eyes lighted up with a burst of joy so pure and sweet it shone like the sun's radiance.

For a moment he was so overcome with relief he felt dizzy.

"Cole?" she said, frowning. "Are you all right?"

"Am I…" His voice all but squeaked. "Are *you* all right? They said the Jeep went off the mountain. They told me…oh my, God," he whispered when he finally caught sight of the bandage on the left side of her forehead.

"What?" Seeing the direction of his gaze, she reached up, touched the bandage and said, "This? It's not as bad as it looks. Just a scrape and it was my fault anyway. If I hadn't tried to lean out the window…" Her words died at the look of stark, raw terror in his eyes.

He walked the few remaining steps to her bedside and lifted his hand toward her face, hesitated, then touched her cheek. His hand was shaking.

"I almost… I've never been so scared in my life."

He meant it. She could read the truth of his words in the depths of his browner than brown eyes. Hope, the kind that springs from a love too deep to ever die, the kind that soars from a dream too special not to become reality, bloomed in her heart. *He does care,* she thought. *More than he knows. More than maybe he's willing to admit, but he…cares!* Where there was caring, there was hope. And where there was hope, they had a chance to build something beautiful and lasting out of the ashes of their past.

"Take me home," she said a second before his lips touched hers in a sweet affirmation of those hopes.

Getting home took another hour, and by the time Cole pulled his truck into her driveway, Jordan was in the throes of a full-blown attack of guilt. But when he helped her out of the truck, promptly swung her up and into his arms and carried her to her front door, the guilt almost overwhelmed her.

He's being so sweet, so tender. If he knew the truth, he'd probably drop me on the nearest street corner.

Jordan's temperament had changed since they had left the hospital, and Cole didn't know why. He *did* know the last thing his green-eyed adventuress wanted was to be treated like an invalid, but at this point any excuse to keep holding her next to him was a good one.

"Put me down," she instructed, none too sweetly.

"You've just come from a hospital where—"

"They keep sick people. And in case you haven't noticed they didn't keep me, so that means I'm not sick. Therefore, you don't have to treat me like an invalid. So, put ... me ... down."

"No."

"Pardon me?" she said, a little shocked by his unexpected answer.

"I said no."

"And just why not, I'd like to ask." Shock was quickly giving way to anger. She started to squirm.

"Because I want to hold you." She stopped squirming. "Because for a few minutes today I seriously entertained the possibility that I might not ever hold you again."

She gazed up at him, her eyes full of understanding, full of hope, as she gently slipped her arm around his neck. She pushed her guilt to the corner of her mind, pulled his head down to hers and kissed him.

No kiss had ever been sweeter, more needed. Or more arousing. So much so, Cole felt the hot fire of her kiss sweep through him like a backdraft. He finally put her down, so he could feel all of her next to all of him. And he wanted that. Dear God, how he wanted it.

Cole felt her body melt against his, felt the giving softness of her breasts pressed against his chest, felt the velvet textures of her mouth. He felt it all, wanted it all.

Jordan felt his thighs hard against hers, felt his hands glide over her back and down to caress her buttocks, felt his mouth on hers, hot and heavy, demanding that she give all of herself to him. She felt everything in her respond to everything in him. She felt their bodies fit together intimately, their hearts beat together wonderfully, and she knew this was the way it was meant to be.

"Let's go inside," she whispered and led the way.

Once inside the rustic cabin, she turned on only half the usual number of lights, not wanting even the glare of light to intrude on the exquisite intimacy.

They stood halfway between the kitchen and living room. "Would you like a glass of wine?" she asked, her voice a little breathless.

"Would you?"

She shook her head. He pulled her back into his arms and lowered his head for another kiss . . . and was promptly interrupted by a rather forceful meow.

Jordan looked down at the toe of her shoe now decorated with a wiggling black-and-white fur ball. "Oh, no. I forgot about the kitten."

Cole stooped, retrieved the furry intruder in one big hand and held it up in front of him. "Hey there, Spot. You almost got squashed." The cat, obviously unenthusiastic about such heights, clung to the sleeve of his shirt and voiced her protest.

"She's been here alone all— Wait a minute." Jordan glanced around. "How did she get out of her box?"

The box in question had been turned over on its side and the kitten's water and food had spilled onto the floor and formed a wet glob. "Oh, poor baby. She must be starving." Spot meowed in agreement.

While Jordan searched for an old but soft, clean towel for the kitten to snuggle with, Cole stabilized the box so it wouldn't tip over. When they had finished, Spot's quarters were again ready for occupancy.

"There you go," Jordan said, placing the small sectioned dish containing fresh food and water at one end of the box. "Home, sweet home."

Cole stooped down, balanced himself on the balls of his feet, picked up Spot and gently stroked the kitten beneath her chin. "Fresh food, warm bed and two great-looking ladies to take care of you. Don't take it for granted, Spot, because it doesn't get any better than this."

"I'm not sure she'll take your recommendation after listening to her stomach growl for God knows how long."

Cole carefully placed the cat into the box, then stood up. "She won't get my sympathy if she doesn't know she's being cared for by the loveliest, most intelligent, most honest woman in the world," he said, his mahogany-brown gaze capturing hers. "Excuse me, *women*."

"Cole . . ."

He leaned over and kissed the corner of her mouth. "And speaking of the other woman, I miss her, but in a way I'm glad she's not here."

"Why?"

"Because," he rested his hands on her shoulders and began to knead the knotted muscles, "it gives us an opportunity to be alone."

Tell him. "Cole—"

"And to talk." He ceased massaging her shoulders, took her hand and led her into the living room. Then he sat her on the couch beside him, turned her facing away from him and resumed the massage.

His fingers were magic, gently kneading the knots of tension from her body, and Jordan fought the urge to melt into him, never move from this spot, never speak of anything but how good his hands felt, how warm and loved she felt. Cole's thumbs pressed into her flesh, rubbing, subduing the tension and subduing her good intentions at the same time. With each stroke, each sweep of pressure by his fingers, her resolve to deal with the truth grew weaker and weaker. *Tell him now,* some still strong-enough-to-resist part of her mind yelled. *Before it's too late.*

She had to tell him…tell him… Her head fell back against his chest, and she half moaned, half sighed with pleasure.

The purely pleasure-filled sound arrowed through Cole straight to his soul. He wanted to hear it again and again. He wanted to hear it while he kissed her, while she kissed him, while he touched her, while she touched him. He wanted to hear it while they came together in the sweet, wild rush of passion that had burned in his memory for so long it was a part of him. He wanted all the sweet sounds she made and he remembered. He wanted her love, her joy, her heart, her soul. He wanted it all, *needed* it all.

And today you almost lost it. Forever!

Suddenly he desperately wanted her to understand how much her joy, her sparkling radiance had meant to him at a time when he thought joy had died, thought his soul had died. Without submerging her into his dark past, he needed her to know she had been his only light.

With his lips close to her ear, he said, "Do you remember that doughnut shop down the street from your apartment in Shreveport?"

"Mmmm," she sighed. The pastry shop in question had been one of their favorite haunts, particularly after hours of lovemaking. They would wander in, arm in arm, giggling like kindergartners, purchase a ludicrous amount of calorie-laden goodies, then take them back to her apartment and feed each other in bed. "Whatever made you think of that?"

"I'll never forget the look in your eyes when you took the first bite of a fresh, still-warm doughnut, then licked the glaze from your lips. I remember thinking how incredible it was that someone could get so much pure joy from anything as simple as eating a doughnut. Last night I saw that expression again while you gazed at your daughter, and again tonight when you first saw me in the hospital. It's an appreciation of things money can't buy, of moments that can't be duplicated." He paused and took a deep breath. "My memory of that expression kept me sane in an insane world. *You* kept me sane, kept me warm when I thought there was nothing left in the world but coldness."

He pulled her against his chest, wrapped his arms around her waist and held her tightly. She could feel his heart drumming hard against her back, the beat reverberating through her body. His arms were steel bands of tension, not to hold her to him, but to hold himself steady. The lethargy that had all but drained her of energy a few moments earlier, vanished.

"You were all I thought about, all I held on to for twenty-one months in a prison cell. When they tortured me until they...broke me... When I wanted to die, you kept me...alive."

Chapter 11

Jordan went still inside, afraid even to breathe. This was the darkness he had alluded to, the darkness she had seen so often in his eyes. She waited for him to resume speaking, praying she had the courage to hear what he needed to tell her.

"Before ... when we were together, I got a call that last morning after you had gone to the studio. You have to understand, Jordan, at that point in my life, who I was and what I did were all tangled up together. I'd never been able to separate the two, never wanted to. Oh, I wasn't crazy enough to think I was invincible, far from it, but somehow I never considered that I might run up against something that would *change* me. Kill me, yes, but not turn me inside out then leave me looking in the mirror at a person I didn't recognize."

He took a deep, unsteady breath and swallowed hard. "That assignment was supposed to last four or five days. I couldn't tell you where I was going. My life wasn't my own.

How could I have asked you to share it? I wanted to talk about forever, but in my line of work forever could have been a year, a week . . . even a day. But I swear, I was coming back to you.

"The assignment lasted almost a month and jumped right into another one. Then another. I couldn't contact you . . . there wasn't any way. Then they sent me to pose as a translator for a large American corporation in one of the Middle Eastern countries. There were—" he cleared his throat "—there were five of us, working late one night when the terrorists attacked. They . . . they killed one of the men and the only woman in the room. Took the rest of us hostage."

Jordan pressed her lips together to keep from crying out, but she couldn't close her eyes tight enough to stop the tears. She listened as he told her about his time in hell. She listened as the man she loved verbally painted her a picture of the kind of human deprivation she had only read about and could never fully comprehend without living through it herself. She listened with her ears, her mind and with her heart, and she heard the deliberate, systematic shredding of a man's mind . . . *one, thin strip at a time.*

Until finally, she heard him die.

All emotion was gone from his voice as he recounted the exact moment when he reached the breaking point . . . then stepped over. He spoke as if relating a story told to him by someone else, and she realized that was the only way he could tell it. Otherwise he would have to relive those moments, and no man should have to serve time in hell twice. When he stopped speaking, the room filled with silence, overflowed with silence. For a long time, the only sound was their ragged breathing. For a long time the only movement was the warm, steady, healing tears flowing from brown eyes, and from green eyes.

"The only thing," Cole whispered, his voice now raw with all the emotion he had tried so hard to suppress, "that kept me going, kept me alive, was thinking about you. Remembering the way you walked and smiled, the way you tilted your head to one side when you asked a question. And the fragrance of your perfume and that lemon-scented shampoo you always used. But most of all I remembered your joy, the way you embraced life. And the way you faced it so *honestly*. I needed that honesty. Because I had lied to myself, I needed it desperately."

Jordan couldn't take any more. She turned in his arms, flung her own arms around his neck and buried her head against his shoulder. The ironclad embrace of moments ago was now loose, almost as though he was afraid to hold her.

"Today, when I thought something had happened to you—"

"Don't . . ." she begged, placing the tips of her trembling fingers against his lips. "Cole, don't . . . I love you, I love you."

His arms closed around her then, tentatively at first, then so tight she barely had enough breath to whisper again, "I love you—"

Her mouth found his or maybe it was the other way around. Either way, they were kissing and that was all that mattered.

The thought crossed Cole's mind that this wasn't real, couldn't be real because he wanted it so much. He tore his mouth from hers. "Jordan . . . I need you."

"No more than I need you," she groaned. She drew back just far enough to look into his eyes. "Kiss me, Cole. The way you remember kissing me. The way you want to kiss me now. This minute."

This time, when his mouth touched hers, he felt the past burn away, felt it go up in a burst of flaming need that surpassed anything memory could contain. This was Jordan. This was the woman he loved, the woman who had loved him as none other. This was right. Cole groaned, angling his mouth more intimately against hers, using his tongue, commanding her with gentle force to part her lips.

Jordan complied. Happily. Greedily. This was Cole. This was the man she loved beyond all else. This was right. She forgot yesterday, forgot she would have to face tomorrow, and the moment of truth slipped farther and farther away. Being in Cole's arms was all she knew or cared about.

Cole shifted his body so she fit intimately between his legs. He tried to bring her closer, but the confines of the narrow sofa prohibited it. He moaned his frustration into her mouth. Jordan tasted his frustration. It was the flavor of need. Hers. His. The need to touch and be touched. The need to feel all of him next to all of her.

"Come upstairs," she said. He needed no further invitation.

As they stepped inside her bedroom, moonlight poured through the massive arched, multipaned window dominating the center of the opposite wall, and spilled across the strikingly colorful Navajo blanket used as a bedspread. They needed no light except the starlight and moonbeams that filled the room and danced over the covering as if engaged in some ancient ritual of celebration inspired by the weaver of the exquisite design.

Standing beside the bed, Cole reached for the buttons on her blouse. Working as slowly as what was left of his reason permitted, he moved from button to button, his knuckles grazing warm, smooth skin, lightly, teasingly. Finally he pushed the blouse from her shoulders, down over her arms . . . and suddenly had to remind himself to breathe.

She was perfection, sculpted in warm ivory satin and lace so soft, so pale it was difficult to discern where the fabric ended and her own satiny skin began. He remembered that she had once told him about her affinity for the moon and how she called upon its silvery subsistence in times of pain and joy. Seeing her now, bathed in the moonlight like a pristine goddess, he understood the complementary relationship. The moon's light showcased her beauty, showering her graceful neck and shoulders and the swell of her breasts with a pearlescence.

Cole's hand trembled as he reached up and stroked her slender throat, then with fingers spread, smoothed his hand down over the curve of one breast, while his other hand unhooked the lacy barrier and discarded it.

Jordan sighed, her body thrilling to the sweet satisfaction of his touch and at the same time craving more. Because she knew the definition of *more* was the kind of oblivion she had found only in this man's arms, only with this man's love. She pressed herself into his palm, luxuriating in the rough texture of his skin next to her yielding softness. Slowly, deliberately, she rubbed herself back and forth against his palm until her nipple pebbled into hardness and sent a streamer of piercing need curling through her, spiraling lower and lower until she felt herself grow hot and moist.

Cole removed his hand and she made a tiny sound of protest, only to have the sound transform itself into a moan of pleasure when his lips touched first one tempting swell, then the other. His tongue moved over her tender flesh, soft and wet, rough and oh so exciting. Need, sharp and hot, sliced through her body until she couldn't draw a full breath.

"Cole...Cole, please..." She groped for the button on his shirt and hastily freed them. The need to touch him, the need to feel his skin beneath her fingers was almost unbearable.

"Your skin—" he lifted a heavy wave of her hair and kissed her earlobe "—is so... incredibly soft."

She tilted her head to one side, giving him greater access to the slender column of her throat while her fingers continued to free button after button until at last, she could touch him the way she longed to. She splayed her hands across his broad chest, threading her fingers through the fan of soft, dark curls.

"That's it. Touch me, baby. Touch—"

Whatever else he intended to say was lost in a mutual moan of glorious satisfaction as she pushed the shirt from his shoulder, slipped her hands around his waist, up to the middle of his back and pulled the upper part of his body full against her. Instinctively Cole's hands cupped her buttocks, pressing the lower half of her body full against him.

Soft, so soft. The feel of her breasts flattened against his chest was the softest, most sensual thing he had ever known. Or was it the softness of her buttocks, filling his hands as he kneaded her flesh? *Soft. Soft.* He wanted to sink into her softness and never leave. Nothing in his memory even came close to the heat of her skin, her body next to his.

Hard, so hard. His chest was hard against her nipples, hard themselves with an ache only he could assuage. The hard ridge of his arousal pressed against her was both the source of the heat that burned higher and higher with each second, and the only control over the raging flame. *Hard. Hard.* She wanted to relish the feel of his hardness deep inside her melting softness until neither cared about memories or dreams or anything but now. This moment. This heat. She ground her hips against him with an urgent need.

"Baby... oh, Jordan. I'm crazy with wanting you."

"Yes," she said harshly.

He reached for the waistband of her slacks. "I have to feel all of you next to all of me. Have to..."

"Yes." She helped him by leaning back just enough for him to manage the zipper, then push the fabric down her legs. She stepped out of the slacks and kicked them to one side. Cole's jeans and shorts joined the slacks a second later.

He had planned to love her slowly, driving them both to the edge of the sweet abyss by degrees until neither could stand the thought of one more instant without the joining, the melting, the exquisite soaring trip to paradise. But he couldn't wait.

Now, touching her from breast to thigh was the worst and most delicious agony he had ever known. Nothing, not even his time in hell compared with the way he wanted her. She was a fire he couldn't put out.

The past called to him, drove him with a hunger that was out of control. She had been a part of him, always as close as his memories, yet so far away that the need to fill her body as she had filled his mind was white-hot, blinding him to finesse, to anything else.

"I can't..."

Jordan felt his control slipping, taking hers with it. Somewhere in the back of her mind, she had thought they would make love long and leisurely, calling into the present all of the lonely and longing moments of the past. But the instant their naked bodies touched, the past was burned away in a blaze of passion so hot, so wild, they were help-less to resist. They were prisoners of the flame with no will of their own.

"I wanted...but I can't wait... Baby, I need you...now."

"Yes," she murmured, his hands moving over her body like flames licking at her skin. "Waited...so long..."

He lifted her onto the bed and settled on top of her. She whimpered her need, her breath coming hard and heavy from her slightly parted lips. Then he stamped his mouth over hers, sealing her cries.

Her head was empty of all thoughts except that she wanted Cole inside her more than she wanted her next breath, her next heartbeat. Then she didn't have to wait anymore.

While his tongue took total, complete and unconditional possession of her mouth, plunging hot and deep, he filled her body, sliding into the center of her silky heat.

She closed around him, silk to steel, flame to fire.

He was hell deep and heaven high. After years of darkness he stepped into the light.

Then all they knew, all they cared about was motion. Wild motion. Their bodies moving together, twisting in the flame, dying in the flame that burst like a thousand suns exploding with each stroke, each gliding, sensual explosion of heat, heat and more heat. Until finally the flame claimed them, made them part of its brilliance, then sent them spinning into the cooling abyss.

When they drifted back to earth, their sweat-sheened bodies glistening in the moonlight, Cole wrapped his arms around her, fitted her snugly against his body and whispered, "I love you."

"Yes," Jordan barely managed to answer.

"There was a time when I didn't think I would ever be able to say that again to anyone, least of all you."

"B-because of what happened when you were a hostage?"

He sighed and held her tighter. "When I walked away from that life, I swore I would never go back. I shut myself away. Away from the pain. Away from you."

"But I—"

"Can you honestly say you would have welcomed me back with open arms three, even two years ago?"

Her silence was his answer. "Don't you see? I couldn't come to you with all my scars."

"Your leg?"

"No. My soul. The wound inflicted to my body healed long ago, but my soul was still raw. And I wanted it that way."

"Why?"

"Because it helped me remember what a coward I was. Helped me remember I had no right to love any woman, especially you."

"But I understand—"

"Now. But you wouldn't have, then. And I wouldn't have wanted your understanding then. Don't you see, Jordan? We had to come to this time, this place even, before we could face our pasts."

"But you still can't forgive yourself."

His answer was to kiss her into silence. His answer was to stroke her body while he stoked the flame they had so recently been a part of. Tonight wasn't for the past. Tonight was for the present. And maybe the future.

But Cole couldn't have given her an answer if he had one. The only thing he knew for certain was that he had been shattered and she made him whole.

He had sold his soul. And she had redeemed it.

The next morning Jordan awoke to find herself alone in bed. A quick glance around reassured her that she was not alone in the house, or at least if she was, Cole was running around the countryside in nothing but his underwear, because his shirt and jeans were hanging from the top of her closet door.

She discovered him in her kitchen, but the search was no great mystery since all she had to do was follow her nose to the delicious smell of bacon frying.

She cinched the belt tighter on her old terry robe, shoved the waves of hair away from her face and was greeted by a disarming sight. Cole, barefoot, the muscles of his powerful legs flexing as he moved about her kitchen. Cole, the sunlight striking his broad back, making light and shadow dance over the muscles in his shoulders. Cole, wearing the sexiest pair of—were they silk? They looked like silk, totally, outrageously sexy—boxer shorts she had ever seen. She didn't remember touching silk last night, but then, she didn't remember the two of them walking into her bedroom or actually lying down on her bed, either, and they most certainly *had* been in bed together.

The shorts were paisley, navy-and-wine-red paisley and fit so well her mouth went dry. For a moment she couldn't breathe. Another man, a less magnificently male man, might not have been able to get away with wearing the print or the silk. Cole got away with it ... and then some. As he got away with cooking breakfast wearing only those shorts. While she watched, he leaned forward slightly, and the muscles in his trim and oh so enticing buttocks flexed. Despite the fact that he slightly favored his leg that had been broken, he was the most beautiful man she had ever seen. Unable to stop herself, Jordan breathed a soft cry of pure appreciation.

He looked up and smiled. "Good morning, gorgeous."

She thought the description better suited to his appearance than to hers. "Good ... good morning."

Without another word, he set the frying pan sizzling with half-cooked bacon off the gas burner, walked across the kitchen, hauled her into his arms and kissed her soundly. Deliciously. Thoroughly. He tasted like coffee and a hint of toothpaste, a not altogether unpleasant combination simply because it came from his lips, flavored his kiss. When he finally released her, she sighed and nestled her head on his shoulder. "I was afraid I might have dreamed you."

"Then I have to say you have some pretty erotic dreams, lady."

"Hmmm. They can't hold a candle to last night."

He held her, caressing her back. Even through the terry cloth she could feel the heat his touch generated, like being infused with the warmth from a slow-burning flame. When she raised her head, his gaze automatically fell to her lips, still moist from his kiss, her full lower lip glistening slightly. Seeing the direction of his gaze, she unconsciously licked her lips, her pink tongue sliding quickly across the aforementioned lip. Unintentional or not, he couldn't resist the invitation and his tongue followed hers into the honeyed sweetness of her mouth.

"You..." He pecked kisses along her jaw. "Are..." More kisses up to her earlobe. "So incredibly..." Then back to her mouth. "Sexy. Did you know that?"

"If you say so." Her breath escaped in tattered sighs.

"Oh, I say so. And I intend to say so, every chance I get." His fingers curled around the lapels of her robe and pushed them back far enough to expose the soft mounds of her breasts. He placed fevered kisses across one enticing swell of tender flesh, then the other, then into the valley between.

Jordan's knees threatened not to support her and she lifted a hand to his chest for support... and found her fingers tangled in swirls of dark hair fanning across his chest.

He raised his head and looked at her, watched the fires of passion dance in her eyes. "Hungry?"

"Starved," she breathed.

He grinned. "How do you like your eggs, fried until they're just done but still hot and soft in the center? Or scrambled, not hard, but firm and still a little wet? Or maybe slipped into steaming water and poached until hot clear through but still soft to the touch?"

My God, Jordan thought. *Even food sounds sexy when he describes it.* She took a deep breath. "Suit yourself."

He thought for a moment, then said, "Fried. Hot and soft in the center."

"Yes," she said, thinking that was an apt description of her body at the moment. A body that longed to be stroked, loved, filled by this man she had once thought she had lost forever. This man who *was* her second chance.

"Then why don't you..." His voice trailed off and she waited for him to say, to hell with the bacon, to hell with the eggs, to hell with anything but you and me. Again. In that big bed upstairs. "Hop into the shower while I finish. Then I'll shower and we'll do something ... fun."

He released her and Jordan almost lost her balance. "Ohhh, you rotten tease, you," she said, her body still flushed, still wanting.

He grinned again, this time wider. "Gotcha."

"And I'm going to get you, mister. I'm going to pay you back, but good."

Now it was his turn to lick his lips. "I can't wait."

Jordan folded her arms across her chest and all but pouted. "How long until breakfast?"

"Ten minutes."

"Good. That gives me time to plot your demise." And with that, she turned and hurried up to take her shower.

During breakfast they decided the something fun would be a simple lazy walk through the meadow behind her cabin and possibly a picnic lunch. Fancy wasn't due home until late afternoon, and Cole had already called to check on the construction site and found things running smoothly, so they had almost the whole day to do with as they pleased.

While Cole showered, Jordan slipped into an airy, sleeveless sundress of soft printed challis. The peach-and-forest-green floral design on a cream-colored background flattered her complexion, and the fabric moved like a whisper around her body when she walked. She wanted to be as beautiful as he thought she was, but knowing that she still had to tell him the truth made it hard for her to look into the mirror above her nightstand and see anything other than ugliness.

Will last night make a difference? Will he hate me more, or love me less when he learns the truth? These last hours had been so blissfully, deliriously happy she wanted to cry because they had to end. In her heart of hearts she knew she couldn't continue to live this inside-out version of the truth. Sooner or later she had to tell him about Fancy. Sooner or later she would have to face whatever his reaction would be. But oh, sweet heaven, how she wished sooner would never come. How she wished they could be together as they had been last night, in each other's arms, in each other's souls, forever.

She had just finished brushing her hair to a lustrous shine and applied a peach gloss to her lips when Cole stepped into the room wearing a bath towel knotted around his trim waist.

Jordan was sitting on a chaise longue positioned beside the huge multipaned bedroom window, the full skirt of her sundress cascading over slightly parted knees and fanning out over her slender legs. An old-fashioned, wide-brimmed straw hat rested partly on one knee, partly on her lap. Midmorning sun shot sparks of red gold through her hair. She looked like a bouquet of freshness just picked from some heavenly garden.

Cole's breath caught in his throat. He had never seen anything more breathtakingly beautiful in his whole life. And she loved him, again. *Still. She still loves me. That much hasn't changed. Please, God, will never change.*

He walked over to her, intending merely to brush a kiss across her peaches-and-cream cheek. But then he looked into the depths of her green eyes and was seduced by the yearning he saw reflected there. A yearning that was part love, part soul-deep need, and all wrapped up in desire. His good intentions vanished.

He leaned over her until his mouth was scarcely a breath away from hers. Then he traced her lips with the tip of his tongue.

She moaned, her tongue searching greedily for his, finding it, drawing it slowly into her mouth the way she wanted Cole slowly entering her body. The want became an out-of-control, hotter-than-hot flame of desire. It sparked, sizzled and flamed through her body like wildfire. She hadn't planned it, hadn't anticipated it, but once unleashed, she couldn't do more than let it consume her. One last time. She wanted this one last time, one last moment of the heaven she had tasted in his arms. Of the heaven both past and present, but possibly never of the future. And heaven, she felt sure, would forgive her. What could it hurt?

Hurt. He wanted her so much he hurt. His body tight with need, he kissed her again and again. Each time letting his tongue coax her, tease her. And each time she took him slowly into her hot sweetness. Then he did it again, only this time she was through playing, this time the flame had been stoked into a blazing inferno. This time she sucked his tongue inside her mouth with such ravenous need, it literally brought him to his knees.

Kneeling in front of her, their lips still sealed in a can't-get-enough-of-you kiss, he snatched the hat from her lap and sent it sailing across the room. In an action light-years away from the abrupt hurling of her hat, he lifted her hands, placing them on the chaise on either side of her body, then his own hands dropped to her feet. His fingers curled slowly around her ankles, rested there momentarily then began an upward sweep as his hands slid up the outside calves of her slender legs, then around to the inside, then back again. Still kissing her, his hands continued upward over her slightly parted knees . . . lifting, pushing the seductively silky fabric with him as he went. Until finally, both his hands resting on her knees, he pulled back. Jordan moaned, and tried to bring him back into her mouth, but Cole had other ideas.

"Look at me," he demanded. She opened slumberous eyes, but nothing about her breathing was languid in any way. Her breathing was heavy, hot, her breasts rising and falling as arousal swept her body, burned her body.

Without another word, holding her prisoner with his eyes, he bunched the fabric of her skirt in both his hands, crushing the material as if it could provide even a momentary release of the tension that held him in its grip. Then he let go of the fabric, his hands once again slipping beneath to continue their seductive journey. His fingers trailed over the satin-smooth skin of her thighs, then glided over her inner thighs, stroking, caressing, sending her headlong toward a madness she craved.

When his knuckles brushed the silky barrier covering the vee at the apex of her thighs, Jordan's eyes widened, and she urgently called his name.

"Stay with me, baby. Stay with me."

Through the silk of her panties he stroked her tummy, her hips, finally to the center of the heat that flamed higher and higher with each stroke, each caress.

Cole leaned forward, urging her knees farther apart, urging her to give him access to that which he sought. And she did. One hand slid over her tummy and around to her buttocks, while the other . . . the other cupped the center of her heated moistness, his thumb gently skating back and forth over the tiny nub that was the furnace of the all-consuming flame.

Jordan closed her eyes as ring after ring of pure, sweet ecstasy expanded in ever-widening circles while at the same time spiraling in on itself, creating more pleasure, more need, more ecstasy. Endless, the pleasure was endless, yet pulling her closer and closer to the point when it would end, must end in sweet glory.

"Almost, baby. Almost. Look at me."

When she did as he commanded, what she saw reflected in his eyes was her own passion, her own overwhelming need. The flames went higher, taking her deeper into the heat, closer to the center of the fire he and he alone controlled, the center of the must-have-or-die fire.

With their gazes locked together, suddenly he leaned into her, forcing her legs even farther apart and pulled her to him in one fierce motion. As her body made startlingly intimate contact with his, he planted his tongue so deep in her mouth, Jordan's breath wedged in her throat. Instinctively she wrapped her slender legs around his waist. Then both his hands were kneading her buttocks, holding her to him, grinding her sweet heat against him until she thought surely this must be what it's like to die from pleasure. But it wasn't enough. She wanted to be closer.

When they finally broke the kiss long enough to take a deep breath, she arched her body, her head falling back in a posture of pleasure so totally feminine, so totally arousing, Cole thought his body might burst from the need to bury himself so deep in her body neither would know where one began and the other ended.

"Cole..." she finally managed to breathe. With her hands on his shoulders, her fingers dug into his flesh while he rotated her buttocks, moving her against him in sweet torture. "Please," she begged. She still wasn't close enough.

"That's it, baby. That's it."

Still holding her to him, Cole rose to his feet and walked toward the bed.

In those few steps the towel dropped from his body and he was splendidly, gloriously naked. In those few steps the friction of her body against his was almost more than she could take, yet more was what she needed. More friction, more heat. More Cole.

And he gladly obliged. With a breathtaking upward sweep, he whisked the sundress up and over her head, and a heartbeat later with an equally breathtaking downward sweep she was free of her bra and panties. Then it was heat to heat, need to need, man to woman as they came together and let the fire consume them, burn down around them, then rise higher and higher until they were the flame. They were the fire.

An hour later, neither remembered talking about a walk in the meadow, much less cared if they did. They made love again, this time slower, gentler, then they showered again. This time together.

"I should call the Dobsons to see if Jill and Fancy are back," Jordan said as they walked downstairs sometime after noon. "Would you like a sandwich?"

"Make that two sandwiches and you got yourself a deal. While you're checking on the beauty, I'll use my mobile phone to call the site. Don't forget Spot," he called as he went out the front door.

She watched him go and realized that she had, once again, put off telling him about Fancy. *You can't go on this way much longer. He has to be told and you're only giving yourself ulcers by prolonging the agony.*

A few moments later, Cole walked back into the kitchen. "Is Fancy back?"

"No answer at the Dobsons', but Jill told me they might not return until around four o'clock. That gives us some time to—what's that?" she asked, pointing to the video case in his hand.

"I think it must be yours—"

"Ohmygod." Jordan put down the knife she was using to spread mustard on a slice of rye bread. "I took that out of my purse the other night when Fancy fell asleep in your truck. The night of the robbery."

Cole eyed the case. "What's on it?"

She shrugged. "A hot-air balloon ride. The client didn't like part of it and wanted it edited."

"Did you have this with you when you left the shop that night?"

"Yes."

"What part of the tape did the client want edited out?"

Jordan licked a spot of mustard from her finger. "We had to take a detour on that trip. Coming over a particularly picturesque lake, we dipped low over the water and accidentally picked up a couple of fishermen. The client loved the lake, but hated the fishermen."

"Did you edit the fishermen out?"

"Actually, I'm not sure. I was in the process of trying to do just that when Barry came in and offered to take over. I left the shop for a little fresh air and when I got back, it was done. Haven't had a chance to view the finished piece."

Cole held up the case. "Can we look at it now?"

"Now?"

"I have a hunch it might be important."

"Sure," she said. Cole was already halfway to the VCR. He hit the power button, shoved the video into the slot, then punched Play. A rainbow-colored hot-air balloon with two passengers and Barry Clark came into view.

"I was shooting from the other balloon and—there—"
She pointed to the right of the balloon. "There are the fishermen." Sure enough, the camera panned over the heads of Barry and the clients, behind their backs and captured the two men standing in front of the Jeep. "Wait a minute," she said, frowning.

Cole hit Pause. "What's wrong?"

"I must have picked up the original tape by mistake. The edited tape wouldn't have the men."

Cole hit the "frame advance" button, and slowly, frame by frame the snippet of the confrontation between the two men played out on the screen. Cole turned to Jordan and asked, "Have you ever seen either one of those men?"

"No."

"You're certain?"

"Positive. Why?"

"Because," Cole replied calmly, ejecting the video. "I think I've just discovered why someone wanted in your house."

"Why?"

"For this." He waved the videotape in his hand as he headed for the door.

Following behind him, Jordan stopped suddenly. "Why would a thief want a videotape of a hot-air balloon ride?"

"Not the ride, my beauty. The men."

Jordan wasn't sure she understood what he was driving at, but she trusted he knew his business and decided to go along with him.

At the door he turned and said, "Can I take this with me?"

"I guess so."

He placed his hands on her shoulders. "Jordan, I think your videotape is going to help me catch the bad guys." Despite what he had told her last night about his hatred for all things connected with his past life, she could see the sparks of excitement in his eyes.

"What bad—"

"The saboteurs at the construction site. If I'm right, and I'm ninety-nine-percent sure I am, then these guys are cold busted, with a video as evidence." At the quizzical look in her eyes, he added, "It's extremely complicated, and I don't have time to explain everything, but I'll be back later and we'll talk."

Jordan simply nodded.

"You sure you're okay with me leaving...like this, I mean?"

"Like this?"

He smiled apologetically. "I had planned to spend the rest of the day with you and the little beauty, then later... Well, I don't want you to feel as if I'm abandoning you—"

"No. Oh, Cole, no," she protested, understanding beginning to dawn. He was afraid she would relate the events of today with the past. "I know you wouldn't be leaving if you didn't think it was very important."

"Very important. So, am I forgiven?"

She smiled, wondering what his answer would be when she asked the same question. "Always."

"God, I love you," he breathed as his lips took hers in a kiss rife with promises of later, of always. "Tell the little beauty I'll see her later." He kissed Jordan again, hard and thoroughly. "Hold that thought until I get back."

Jordan watched him drive away and wondered if he would be so loving, so excited...later. Later when she told him the truth. Later when he learned that Fancy was his child.

When the doorbell rang thirty minutes later, she dashed to the door, hoping it was Cole, but he wasn't standing in her doorway.

Barry was.

"Hey, can I come in?"

"Of course." They had barely spoken since their last confrontation regarding Cole. The last thing Jordan wanted was to lose Barry's friendship, but she had no intention of allowing that friendship to interfere with her relationship with Cole.

"So, how you doin'? I mean, you're okay, right? Other than a bump on the noggin." He pointed to the bruise on her forehead that now lacked a bandage.

"I'm fine. Good as new."

"Yeah, well. When I talked to you in the emergency room you sounded all right, but I wanted to check for myself. I would have been here sooner, only..."

"Only what?"

His gaze darted away, then back again. "They, uh, told me at the hospital that Forrester took you home and I figured..." He shrugged. "You know."

"I see," she said, a little annoyed that his opinion of Cole was still slightly tainted.

"And, I wanted to drop by and see how the Munchkin liked her overnighter."

"She's not back yet. I was just polishing off a sandwich. Would you like something to eat?" she called over her shoulder as she walked back into the kitchen.

"No, uh, no thanks, sugar." He didn't follow her, but ambled around the living room.

Jordan smiled. He was back to calling her "sugar," so the rift between them couldn't be too wide.

"By the way," he said, elevating his voice to carry the distance. "I mailed that make-good to the client."

"Thanks."

"Say, sugar. You didn't happen to see the original for that piece, did you? I don't know what happened to it after you left."

Jordan stuck her head in the room. "I picked it up by mistake."

"Really."

"And you're not going to believe this," she said, excitedly.

"Believe what?"

"You and I may have solved a mystery."

"No kiddin'?"

"It seems we accidentally captured some men on the video that Cole thinks may lead to whoever is behind the sabotage at the bobsled site."

"I'll be damned," Barry said, sounding surprised.

"Wouldn't that be great, Barry? Then maybe this awful struggle over the land could be put to rest. Maybe we could get on with making sure the environment suffers the least amount of damage possible."

"Yeah, great. Say, sugar—"

The ringing of the phone cut him off.

"Cole," Jordan said happily into the receiver a moment later. "Of course I can. You mean, right now? Well...hold on a minute." She covered the receiver with her hand and turned to Barry. "Do you have time to hang around until Fancy shows up? Maybe another half hour. Cole wants me to meet him at the shop so I can dupe the tape before something happens to it."

He slipped his hands into his pocket and shrugged. "No problem."

"I'll be there in twenty-five minutes," she told Cole, then hung up. Jordan snatched up her purse, gave Barry a peck on the cheek and said, "Thanks. You're a lifesaver."

By the time she made not one but two copies of the tape and she and Cole drove back to her cabin, the time for Fancy's arrival was long past.

When they pulled into the driveway, Barry's Jeep was nowhere in sight, but Jordan didn't consider that strange. He had probably driven Fancy into Fairplay for an ice-cream cone or soft drink.

But when she and Cole stepped through the door, the living room was also empty. Without reason, an icy dread gripped Jordan. An internal warning system activated by every parent's worst fear—the fear that *something* has happened to their child, set alarm bells jangling in her head.

"Barry must have taken her into Fairplay," she said, feeling more and more uneasy by the minute.

"I don't think so." The ice in Cole's voice could have lowered her air-conditioning bill.

"What do you—" Turning to face him, she caught sight of a note in his hand.

When he looked into her eyes, Jordan was overcome with a dark sense of foreboding. "Cole?" When his answer was a look that redefined the word *rage*, Jordan panicked. "Cole, what is it?"

"The son of a bitch has kidnapped Fancy."

Chapter 12

"K-kid-kid..." Jordan couldn't even bring herself to say the word. She was certain she must be in the throes of some bizarre nightmare, because she could swear that he had just told her in a very calm, collected voice that someone had abducted her child.

"Cole?" She stared at him, as if she expected him to awaken her from the horrific dream.

"God, baby, I'm so sorry." He held out the note. "It's true."

Her stunned gaze traveled from the piece of paper in his outstretched hand to his face, then back to the note. "No." She shook her head vehemently. "You're wrong. She's all right. Barry took her to get ice cream or a so-soda ... No." She kept shaking her head.

"Jordan—"

"No. No."

Cole could see her struggling with the truth, knew it was only a matter of minutes, maybe seconds before panic beat down the wall of denial that was her only protection. "Jordan," he insisted quietly, contending with his own outrage and the anger that was seething inside him like hell's own fury. He hauled her into his arms and held her tight, tighter. "Listen to me. We'll find her. I promise you."

Find her... find her. Jordan tried to shove the realization from her mind. *Fancy's gone. We'll find her... find her... find her...*

"No." She clutched Cole's shirtfront as the terrifying truth seeped into her consciousness. "Nooooo!" she cried as denial finally surrendered to gut-wrenching reality. Then she sagged against him, sobbing helplessly.

He held her tighter, stroking her hair.

"Fancy, Fancy," she whispered desperately.

"We will find her. And when we do, I promise you Clark will pay and pay dearly." Jordan felt the muscles in Cole's arms tighten with every word.

The tiny part of her mind still capable of rational thought, questioned why Cole was talking about Barry. Barry wouldn't hurt Fancy. He couldn't... "B-Barry?"

Cole released her just enough to look into her eyes. "I know this is going to be hard for you, but Barry is the one who took Fancy."

"Barry? I—I... don't understand. Why would Barry, of all people, want to harm my little girl?"

"Blackmail."

The word exploded into the quiet of the room and Jordan almost reeled from the impact.

"It's all here in the note," Cole explained. "They'll return Fancy in exchange for the tape that you accidentally took of the two men. One of those men is Bob Riley, a supervisor on the bobsled construction project. And I believe he's responsible for the sabotage."

She stared at him, frowning. So much had happened in the past few moments she was having a difficult time putting everything in order. Barry took Fancy. But he'd trade her for a video. A video of two men planning sabotage. But why would Barry be involved with men like that, unless...

"He's part of the sabotage," she said, scarcely able to believe what must be the truth. "He's been involved all along."

"I think so."

Still clinging to Cole, Jordan winced as if she had been dealt a physical blow. Certainly the pain couldn't have been any more real if someone had picked her up and slammed her into a wall. "Why?" She looked at Cole, her eyes begging for some reason that would help her make sense out of a situation that defied sensibility.

"He's gone off the deep end over the ecology issue. You said yourself his attitude was almost militant. I think he's linked up with a group called Alpha and Omega, and I wouldn't be surprised if Riley is connected to them as well. They're a hard-line group of environmentalists who will stop at nothing to get their message across, including terrorism." Cole didn't add that these same people were also suspected of murder and arson. She had been traumatized enough in the past ten minutes. There was no need to paint a blacker picture.

"They...they want to destroy the evidence," she said, some of the fog finally beginning to lift.

"Yes."

"And then it would be your word against this Riley, this supervisor's."

"That, but more importantly, the tape also makes it possible to identify the other man."

"Other man?"

"The man Riley is talking to works for the construction company that lost the bobsled project to Great Northern. We're talking federal offense on a grand scale, and lots of payoff money, not to mention the civil lawsuits Great Northern could bring."

"Are…are these people…dangerous?" When he didn't meet her gaze directly, she demanded an answer. "Are they, Cole? Tell me?"

"They play hardball, Jordan…" She closed her eyes and fresh tears slid down her cheeks. "But that doesn't mean they would hurt Fancy." *Not until they get their hands on the tape, anyway.* "And I don't think Barry would let them."

Her eyes flew open. "You don't—"

He shook his head. "I wouldn't be surprised to find out that your friend is being used. And I doubt very seriously that he's aware of who he's dealing with or what's behind all of this. My guess is, he doesn't know the machinations concerning the building contract. For what it's worth, I think Clark's only interest is saving the planet, and I don't think he would let any harm come to Fancy."

"Oh, please, God." She closed her eyes again. "Let that be true."

He took hold of her, his fingers biting into her upper arms. "Jordan, look at me."

She did, and the look in his eyes was every bit as compelling as it had been hours earlier, only now the desire in his eyes was for revenge.

"I'm going to find Fancy. I'm going to find her, bring her home and put her into your arms myself. And she's going to be all right, do you hear me? I'll move heaven and earth if I have to, but I'll bring her home to you safe and then I'll make sure no one ever hurts you again. No one." He pulled her fiercely into his arms and whispered into her hair. "Ever."

She believed him. Not only because she wanted to, but because she knew he meant every word. The man she loved, past and present, didn't make weak commitments or idle threats. Jordan let her body slump against his, let him pour his strength into her, willing herself to believe his words. His strong arms, his calm voice, his *presence* were the pillars of hope in a seemingly hopeless situation, and she held on for dear life. Fancy's life.

"How... how will you find her?" she asked, her breath warm and moist against his shirt, her hope as fragile as her voice.

There was a long pause. With her head against his chest she felt his heartbeat fast-forward, drumming hard. She felt his chest expand as if he were filling his lungs with much-needed air, then he slowly released the breath.

"I have contacts."

The three words sounded like a death knell in the quiet room. "They can help, but they won't do the hard part. I will. I can move faster on my own, and God knows I've had the practice."

For the first time Jordan began to realize how all of this might affect Cole. She lifted her head and met his gaze.

"I can't ask you to—"

"I told you. I'll move heaven and earth to find Fancy. Whatever it takes."

"But last night, you said—"

"I said a lot of things last night. One being, I love you. What I didn't add was that I love Fancy, too."

At his words, Jordan's heart, the heart she thought couldn't be bruised any more than it already had been, splintered into a thousand painful pieces.

"When I was..." He swallowed hard. "All the hours in my cell, dreaming of you, remembering you, holding on to you, we were always together, just the two of us. And I guarded that intimacy, that *privacy*. I didn't want anyone or anything to intrude on the special love we shared. It's strange." He brushed a wayward strand of hair from her tear-dampened cheek. "Looking back, I should have been jealous when I learned you had a child, but I wasn't. Because she was part of you. But from the moment I saw her, she worked her way into my heart almost as if she were a part of me, too."

Jordan watched his face, saw the love and pain in his eyes, and she remembered thinking to herself that no man should have to live through hell twice. Yet that was exactly what Cole was about to do. He was going to step back into a mind-set that he equated with the death of his soul.

And he didn't even know he was walking back into hell for his own child.

She couldn't let him go out the door without telling him. No matter what happened, no matter if he turned his face from her and never looked back, he had a right to know that the prize he sought was as much his as hers.

Unable to stem the flow of tears, she placed a trembling hand against his cheek, very much the same way she had the first day they kissed in the meadow. In a voice filled with equal parts of pain and hope, she said, "She is part of you."

He sighed, his own emotions tumbling wildly. "Thank you for saying that."

"Cole—"

"I do love her, Jordan."

"Cole..." Her fingertips touched his lips to silence him. "Fancy is as much a part of you as she is of me. She's yours. She's your daughter."

In a time and space already filled with unbelievable words and emotions, one more crowded in. He looked into Jordan's eyes, searching for hope, searching for the truth. And he found it.

"Mine?"

"Yours. She always has been, always will be."

"But your husband—"

"I never had a husband." *Oh, dear Lord, how can I make you understand what I didn't even know myself until you came back into my life...our lives?* "When you left...when I found out I was pregnant, I was out of my mind with happiness...and worry. Happy I was carrying your child and worried sick because you had disappeared. When I...when you didn't come back and I learned you had lied..." Her voice shook with the force of her emotions, and she prayed he would understand and forgive. "There was a time when I tried to convince myself that I hated you. That you had lied to me. That you got what you wanted and that's all I meant to you." At the smoldering fire of rage she saw building in the taut muscles of his body, Jordan tried to make him understand. "I needed you and you weren't there. I loved you," she said, desperate to reach him. "And you...were...gone. I needed someone, even if he was make-believe. But even then, whether I wanted to admit it or not, in my heart the man I fabricated was always you. In my heart there was never really anyone else..." Her voice trailed off again.

"What were you going to do? Let me go on indefinitely believing she was another man's child?"

"No! No. I was going to tell you—"

"When?"

"I—I...I tried to tell you last night."

"But you didn't try very hard, did you?"

"No," she admitted shamefully, dropping her head.

There was a long pause before he spoke again, and when he did his voice was colder, harder, more distant than anything she had ever known. "Why should I believe you?"

Her head snapped up. "Because it's the truth."

"You lied before. Why should I believe you now?"

"In the beginning I lied to protect myself, to pamper my own insecurities. Later, I realized what a mistake I had made, but it was too late. Everyone thought I had a husband and Fancy had a father, so—"

"So you conveniently killed him off."

On his lips it all sounded so juvenile and self-centered. "Yes."

"And when we met again. When we... Why didn't you tell me?"

"When I saw you again, I was afraid."

"Afraid?"

"Of what you might do. Afraid you might take her away from me..."

Incredulously his lips drew back in something that could have been a smile, but only if the observer was generous. "The woman I thought of as honest to a fault. The woman I would have bet my life would never lie."

"Cole...please. I know you must hate me. I can see it in your eyes, but please, please...don't take out your feeling for me on—"

"How dare you even *think* I would be that heartless!" He grabbed her by the arms, almost shaking her. "If I would have gone the distance to find her when I thought she belonged to someone else, do you think I would walk away from my own daughter just because her mother is a consummate liar?" He shoved her away from him. "I'll find her, Jordan. And when I do, you'll have every reason to be afraid of what I might do." He stormed out of the house.

Chapter 13

Jordan had no idea how long she stood in the middle of her living room, staring at the door Cole had slammed so hard it rattled on its hinges. She had no idea how long she would have to remain there until the numbness faded, until she could pick up enough pieces of her heart, not to go on living but merely to go on to the next minute, the next necessary heartbeat. But even if she could find all the broken pieces of her heart, which she doubted was possible, even if she could move to the next instant, how did she deal with the pain? How did she stay afloat in the cold, deep ocean of mind-splintering pain?

Then she realized it was too late. She was going down for the third time.

Finally, haltingly, she took a step, but she couldn't have said whether it was forward or backward. She didn't want to sit, but she didn't want to stand. She didn't want to cry, but neither did she want to hear the oppressive silence. She didn't want to stay in the house, but couldn't bear to leave. She wanted ... she wanted ...

To run. To scream. To raise her fists at God, or Fate, or whoever was controlling her destiny. She wanted Fancy and she wanted Cole. She wanted ...

The doorbell cut into her silent tirade. Barely able to direct her legs to carry her across the floor, she opened the door and felt the rest of her already-shaky world slip out from under her.

"Jordan," Barry started, a wild, nervous look in his eyes. "I have to—"

"You bastard," she hissed. For the first time in her life, Jordan wished she had a gun. For the first time in her life, she knew what it meant to want someone dead and to want to do the killing.

He pushed inside and closed the door. "Jordan, she's not hurt. You know I would never let anyone hurt her. But it was the only way—"

"You're insane."

"No, I'm just doing what I think is right."

"By taking Fancy? How could you *do* that? How could you come in my home and take my *child?*" Her voice had risen to almost hysterical levels.

"Trust me, Jordan. Nothing will happen to Fancy."

"Trust you?" she screeched. "You *are* insane."

"All they want is the tape. Give it to them and they will let Fancy go. I promise. Just give me the damned tape and I'll bring her home."

"You're a fool."

"Jordan—"

"Don't you know they're using you?" She doubled her hand into a fist and waved it in his face. "Don't you know you've committed a felony for people who couldn't care less about your precious cause?"

"You're wrong."

Now driven to have him understand the scope of what he had done, she grabbed his arm. "Your contact, who is he?"

"I can't tell—"

"Bob Riley." When he didn't answer, she all but shouted, "Isn't that right?"

"Yes," he admitted grudgingly.

"And Riley has you believing he only wants to save the environment, hasn't he?"

"Of course."

"Did he tell you who the other man was on the tape?"

"A supporter. Just a guy interested in saving—"

"Well, he's lying." She spit the words out with all the venom she could manage. "The man on that tape works for the construction company that Great Northern beat out for the bobsled contract."

Barry stared at her. "No."

"Yes. Cole recognized him."

"Can't be—"

"Oh, yes it can. And you took my baby to those... those..." She couldn't complete the sentenc because the thought was too painful.

Barry shook his head, then he backed up several steps and dropped onto the sofa. "We're only trying to protect the environment. You're wrong about Riley, he's—"

"What if I'm not? What if Riley is lying to you and I'm telling you the truth?" Jordan dropped to her knees beside him. "Help me, Barry. Take me to Fancy. Right or wrong, she doesn't deserve to be involved in any of this. Where is she? Tell me where my baby is."

He looked into the desperate eyes of his friend and knew she was right, at least about one thing. They had been wrong to involve a child, and suddenly he didn't like himself very much because he hadn't been strong enough to say no to making Fancy a pawn in their plan. "I'll take you," Barry said, "I'll take you."

Cole drove straight to the construction site. If Riley was anywhere around, he was going to have to do some fast talking, and Cole didn't care how he got the answers. He hung up the mobile phone and made several mental notes about the information he had gleaned concerning Riley and his cohorts. He knew what motivated men like Bob Riley—money, pure and simple. What he didn't understand was how a man who, according to his background information, was as intelligent and street smart as Barry Clark, could be sucked in by such an obvious ploy. Both of these men had been run through the grinder as far as constructing a security profile was concerned, and no one in Cole's organization had noticed even the most minute glitch. Under the circumstances, that fact alone made him question whether or not some of his own people might be involved. He had called in a few markers, several in fact, and they were worth calling because they would produce the kind of details he needed. In a matter of minutes he would have it all: names and addresses, possible contacts. Hell, he would have the number of their last laundry ticket if he needed it. And he just might.

Alpha and Omega had a track record of working underground until they could set up a major media-attention-grabbing event. Judging by the way incidents had escalated, Cole was certain such an event was imminent, so imminent the saboteurs couldn't waste time with subtleties. Everything, including Fancy's kidnapping, underscored urgency.

Fancy.

Every time he thought about her, thought about the fact that she was his child and that she was in danger, the word *urgent* was hardly sufficient to describe his overwhelming need to go tearing out into the night looking for her. But Cole, of all people, knew tearing out into the night was *not* the way to find his daughter.

His daughter.

That sweet-faced, innocent-eyed little beauty was his. His child. His flesh and blood. The thought filled his heart with such warmth and joy it was almost too much to be contained. He could close his eyes and remember every detail of her turned-up nose, her mop of red curls, her big brown eyes . . .

Fancy's eyes *were* brown. The same color as his. Why hadn't he ever noticed the color of her eyes before? Why hadn't he ever *thought* she might be his? Then he remembered the day Barry had told him about Fancy. For a split second he *had* considered just such a possibility, but according to Barry the timing had been wrong.

Of course, now we know it was all a lie. Jordan's lie. The years he had missed! Her first step, first word. Her first birthday and first Christmas and all of the thousand other little everyday first moments that come in a child's life— He thought of all the opportunities she'd had to tell him the truth, all the opportunities she had conveniently sidestepped or ignored altogether, like the day at the restaurant when he had asked her about using her maiden name. What a gullible fool he had been.

Cole shook himself free of the debilitating thoughts. He had to concentrate on the job at hand. He had to find his daughter. There would be time enough later to deal with Jordan's lies. Thinking about how far-reaching and complicated her lies were, rage bubbled through his veins like molten lava. At the same time, the pain of her betrayal was like a dull knife, slowly dissecting his soul. If he was a betting man, Cole would have given four to one odds that the anger would win out over the pain, but then he had never been much of a gambler when it came to his heart. Whether he liked it or not, for now he would have to work with Jordan in order to find their child, but he sure as hell didn't have to make it easy for her.

He pulled the truck up to the security checkpoint and flashed his identification.

"Good evening, Mr. Forrester," the guard said even before Cole's ID was shoved under his nose.

"Has Bob Riley been through tonight?"

"No, sir. Haven't seen him since early this morning. You want to leave a message?"

"No thanks. My message has to be delivered in person." With that, Cole popped the gearshift into reverse, backed up, the rear wheel spitting gravel, then changed gears and peeled out onto the road leading away from the construction site. Headed for Jordan's cabin.

When he pulled up at the foot of the stairs leading to Jordan's front door, Cole noticed only one light shone from the cabin. After their confrontation he thought she might have called the police anyway, and he half expected to find them crawling all over the place with the FBI not far behind. He was relieved to see that she had the good sense to believe that no one could do as good a job at finding Fancy as he could. God knew he had enough training in the kind of work that not only took up where regular police work stopped, but went down some dark alleys only a man with a lot of experience or a death wish would tackle. Cole had a *lot* of experience.

Had, he reminded himself. It had been over two years since he had lived with an agent's mind-set, with a watch-your-back-at-all-times point of view. A long time since he had lived with an operative's version of the golden rule: Do the other guy before he does you. The thought of returning to that blackness that had once been his life was hateful, but there was no other way.

His long legs took the stairs two at a time, not just because he was in a hurry, but also because even those seconds of physically stretching his muscles helped uncoil some of the tension in his body. Tension he feared would interfere with the distance he intended to keep between himself and Jordan.

He knocked on the door and received no response. He knocked again, louder this time. Still no answer. Out of nowhere a breeze whipped around the cabin and blasted his face and neck. The hair at the nape of his neck stood on end. Or was it a sixth sense warning him something was very wrong? A shiver of dread skated down his spine, the same kind he had learned to respect years ago when his life depended on no more than a hint of danger.

He walked back down the stairs, retrieved a flashlight from his truck and began to examine the several sets of tire tracks in the gravel-ground-to-powder driveway. His own truck tracks were clearly visible, so were Jordan's Jeep, which led up to the closed garage door, then disappeared. And a third set he couldn't identify. Then he noticed there were no tracks leading *out* of the garage, and when he checked the small windowed door on the side of the garage, he discovered the Jeep was still inside.

She's gone but her car is still here. Where would she go? And with whom?

His ever-trustworthy sixth sense came to full alert. Jordan was in trouble. He could feel it in his gut.

Cole walked back to the tracks. Squatting low to the ground, balancing himself on the balls of his feet, he held the light steady and studied the curve of the driveway and the position of all the visible tire tracks. As best he could determine, someone had parked in the driveway between the time he left Jordan less than an hour earlier and the present. And judging by the extra-wide, deep tracks, that someone was driving a vehicle requiring tires specifically designed for four-wheel driving.

Jordan's words the day of her near miss on the mountain flashed across his mind. *Barry is the four-wheel daredevil. Got a cabin somewhere near the summit of Hoosier Pass...*

Cole stared at the tracks trapped in the beam of his flashlight and knew... *knew* who Jordan had left with.

Barry Clark.

The bastard has them both!

He walked back to his truck, jerked up the mobile-phone receiver and punched in a number.

"Reed Sheridan," the voice at the other end of the line said.

"Reed, it's Cole."

"Cole, everything okay?"

"I need a favor. I need you to call that obnoxious mayor, what's his name?"

"Will Burke?"

"Yeah, that's it. Get him to dig through the county tax records, building permits, whatever it takes for him to find the location of a piece of property owned by a man named Barry Clark. East of Breckenridge."

"You do realize, don't you, that it's almost seven o'clock in the evening and the city and county offices are closed?"

"I know that," Cole snapped. "And I also know Burke should get down on his knees and give thanks to whatever God he prays to that this damned bobsled run ever got off the ground. He owes you, and Great Northern." Then in a calmer voice he added, "I also know that Fairplay city records, and for that matter, Park County records, are housed in a building not much bigger than a convenience store, so it shouldn't take him long to find what I need."

"Cole, what's going on?"

"I don't have enough time to give you details, but I believe I've got a lead on the men responsible for the sabotage at the site . . . and a kidnapping."

"A kidnapping?" Reed said, shocked. "Connected to the sabotage?"

"Yeah. A little girl."

"Oh, my God. Whose child is it?"

"Mine."

There was a long pause at the other end before Reed answered. "How much time have you got?"

"I don't know," Cole said truthfully.

"You'll have what you need in the next half hour or I'll personally kick Will Burke's butt from here to hell and back."

"And Reed . . ."

"Yeah?"

"Tell Burke it's for Jordan Lockridge, and you'll probably get quicker results."

When he hung up, Cole felt the first surge of hope since he had learned of Fancy's disappearance. *You'll find them. And they'll be all right,* he assured himself. *They have to be.*

And if they aren't?

The possibility was too horrible even to contemplate, and Cole summarily dismissed such foreboding thoughts as he drove back to the construction site. A short time later he had swapped his truck for one of the four-wheel-drive vehicles in the project's motor pool. He climbed inside the Jeep, slung his portable mobile phone, and his gun onto the seat, and headed for Hoosier Pass.

"Mommy," Fancy called, the instant Jordan stepped through the doorway of Barry's two-room cabin.

Jordan dashed across the floor, snatched Fancy into her arms and held on for dear life.

"I go home?" the child whined.

"Shh, baby," Jordan said, trying to soothe her. "It's all right. Mommy's here."

"I told you she was just fine," Barry said as he closed the door.

"He probably told you too damn much." From a table in the far corner, the man Jordan recognized as Bob Riley glared at her.

She hugged Fancy tighter.

"You get the tape?" Riley asked, closing the magazine he had been reading.

Barry held up two tape cases. "And the copy."

Riley lighted a cigarette. "Is that the only one?"

Barry gave Jordan a questioning look, silently asking for an answer to Riley's question. When she nodded, he turned to the other man and said, "That's the only copy."

Having witnessed the unspoken exchange, Riley scowled. "Are you going to take her word? Christ, she's sleeping with Forrester."

"If she says there's only one copy, then there's only one," Barry said defensively.

Jordan's gaze bounced between the two men, and she prayed Barry's trust in her would be enough to convince his accomplice. Riley seemed to consider whether such trust was even possible, then pointed a finger at Barry, saying, "You better hope she's telling the truth, or it'll be your ass."

"So," Barry said, nervously. "We can let them go now."

Riley took a deep drag of his cigarette. "No."

"What do you mean, no? We've got what we need. Let them go."

"Can't."

"What the hell are you trying to tell me?"

"What do you think I'm trying to tell you?" He pointed at Jordan. "She can ID us, man."

All the color drained from Barry's face. "But she won't," he said, nervously. "Will you, Jordan?"

She shook her head.

"See? And I told you. You can trust her. If she says she'll keep her mouth shut, she will."

"Man, you really are a bleeding heart, aren't you?"

"Hey, Jordan and Fancy have nothing to do with what you and I are trying to accomplish."

"I told you, man. They can ID us. All I'm waiting for is the go-ahead." Then calmly, Riley went back to reading his magazine.

"What go-ahead?"

"From my contact." Riley pointed to the portable phone on the table.

Jordan's eyes widened. Not only had she not noticed the phone before that moment, but neither had she seen the rifle, its barrel propped against the opposite side of the table.

"I told you from the beginning we had help."

"From who?"

"What difference does it make?"

Barry looked Riley in the eye. "Suddenly it makes a great deal of difference. Your contact couldn't by any chance work for Great Northern's competitor?"

Riley's only answer was a hard stare.

Barry looked at the other man, and Jordan saw the shock in his eyes turn to realization. The horrifying realization of Riley's plans for Jordan and Fancy. Barry glanced over at them, his eyes wide with terror. His mouth opened as if he intended to speak, but no words came out. In his eyes, she saw the truth of their situation, and talons of fear clawed at her insides. *Help us, Barry,* she pleaded with her eyes as she hauled a yawning Fancy into her lap and began to rock . . . rock, back and forth. *Help us, please.*

Struggling to keep her mind clear and her emotions in check, Jordan tried to think about all of her options, about all of the possibilities and probabilities.

There has to be a way out of this. I can't just sit here and wait for them to kill us.

Even though Barry was certainly no weakling and he had promised to protect them, she suspected he was no match, physically, for the brawny construction supervisor. And if she was honest with herself, she had to face the possibility that she and Fancy might not get out of this situation alive.

No! She quickly rejected the self-defeating thought. *We're not going to die. Somehow, someway . . . Cole!* Hope surged through her. *Cole will find us.*

She prayed he would remember that she had told him Barry was a four-wheel daredevil and that he had a cabin east of Breckenridge. She prayed that one piece of information would be enough to point him in the right direction for a rescue attempt.

Strike "attempt." Think positive.

Then suddenly, the words Cole had spoken when they discovered Fancy missing, came back to her.

I have contacts . . . I'll move heaven and earth . . . bring her back and put her in your arms . . . I love you. I love Fancy, too.

She didn't know how Cole would find them, but she knew he would. Not for her, but for Fancy.

I'll find her, and when I do, you'll have every reason to be afraid . . .

As she rocked her child, tears trickled down her cheeks and Jordan faced the one certainty she couldn't shove to the back of her mind. The one certainty she had seen in Cole's eyes when he learned of her lie. The one certainty she would have to live with the rest of her life.

He could never forgive her.

And when this nightmare was over, another would begin. Another blacker, more soul-rending nightmare, even than facing death.

She would have to fight the man she loved for the child their love had created.

Chapter 14

Reed Sheridan was as good as his word, but Cole had to wonder about the condition of Will Burke's rear end, given the incredibly short time it took Reed to get back to him with the information he needed. Without a survey or map, that information and his own determination would have to be enough. Fortunately there were so few cabins in the area, he had better luck than he anticipated.

The cabin was isolated, so isolated that a light, even one flickering through darkness relieved by moonlight scattered through the trees, could be seen at a great distance. So, when Cole drew to within a quarter mile of the location Reed had described via Burke, he parked the Jeep and killed his headlights. Then he reached into the passenger seat, picked up his pistol, checked the clip and tucked it into the waistband of his jeans. He wasn't taking any chances.

And he wasn't waiting for the backup that Reed had promised was on its way.

Cole made his way around so that he came up on the back of the cabin. Hardly more than a hunting shack, light spilled from the cabin's two front windows and a side window, but he wasn't close enough to see inside. Stealthily he drew closer, moving like a shadow, until he was right next to the side window. With his head turned toward the window, pressing his body as close to the building as he could, Cole was able to see across the room at an angle.

His heart almost shot out of his body with a surge of fear when he saw Jordan, sitting on a cot on the far side of the room, holding Fancy's limp body in her arms. Only after he forced himself to look harder did he realize that the child was probably sleeping. As if to confirm what his eyes were seeing as truth, at that moment Jordan shifted Fancy slightly in her arms and the child snuggled closer to her mother.

Cole's knees went weak with relief, and nervous perspiration beaded across his forehead and upper lip. *They were all right. Scared to death, obviously, but all right.* But when he focused his attention on Jordan, the terror in her eyes made him want to cry out his rage at the pain and fear she was suffering, made him want to throw himself through the window and strangle both men with his bare hands. The way she held her slender body, the tilt of her head, were window-dressing bravado. Cole had never seen anyone more courageous in his life.

He forced his attention back to Riley, who was now facing away from Jordan, Fancy and Barry on the opposite side of the room. The thought struck him, that they were divided. If he drew an imaginary line down the middle of the tiny room, Bob Riley was on one side and Jordan, Fancy and Barry were on the other. It was a little thing and hardly strong enough evidence to assume that Barry was now in Jordan's corner; yet, Cole's instincts told him it counted.

And he had learned the hard way to listen to his instincts.

While Cole watched, Barry rose from his chair and approached Riley, and although their voices were slightly muffled with the help of gestures and inflection, he made out the gist of their conversation and what he heard was music to his ears.

Barry was scared. Not only did Cole hear the fear in Barry's voice, but he also saw it in the cameraman's eyes. Riley, on the other hand, was hard-nosed and clearly disgusted with Barry's obvious change of heart.

And just as clearly intent on getting rid of Jordan and Fancy.

On a cold day in hell, Cole thought, vivid images of extremely vicious things he would like to do to the burly supervisor flashing through his mind.

The two men continued to argue until finally Riley yelled at Barry to shut up or he might wind up joining his friends. The look of total shock on Clark's face was unappreciated by Riley because he yanked the cigarette out of his mouth and threw it on the floor. In one motion, he looked down, crushed out the still-lighted cigarette and turned away... in Cole's direction.

Cole jerked his head back, but not quickly enough. He was almost certain Barry had looked over Riley's shoulder just as he turned.

Cole's heartbeat jumped into overdrive, hammering against his ribs. He pulled out the pistol. Glancing around for suitable cover, he estimated the distance between his location and the Jeep parked in front of the cabin, made his decision and moved. He had barely made it to a crouching position on the passenger side of the Jeep before the door to the cabin opened and Barry Clark stepped into the night.

Years of training deliberately shoved to the dark regions of Cole's unconscious now came rolling back, clicking neatly into place. With an ease that would have shocked him had he stopped to think about it, Cole willed his body into a steel-nerve state of calmness, prepared for whatever the next few moments brought. Prepared to do *whatever* the situation demanded. Prepared to save Jordan and Fancy, no matter what the cost.

"I'm just going to get a blanket out of my Jeep for the kid." Clark's voice wafted clear and strong on the night air, followed by the sound of gravel crunching beneath his feet as he came closer and closer, heading for the driver's side of the jeep. The footsteps stopped, then started again... changing direction toward the back of the vehicle that was Cole's only cover.

Cole heart a rustling noise that sounded as if the Jeep's canvas flap had been shoved out of the way, then...

"Forrester?"

Cole didn't answer.

"Forrester!" Barry whispered urgently. "I know you're out here." At Cole's continued silence, Barry uttered several colorful expletives, punctuating his frustration and desperation.

"Look, you got no reason to trust me, but dammit, I don't wanna see them hurt any more than you do. Riley's got a rifle. He's just waiting for a call... somebody, I don't know who, to give him the go-ahead. You've got to do something!"

Now or never, Cole thought, again opting to rely on his instincts. "Where's the rifle?" He thought he heard Barry sigh with relief.

"Leaning against the edge of the table, about three feet from the window where I saw you."

"Can you get it?"

"Doubtful. He knows I'm not with him now."

There was a long pause, before Cole said, "Then you've got to send him to me."

"H-how?"

"Tell him you thought you saw lights in the distance. Thought you heard someone moving around in the brush."

"He'll come with the rifle."

"I know."

"But what if—"

"Just do it."

The cold steel in Cole's voice put an end to any further protest. Barry yanked the blanket out of the back of the Jeep and went back inside the cabin.

After what seemed like an eternity, the cabin door opened and Cole heard footsteps again...the footsteps of a much heavier man. Riley.

With the pistol in his hand, Cole waited.

The instant the door closed behind Riley, Barry raced to Jordan and Fancy.

"Cole's outside," he said, breathing hard.

"Oh, my God." Terror streaked through Jordan. "Riley has a gun!"

"So does Cole."

No, her mind screamed, *oh please, dear God—*

A single shot rent the night air. Then nothing. No sound at all.

Seconds crawled by like centuries while images of Cole tortured Jordan's mind like knife points flicking at her flesh—Cole lying bleeding, Cole, his life ebbing away, dying. *Cole...Cole...Cole...*

The cabin door flew open and banged against the wall. Instantly Barry stepped in front of Jordan and Fancy, making himself a target if necessary. A heartbeat later he stepped aside.

* * *

An hour later, safe inside her home, gazing down at Fancy now securely tucked into her own bed, Jordan could almost make herself believe the nightmare of the past few hours had never happened. Almost. Until she closed her eyes and relived the moment she looked up and saw Cole standing in the doorway. She might forget the events that followed: the arrival of the police, Riley in the back seat of a police car, holding his wounded right arm as the car disappeared down the mountain road, and Barry being taken into custody. She might, with time, forget all of it.

But she would never forget the sight of Cole, standing in the open doorway, the pistol still in his hand, glaring at her as if he hated her.

And why shouldn't he? Because of her, he had been forced to step back into a mind-set he abhorred, a mind-set so closely connected to his dark past that he feared for his soul. And if that wasn't enough to guarantee his hatred, she had lied to him about Fancy.

Carefully, so as not to wake her, Jordan sat down on the side of Fancy's bed, picked up a dainty little hand and placed it in hers. She held on gently, securely, the way one might hold on to a treasure so fragile it could be shattered by a whispered breath. The way one might hold on to a dream they feared lost.

Downstairs, Cole stood in front of the full-view double doors leading out to the patio, staring into the night. He saw the moon hanging in the sky like a silver jewel, but was untouched by its pale glow. He saw the thousands of stars scattered across the darkness, but was unaffected by their twinkling beauty.

He had thought the worst of this terrifying night was over when Bob Riley and Barry had been arrested and taken away. But he was wrong. The worst was yet to come. When

Jordan came downstairs they would have to deal with everything that had brought them to this moment. The past, the lies, the unforgiveness . . . his and hers.

No. That's not true. She forgave you.

Still staring out at the night, he suddenly saw his reflection in the glass doors. The reflection of a man unable to offer others what he couldn't or wouldn't offer himself—forgiveness. And he remembered snippets of conversations, phrases Jordan had spoken, trying in her own way to tell him, to explain about Fancy and the circumstances of her make-believe father.

He gave me something I desperately needed . . . someday I'll tell you about my husband. And most importantly. *In my heart, the man I created was always you.* He had been as quick to judge her, to withhold forgiveness from her as he had from himself. And he had been equally unfair on both counts.

But the insane part of all this was that he had almost succeeded in keeping the vow he had made years earlier, the vow to stay out of Jordan's life. Not out of any driven need to do the right thing, but out of his own obstinacy. And that obstinance had almost cost him the only important people in the world. When he thought of how close he had come to losing Jordan *and* Fancy, he started to shake.

Please let me have half the courage she displayed tonight, so I don't lose her twice in one lifetime.

"Cole?"

At the sound of her voice, her tremulous voice, he turned.

"She's . . . asleep, but you can look in on her if you like."

They had opted to leave the downstairs dark when they arrived for fear the lights would wake Fancy. Cole had not seen fit to turn them on. The entire downstairs was illuminated only by moonlight. Rivers of it, oceans of it, flowing in sweet silver streams, washing the room in an alabaster glow. The almost-stark whiteness cast Cole's features in shadows so that she couldn't read the expression on his face.

"You think she's all right?" His voice, deep and calm, seemed to materialize out of the dark. "I mean, you don't think she'll be...you know, traumatized by what happened?"

"I don't know. She trusted Barry, and she was with him the entire time, except for the half hour when he came for me, so hopefully not. Besides, children are resilient little creatures. They bounce back remarkably..." Her voice trailed off as she fought back tears. "But, of course, you couldn't know that, could you, because you've never had...I've never given you the opportunity..." She turned away, unable to bear standing in a moonbeam spotlight, exposing her pain to a man who had been, was still and would always be, her love, her life, but who no longer wanted her.

"Jordan—"

"I'm so sorry, Cole." Grateful he couldn't see the tears streaking her face, she fought to keep her voice from sounding as desperate as she felt. "I've made so many mistakes. Mistakes you've paid for. Excluding you from Fancy's life, then causing you to face your worst fear. My God, I almost cost you your life tonight. How can you ever—"

Before she could finish, he spun her around and into his arms. Strong arms. Hold-you-forever arms.

"Don't," he breathed. "Don't say it." Cole buried his hands up to his wrists in the silky texture of her hair, tilting her head back until she was forced to look into his eyes. "It's me who should ask forgiveness. I should get down on my knees and beg you to forgive me for being the biggest fool in the world."

She stared into his eyes, too stunned to speak.

''We both made mistakes four years ago, but we got a second chance. And tonight we got a third. Oh, baby, don't you see? We keep running away from each other, from ourselves, only to wind up right back where we started...needing each other, loving each other. We've wasted—'' he kissed her lips, gently, sweetly ''—so much time. Jordan, Jordan...'' His tongue probed the seam of her lips and tasted tears, tasted forgiveness. ''You're my light, my hope. Without you I'm lost in the darkness.''

She stood on tiptoe, wrapped her arms around his neck and poured all her love, all her hope into the kiss that was a question, then an answer, then a promise.

Early-morning sunlight poured through the massive multipaned window of the bedroom like gold through a sieve, dusting the lovers in pearlescent light. Standing in front of the window, reveling in the pale golden glory as they reveled in their embrace, Cole and Jordan greeted the day after talking and loving the night away.

''You think I should leave?''

Cole wasn't quite certain how Fancy would react if she walked in and found a man in her mother's bedroom, particularly if that man was barefoot and wearing nothing but a pair of jeans. He didn't want Jordan to have to deal with an uncomfortable explanation.

''No,'' she insisted, snuggling closer to him, her head resting on his chest. ''No more pretense.''

Loving the feel of her warm, moist breath against his bare skin, he sighed. ''Are you sure?''

From her deliciously relaxed position she gazed up at him. ''As sure as I knew you would come for us last night. As sure as I knew nothing, not even your own fear, would keep you from Fancy.''

''And you.''

She smiled. "At the time I wasn't so sure about that."

He turned, pulling her full against his body, wishing her terry robe wasn't between her body and his. "I said some cruel things to you, things I'll regret for the rest of—"

She placed her fingertips against his lips. "No regrets, remember?"

"My only real regret is that I shut myself off from you and the rest of the world for four long years. I thought breaking under the pressure and torture while I was a hostage somehow labeled me unclean, unfit for society. If I couldn't forgive myself, how could anyone else forgive me?"

"You were only human, Cole."

"I know that now. But I was convinced my scars were too deep and too ugly to expose to the rest of the world, especially you. It's taken me a long time to realize I could no more separate myself from my past than I could stop loving you. I thought that by shutting myself off from the past I would be free of it."

"Like you said, we wasted so much time."

"And I'm going to spend the rest of our lives making it up to you."

"Making it up to each other."

"Love me, Jordan. Don't ever stop."

"Never . . . never . . ."

Their lips met in the sweetest of kisses, the most solemn of promises. And they would have followed with the sweetest consummation of that promise had it not been for one small detail.

"Mommy?"

Instantly Cole and Jordan moved apart.

"Uh . . . morning, sunshine," Jordan said, a bit nervously.

Fancy's big brown eyes were riveted on the man beside her mother. Jordan glanced from her daughter to Cole, and had to smile at the look of sheer terror on his face. Last night he had single-handedly faced a gunman, and now he was positively shaking over dealing with a wide-eyed three-year-old. But she took one looking at the yearning hidden beneath that fear and knew the only way to handle the situation was honestly.

"Come here, sweetheart," she said, holding out her hand to Fancy.

The child complied, never taking her eyes off Cole. Even when Jordan lifted her onto the bed and wrapped an arm around her little shoulders and Cole joined them on the wide bed. "Fancy, Mr. Forrester would like to be with us from now on. Would that be all right with you?"

Fancy turned and looked at her mother. "Do we gots to give away Spot?" the child asked, obviously thinking the house might be overcrowded and someone would have to go.

"No," Jordan assured her. "We'll keep Spot. But Mr. Forrester will be here, too. He'll stay with us the way..." Her gaze met Cole's. "The way a real daddy does. Would you like that."

"Uh-huh." Smiling, Fancy turned her attention back to Cole. "You stay, Mr. Forrest-der?"

Cole almost couldn't speak around the lump in his throat. "I'd like to stay very much, beauty."

The beguiling little girl looked from Cole to her mother, then back to Cole and gave them her two-word seal of approval.

"Okee, dokee."

Two pairs of eyes misted, one green, one darker than dark brown; two hands clasped and fingers entwined behind Fancy's back, a symbol of the entwining of their lives, their love.

While sunlight touched the trio with the kiss of a golden

future, Jordan gazed into Cole's eyes and knew she would
never again have to run to the moon for comfort, so long as
she could run to his arms.

*   *   *   *   *

AMERICAN HERO

Every month in Silhouette Intimate Moments, one fabulous, irresistible man is featured as an American Hero. You won't want to miss a single one. Look for them wherever you buy books, or follow the instructions below and have these fantastic men mailed straight to your door!

In September:
MACKENZIE'S MISSION by Linda Howard, IM #445

In October:
BLACK TREE MOON by Kathleen Eagle, IM #451

In November:
A WALK ON THE WILD SIDE by Kathleen Korbel, IM #457

In December:
CHEROKEE THUNDER by Rachel Lee, IM #463

AMERICAN HEROES—men you'll adore, from authors you won't want to miss. Only from Silhouette Intimate Moments.

CHRISTMAS Stories 1992

...rience the beauty of Yuletide romance with Silhouette
...stmas Stories 1992—a collection of heartwarming stories by
...orite Silhouette authors.

JONI'S MAGIC by Mary Lynn Baxter
HEARTS OF HOPE by Sondra Stanford
THE NIGHT SANTA CLAUS RETURNED by Marie Ferrarella
BASKET OF LOVE by Jeanne Stephens

...so available this year are three popular early editions of
...houette Christmas Stories—1986, 1987 and 1988. Look for
these and you'll be well on your way to a complete collection
of the best in holiday romance.

Plus, as an added bonus, you can receive a FREE keepsake
Christmas ornament. Just collect four proofs of purchase from
any November or December 1992 Harlequin or Silhouette series
novels, or from any Harlequin or Silhouette Christmas
collection, and receive a beautiful dated brass Christmas
candle ornament.

Mail this certificate along with four (4) proof-of-purchase coupons, plus $1.50 postage and handling (check or money order—do not send cash), payable to Silhouette Books, to: **In the U.S.:** P.O. Box 9057, Buffalo, NY 14269-9057; **In Canada:** P.O. Box 622, Fort Erie, Ontario, L2A 5X3.

ONE PROOF OF PURCHASE	Name: _____
	_____
	Address: _____
	_____
	City: _____
	State/Province: _____
SX92POP	Zip/Postal Code: _____
	093 KAG

COME BACK TO

CONARD COUNTY